Blood Moon

Also by Level Best Books

Available at
www.levelbestbooks.com

Cover photograph by Teresa Moylan

Best New England Crime Stories

Blood Moon

Edited by

Mark Ammons
Katherine Fast
Barbara Ross
Leslie Wheeler

Level Best Books
Somerville, Massachusetts 02144

Level Best Books
411A Highland Avenue #371
Somerville, Massachusetts 02144
www.levelbestbooks.com

text composition/design by Katherine Fast
cover photo © 2012 by Teresa Moylan
Printed in the USA
anthology © 2012 by Level Best Books
"Epitaph" © 2012 by Mark Ammons
"Out to Sea" © 2012 by VR Barkowski
"The Cornfield" © 2012 by Judith Boss
"No Corners" © 2012 by John Bubar
"The Exhibitionist, A Love Story" © 2012 by Stuart Cohen
"Kept in the Dark" © 2012 by Sheila Connolly
"The Project" © 2012 by Frank Cook
"Driving Miss Rachel" © 2012 by Ray Daniel
"The Cat and the Blue Moon" © 2012 by Randy DeWitt
"Suicide by Engagement" © 2012 by Stef Donati
"Mr. Fussy" © 2012 by Christine Eskilson
"Free Advice" © 2012 by Katherine Fast
"The Sounds of Silence" © 2012 by Kate Flora
"Hit and Run" © 2012 by Judith Green
"Big Water" © 2012 by Woody Hanstein
"The Pendulum Swings, Until It Doesn't" © 2012 by J.A. Hennrikus
"Strictly Male Fantasy" © 2012 by Daniel Moses Luft
"Burning Desire" © 2012 by Cheryl Marceau
"The Prize" © 2012 by Peter Martin
"Super Thesaurus" © 2012 by Ruth M. McCarty
"A Regular Story" © 2012 by Peggy McFarland
"Death from a Bad Heart" © 2012 by B.B. Oak
"The City" © 2012 by Pamela A. Oberg
"The Oldest Man in Town" © 2012 by Adam Renn Olenn
"Shades of Gray" © 2012 by Stephen D. Rogers
"House Calls" © 2012 by Barbara Ross
"The Clue Nobody Saw" © 2012 by Annette Sweeney
"Double Wedding" © 2012 by Mo Walsh
"Freebie" © 2012 by Leslie Wheeler
"Acts of Balance" © 2012 by Nancy Means Wright
"The Trunk" © 2012 by Virginia Young

ISBN 978-0-9838780-2-5
Library of Congress Catalog Card Data available.
First Edition
10 9 8 7 6 5 4 3 2 1

Blood Moon

Contents

Contents

Contents

Introduction

We are pleased to bring you *Best New England Crime Stories 2013: Blood Moon*, Level Best Books' tenth anthology. This anniversary edition is our biggest and best *evah*. (As we say in these parts.)

What do New Englanders do when the winter is mild? Write fiction, apparently. Submissions in 2012 ran 50% higher than last year, creating the toughest set of decisions we've had to make as editors. But we soldiered on, and, as a result, *Blood Moon* contains thirty-one of the best and most varied stories we've had the pleasure of publishing.

Here are some fun facts about our submissions. As before, Massachusetts led the way with the largest number (53%). Next came New Hampshire with 13%, then Maine with 11%. Connecticut and Vermont tied for fourth place (9%), and Rhode Island went from zero last year to 5%. The breakdown in terms of gender was 58% female, 40% male, 2% undecided. (Not that there's anything wrong with that!)

We had seven pairs of husbands and wives who submitted stories and one parent-child pair, giving new meaning to the family plot.

Several themes run through this year's submissions. It was a great year for historical mysteries and for incorporating figures and events from the past into current day stories. Two excellent examples are "Death from a Bad Heart" by B.B. Oak and "The Trunk" by Virginia Young.

Sketchy characters exhibit highly questionable business practices in "The Project" by Frank Cook, "Kept in the Dark" by Sheila Connolly and "The Exhibitionist, A Love Story" by Stuart Cohen.

Law enforcement personnel have something to learn in Ray Daniel's insightful "Driving Miss Rachel," in Annette Sweeney's delightful sci-fi romp, "The Clue Nobody Saw," and in Woody Hanstein's powerful "Big Water."

Cops aren't the only enforcers you find in these crime stories. Bartenders fend for themselves in Peggy McFarland's gripping "A Regular Story" and in Daniel Moses Luft's twisty "Strictly Male Fantasy."

Older folks show their mettle in "The Oldest Man in Town" by Adam Renn Olenn, "The Prize" by Peter Martin, and "The Sounds of Silence" by Kate Flora. But let's not forget the treachery of the young, represented here by Nancy Means Wright's richly atmospheric "Acts of Balance."

Classic tales get a distinctly perverse twist in "Shades of Gray" by Stephen D. Rogers and "The Pendulum Swings Until It Doesn't" by J.A. Hennrikus.

Romantic partners have each other's backs in Mo Walsh's hilarious "Double Wedding," and in Judith Green's sweet and strong "Hit and Run." Both stories feature popular characters from previous Level Best volumes.

Relationships of a much darker nature are portrayed in "Burning Desire" by Cheryl Marceau, "Super Thesaurus" by Ruth M. McCarty and "House Calls" by Barbara Ross.

Men who expect to die begin offbeat affairs in John Bubar's fantastic "No Corners," and Stef Donati's satisfying "Suicide by Engagement."

Leslie Wheeler and Katherine Fast each weave a cautionary tale about the perils of accepting something for nothing in "Freebie" and "Free Advice," respectively. Or maybe you don't wait to be offered something for free. You just take it, as in Christine Eskilsen's clever "Mr. Fussy."

Probably because of this year's title, we were the happy recipients of a flood of great stories with paranormal elements. Two are included in this volume, "The City" by Pamela A. Oberg, and "The Cornfield" by Judith Boss. Six submissions had the word "moon" in their titles. The one we picked was Randy DeWitt's story of revenge on a snowy night, "The Cat and the Blue Moon."

As always, we are honored to begin the collection with this year's Al Blanchard Award winning story. We think you'll find "Out to Sea" by VR Barkowski as breathtaking as its Monhegan Island setting. And, in something that's become a bit of a tradition, we end with Mark Ammons' micro-flash, this year entitled "Epitaph."

We've included stories from many acclaimed New England authors as well as startlingly fresh tales by writers never before published. The stories are noir and nuanced, hideous and hilarious, happy, sad and barking mad. We're sure you'll enjoy them all.

Ten years is a long time for a labor of love like Level Best Books to last. Not just the love of editors past and present, but also the love of scores of authors and thousands of fans who've purchased and devoured these volumes. We're honored to be part of the tradition.

Mark Ammons
Katherine Fast
Barbara Ross
Leslie Wheeler

Out to Sea

VR Barkowski

Twelve miles of Atlantic spanned the distance between Port Clyde and Monhegan Island, one hour of pure, unadulterated nautical hell. Inside the ferry *Laura B.*, Vivienne Jamison sat huddled in a corner, her life's purpose reduced to not sharing her partially digested breakfast with the handful of other passengers. There was a reason the Algonquin called the island *Monchiggan*, "out to sea."

Vivienne's father always told her to avoid seasickness, keep her eyes on the horizon. She peered out a window as milky as a cataract and saw nothing but the violent pitch and massive green swirl of open ocean. That was the thing with her dad's advice, it always sounded good, but when time came for practical application, it usually fell short. Not unlike the man himself.

The ferry rounded tiny Manana Island and suddenly, Monhegan lay in front of her, its clusters of shake cottages clinging to the eastern shore like shipwreck survivors to a life raft. The engines powered down and the ferry docked with a jolt. Vivienne stood, strapped on her backpack and stumbled from the boat.

A brief inspection of the wharf revealed a surplus of lobster traps but no Mr. Britton. She zipped the collar of her parka against the chill and walked as swiftly as her unseaworthy limbs would carry her. There were no cars on the island. No paved roads either. When she heard the soft crunch of footsteps behind her, an instinctive quake shimmied along her backbone. *Idiot*. Monhegan had a year-round population of sixty. She was more likely to be swept away by a rogue wave than mugged. She stopped and turned, but with a body still set to ocean sway, she buckled like a weak hinge.

A tall, slender man with a perfect face and strong hands kept her from landing on her ass.

"You all right, Vivi? Crossings can be dicey this time of year."

Vivi? No one had called her Vivi since she'd moved off the island what seemed like a thousand years ago. Her gaze locked on his, and her pulse leapt. Who the hell was this guy?

"You probably don't remember me. We met briefly in Boston at your sister's funeral. I'm Ephraim Britton. My firm handled Elena's estate."

She remembered Ephraim Britton. He was a balding, middle-aged attorney with a paunch.

Seemingly reading her confusion, he added, "Ephraim Britton *the fourth.* I'm the other Britton in Britton & Britton. I had business on the island. My father asked me to stay over and check on Elena's—your—house and deliver the keys."

His eyes brushed over her, lingering in places that made Vivienne warm.

"You look just like her," he said.

"El and I were twins, Mr. Britton. That's the way it works." He still had hold of her. She took back her arm and squared her shoulders. "Thank you for going to all this trouble. I told your father it wasn't necessary."

"Please, call me Ephraim. I—we—that is, the firm wanted to make sure the cottage was . . ." He looked up at the sky as if he might pull the right word from the heavens. "Clean."

Clean. Did he mean dusting the knickknacks and giving the rugs a good vacuum or scouring El's blood out of the bathtub?

"You have a reservation at Hitchcock House?" he asked.

"I've decided to stay at the cottage. Makes more sense since I'm here to pack up my sister's things."

Mild concern crossed his face and he checked his watch. "The return ferry doesn't leave for a couple hours. I'll walk with you. May I carry your pack?"

Young Mr. Britton seemed inordinately solicitous for a lawyer who'd already been paid. Vivienne wondered about his motives. She'd made no secret of her desire to sell the cottage. Year-round properties on Monhegan were in short supply, and she'd lay odds Britton had his sights on the real estate transaction. Then again, she was lousy at reading people. Her sister, for example. Vivienne never dreamt El would take too many pills, open a vein and leave her saddled with a century-old house on this godforsaken Maine outpost.

At Vivienne's request, Britton left her at the front door of the cottage but not before promising a return visit "to check on things." The place looked much as it had when it belonged to Vivienne's grandparents, a weathered shingled box with a porch, capped with a hoary old roof in need of replacement. She dropped her pack on the stoop next to a pile of moving boxes and climbed the rise behind the cottage. Even in the October pall, the island's wild beauty was heart stopping, its frayed coastline and dense forests of gnarled pine hemmed by the unbridled Atlantic. Growing up on the island, she came to this spot to watch the sun rise over the water. In the late afternoon, she'd return to watch it set. Standing there again, she felt the intense, suffocating loneliness she always associated with Monhegan. As a teenager, she couldn't wait to escape, even while her sister vowed to stay forever. If it were true twins shared a spiritual bond, then why hadn't Vivienne sensed El's desperation? Tears caught in her throat and she pushed back at her guilt with anger. *After what Daddy did to us, how could you leave me alone here, El? How could you?*

Vivienne expected the cottage's interior to be as she remembered, worn and scruffy, dark with faux wood paneling and crowded with shabby furniture. The reality stunned her. Outside, winter lay in wait, but inside it was summer, brilliant yellows and electric blues, lush greens and warm ochres, every room a canvas for El's gifted brush. A mural of White Head covered one wall, a painting of a Monhegan sunset decorated another. The cottage radiated happiness, not a hint of whatever had siphoned El's joy so utterly she took her own life.

Vivienne left her pack in the great-room and climbed the stairs to El's attic studio. The familiar scent of oils, turpentine, and bergamot tugged at her memory. Unfinished canvases sat propped on chairs, crammed under the worktable, leaning against walls. Half-empty tubes of paint and soiled rags littered the floor. She pictured her own über-contemporary office in Boston, with its efficient clean lines and custom walnut drafting table. A reminder the only thing she and El had in common was their reflection in the mirror.

Why, El?

Vivienne yanked the chain on the overhead light and began to flip through canvases in search of answers.

"She was so talented."

Vivienne jumped at the voice and whirled around, heart hammering. A woman stood in the doorway, small and fine-boned, with black hair and the most direct gaze Vivienne had ever encountered.

"Damn," the woman said under her breath. "I didn't mean to startle you. I'm sorry. The front door was wide open. I knocked, but it's impossible to hear up here." She took several steps into the room.

Vivienne, certain she'd closed the door, backed away.

"I'm Beth Strickland, Elena's neighbor."

Beth Strickland. Vivienne exhaled. Beth found El's body.

"I noticed you outside with that lawyer." Beth's blue eyes filled with tears. "When you didn't answer the door—I'm sorry, I shouldn't have barged in." Her voice sagged with emotion.

What? Had she expected to find another dead Jamison sister? "How about a cup of tea?" Vivienne said in a quick preemptive strike, afraid the woman might burst into sobs if she didn't act fast. "I know I could use one. I'm Vivienne by the way."

Beth's smile was wide and genuine. "I'd love one. Would you mind if I called you Vivi? Elena called you Vivi—it's how I think of you."

"Sure. Vivienne is a mouthful." True enough, but no one off the island seemed to have trouble with the name.

Fifteen minutes later they were seated at El's Lilliputian kitchen table with mugs of hot tea and a plate of stale shortbread.

"Do you live on Monhegan full-time?" Vivienne asked.

"This was my first summer here. In fact, I'd planned to catch the ferry home today, but I wanted to introduce myself. I'll leave tomorrow." Beth held her fingers to the corners of her eyes and let out a stuttered rush of air. "I'm so sorry I missed the funeral. I was a wreck. It's still hard being in the house after . . ." Her voice trailed off.

Vivienne stared into her cup. "El and I weren't close. Truth is, I didn't know what was going on in her life." She inhaled slowly, summoning the courage to ask the question tormenting her. "Do you know what happened? Why El—?"

Beth pursed her lips, her words halting as if afraid of saying too much. "There was a man." She met Vivienne's eyes and paused.

"Elena said after your mom died, your father committed suicide?"

"My father was bi-polar," Vivienne said. A lie she'd told so many times she almost believed it. An explanation for why Edmund Jamison's eight-year-old twin daughters weren't reason enough to go on living after his wife died of cancer. Would El have thrown her life away over a man? Hadn't their father taught them not to pin their hopes on such an unsteady foundation? "El was seeing someone on the island?"

"I'm not comfortable talking about this. It's none of my business."

"Beth, please, if you can tell me anything—"

The woman lowered her eyes and bit her lip. "The attorney, the one you were with today."

"Ephraim Britton?" Hollowness gnawed at Vivienne's insides.

"They ended badly."

From where Vivienne sat, El ended badly. Britton, on the other hand, looked to make a nice chunk of change off the deal.

Beth's gaze slid away. "I saw what the relationship did to Elena. That was enough for me."

It was nowhere near enough for Vivienne, but she didn't know Beth well enough to press the point, so she let the matter drop.

Not able to sleep her first night in the cottage, Vivienne resorted to a sleeping pill. The sedative left her tense and emotional. Standing in the shower the next morning, she tried not to think of El bleeding to death a few feet away. Under the needle spray of water, she could almost believe her tears weren't real.

El's furniture would be sold along with the house, but Vivienne still needed to deal with her sister's personal effects. Armed with a stack of moving boxes, she headed up to the studio. At half past noon, she finished packing paint supplies. Drained, she followed an anemic rill of light to the attic window and gazed east to a sky low and heavy with dark clouds. *Damn.* She washed up, shrugged into her coat and headed to the village before the town battened down for the storm.

Just off the main road, an old woman called out to her and waved from the yard of a small rundown bungalow. Stooped, white-haired, and wrapped in a thick swaddling of cardigans, she seemed as fragile as spun glass. "You must be Elena's sister. I'm Judith Porter. That's my husband, Charles."

Charles sat on the porch, swallowed by an oversized rocker. He got to his feet and gave Vivienne a salute.

"Vivienne Jamison." She held out her hand to Judith.

The woman squeezed instead of shaking, her crepey skin warm and dry, comforting in the chill air. "Vivi, of course. We were so sorry to hear about Elena. Such a sweet girl and so talented."

Charles walked up behind his wife. "Lovely young lady. Always smiling."

Not always, Vivienne thought reflexively.

Judith's gentle gaze turned hard. "At least until Beth Strickland arrived on the island. Jealous, that one. Forever talking behind Elena's back."

The old woman's tone sent a shock through Vivienne. "Jealous?"

"Leviticus 19:16, 'Do not go about spreading slander among your people,'" Charles said, throwing Judith a wary glance.

"Proverbs 31:8, 'Speak up for those who cannot speak for themselves . . .'" Judith turned her back on her husband and pinned Vivienne with sharp eyes. "Let's be thankful the Strickland woman's gone and taken her forked tongue with her."

Forked tongue? Seriously?

Charles cleared his throat. "Elena told us you're an architect. She was so proud of you."

Yet another of El's secrets. "Architect and urban planner," Vivienne said.

"Beautiful *and* brilliant. My kind of woman." Charles winked, his smile revealing an ample set of too-white false teeth.

Judith chuckled and jabbed Charles with her elbow. "Ignore him, Vivi. We understand you're getting the cottage ready to sell. If we can do anything to help, dear, let us know."

Vivienne thanked them. The wind began to pick up, and black clouds boiled the sky. She could smell ozone. "The squall's going to hit soon, I'd better hurry."

The storm landed late afternoon and blew itself out over night. Dawn delivered a magnificent fall day, clear and crisp, with a stiff breeze that carried the piney fragrance of the forest and the salt of the sea. Vivienne borrowed a wool scarf and galoshes from El's closet and hiked the steep, muddy path to the cemetery.

Located just below the museum, the graveyard overlooked the village and dark rise of Manana Island. Beneath a cobalt sky, with the lighthouse rising like an augury, the view took her breath away. *The Monhegan bait and switch.* Under clear skies and a shining sun, nowhere was more spectacular. During the long, gray bone-chilling months of winter, the island became a Down East Alcatraz. Vivienne's father, a lifelong Bostonian, loathed Monhegan and refused his wife's last request to be buried on the island where she was born. Unfortunately, that didn't stop him from blowing his brains out and abandoning his daughters here.

Vivienne crouched in front of her grandparents' headstone, closed her eyes and traced the engraved letters with her fingertip. They were good, kind people, who raised her and El with love. Vivienne's heart ached from missing them. She wiped away tears.

"Everything okay?"

Her eyes snapped open, and she jumped to her feet nearly slamming into Ephraim Britton the younger. She caught a hint of his cologne, a faint whisper of sandalwood. "I wish you'd quit sneaking up on me."

He reached out and thumbed a tear from her cheek and jerked his hand back as if he'd been burned. "Sorry, that was out of line. It's just that you look—I'm sorry. It's easy to forget."

"Did my sister cry a lot, Mr. Britton?" she asked, her voice cold.

"Call me Ephraim. If you're asking me why Elena took her life, I don't know."

"You were involved with her."

His eyes widened. "I'd like to think we were friends."

"Is that why you're here? Because you and El were *friends*?"

"I'm here because I want to help. This can't be easy for you."

"I can manage," Vivienne said, aware she sounded like a recalcitrant five-year-old. "How did you know where to find me?"

"Best guess. I didn't pass you in town. No answer at the cottage. His gaze swept over her. "It's beautiful up here."

She felt her face flame. "El and I used to come up here when we were kids. Perfect place to spy on the village." She laughed at the memory.

"You should smile more. It suits you."

Ephraim Britton was a charming man. Beth Strickland's forked tongue notwithstanding, Vivienne suspected the woman may have been right.

"Is it true you hate Monhegan?" he asked.

"Hate is complicated. My feelings are simple. Monhegan is not of this world. I am. I never belonged here."

Neither of them spoke on the walk back to the cottage, the weight of the silence heavy between them.

The moment Vivienne stepped into the great-room she noticed the rolltop desk. Papers once neatly stacked were now strewn across the desk's surface, drawers pulled out, documents spilling to the floor. She turned to Britton, furious. "You had no right to go through my sister's things."

He flinched as if she'd slapped him. "Until two days ago, I had a key. Why would I break in and ransack a desk?"

"I didn't lock the door. No one locks their doors on Monhegan."

"Well, it wasn't me. Any guess at what they were looking for?"

"No, and no clue if they found it either." Nothing else in the house appeared disturbed, but Vivienne couldn't shake a lingering unease. "Why be so obvious about it?"

"Maybe I interrupted the search when I knocked," Ephraim said, helping her gather papers off the floor. "Might be a good idea to lock your doors for the time being."

Vivienne drew in a breath and pointed to the couch. "Sit. Tell me about you and El."

He put a hand on the small of her back and steered her to the sofa. "Not much to tell. I met Elena at a gallery opening in Rockland. We started talking wills, ended up going out a few times. Then it was over."

The hairs rose on the back of her neck. "What do you mean, *over*?"

He colored. "I mean she wasn't into me."

Bull. Ephraim Britton fell into the sweet spot between James Bond and a golden retriever, exactly El's type.

"*Quid pro quo.* Who told you Elena and I were involved?"

"Beth Strickland. She said the relationship ended badly. Hinted you had something to do with El—you know, doing what she did." Why couldn't she make herself say the words out loud?

Ephraim studied her. "Are you talking about the neighbor who found Elena? I never met her. Strickland told you five months after Elena kicked me to the curb, she was so distraught, she couldn't go on?"

"Not exactly, but something along those lines."

A flush of anger rode high on his cheekbones. "I need to talk to this woman."

"She left the island yesterday." Vivienne fidgeted on the overstuffed cushions. She wished she hadn't mentioned Beth.

Ephraim rubbed a hand over his mouth and sat back. "This is none of my business, so you're welcome to tell me to go to hell, but why are you selling the cottage? Do you need the money?"

"No, but I don't need a house on Monhegan Island either."

"The cottage has been in your family for generations. I doubt Elena would have left you the place if she thought you'd sell."

Vivienne stifled a laugh. "I doubt El would have left me the place if there'd been anyone else to leave it to. Don't you already have buyers on the hook?"

Ephraim leaned toward her, their faces so close that for an instant she thought he might kiss her. Without thinking, she closed her eyes. He caressed her cheek and whispered, "Keep the house, Vivi. Monhegan is more than who you were. This island is part of who you are."

Heat crept up her neck and into her cheeks. "Maybe I will."

After Ephraim left, Vivienne wandered the cottage, her mind sifting through memories as bright and clear as the ring of crystal. She and El racing up the stairs, sitting on the porch repairing lobster traps with Gramps, watching the daily torrent of summer visitors from the attic window. As girls, Vivienne and El had been inseparable even when not captive in Monhegan's single room schoolhouse. But Monhegan had no high school, and when the girls left the island for ninth grade, their uncomplicated world morphed into something foreign and unknowable that pushed them apart and dropped them on either side of an unbreachable divide. Ephraim had a point. In spite of El's changes, the cottage was still the house they grew up in.

The clock above the refrigerator read five minutes after two. She'd invited Ephraim back for dinner and promised lasagna, which meant she'd better get to the grocery store.

As she passed the Porters' bungalow, Charles waved from his

porch rocker. "Vivi! Out enjoying our beautiful autumn weather?"

"I am. What a glorious day."

He stood and pulled a second chair closer to his own and patted the seat. "Come, sit with me for a few minutes. Keep me company."

She smiled. In fall, after the exodus of summer visitors, the island always felt particularly lonely. She climbed the steps and settled in beside him. "Charles, did you happen to spot anyone up near my cottage this morning?"

"No one but that lawyer fella. *Your* cottage is it?"

My cottage. The words came so naturally, she hadn't even noticed. She sighed. "I've decided not to sell."

A worried crease settled between Charles's brows as Judith stepped out on the porch. With her thin white hair scraped tight into a knot, the old woman appeared more frail than ever. Vivienne stood to give her a seat, but Judith shook her head and gestured for her to stay.

"Ran into the Strickland woman in the village this morning. We thought she'd left the island," Judith said, her voice taut as a bowstring.

"Beth is still on Monhegan?" Vivienne flashed on El's violated desk.

"Unfortunately," Judith said, then brightened. "What brings you by, dear? Do you need help with the house?"

Charles reached out and took Vivienne's hand in gnarled fingers. "This stunning creature is here at my request. Vivi just told me she's decided not to sell the cottage."

Judith cocked her head. "You're sure you want the responsibility?"

"I can hardly believe it myself, but yes, I'm sure." Vivienne pulled her hand away from Charles and got to her feet. If she didn't get back to the cottage with food soon, she'd be feeding Ephraim grilled cheese.

At Carina, she struggled to focus on groceries, but her thoughts strayed to Beth. Why had Beth lied about leaving Monhegan?

Once dinner was in the oven, Vivienne sat down at El's desk. If there was anything worth finding still here, she intended to root it out. After she'd examined every scrap of paper and stray sales receipt, she pushed the old rolltop away from the wall. A crumpled slice of paper fell to the floor. She smoothed the sheet and read.

E:

This is your last warning. Do not try to contact me again. Keep away from me and keep away from my family. If you continue to insinuate yourself into my life and business, I will make certain you regret it. For your own sake, I hope you will seek the psychiatric help you so desperately need.

The signature belonged to Ephraim Britton IV, the lying son of a bitch.

"You are not welcome here." Vivienne tried to slam the door in his face, but Ephraim wedged his foot in the jamb.

"You invited me to dinner."

"Before I knew what a lying bastard you are." She wadded up the note and shoved it at him.

"Where'd this come from?"

"El's desk, if it matters." Again she tried to shut the door, but his foot wouldn't budge.

"It matters," he said, in a tone so dark and intractable, an electric chill rippled along her nerve endings. "Look at the date. I didn't know Elena two years ago. I wrote this to a woman named Elizabeth Shockley. There were incidents."

"*Incidents*? What kinds of *incidents* warrant a threat, Ephraim?"

"Stalking. She harassed my family, broke into my home. I wrote this after she poisoned my dog. Threatening? I hope to hell it was. I ended up petitioning for a restraining order a week later. How did Elena get this?"

The tremor in his voice and desperation in his eyes caused Vivienne to relax her hold on the door. A niggling sense of something very wrong settled over her. *Elizabeth Shockley. Elizabeth. Beth. Beth Strickland. Coincidence?* Had Beth planted the note, or possibly given it to El? That would explain why El turned away from Ephraim. "What did she look like, this Elizabeth Shockley?"

"Dark haired, petite, intense. Why?"

"You said you never met Beth Strickland. What if Beth and Elizabeth Shockley are the same person? Judith and Charles down the road—"

Ephraim raised a brow. "The Porters? The old couple interested in buying your cottage?"

Buying my cottage? "Judith met up with Beth in the village this morning. Beth lied about leaving Monhegan. She's still on the island."

"Turn off the stove and let's go," he said, jaw clenched, vein pulsing at his temple.

Beth Strickland answered the door wearing a flannel robe, her hair tousled from sleep. When she saw Ephraim, her eyes flooded. "You know."

Ephraim grabbed her arm and shoved her backward into the house.

"You're hurting me."

"What are you doing on Monhegan? Why did you lie about leaving? What's going on, Elizabeth?"

"Nothing's going on," she said through tears. "The storm cancelled yesterday's ferry."

"You broke into Elena's cottage." It was a statement, not a question.

Beth shook her head violently, sobs crescendoing. "Last night I remembered Elena still had the note. I had to get it back. I didn't break in. The door wasn't locked. When I heard someone knock, I got scared and ran. I didn't take anything, I swear. I've been good, Ephraim. I visit my therapist every week. I've kept my distance."

His laugh was a mirthless bark. "Yeah? Then why are we having this conversation?"

Beth stared at her bare feet. "I saw you and Elena at a restaurant in Port Clyde last spring. I guess I was jealous."

Ephraim caught her face in his hands and forced her to meet his eyes. "Look at me when you talk to me."

Vivienne put a hand on his arm. "Take it easy, Ephraim."

"I followed Elena to Monhegan," Beth said. "We became friends."

"You lied to her," Ephraim said.

"Only at first. I told her you and I dated, warned her that you threatened me. I showed her the note, and she stopped seeing you."

"Did you hurt her, Elizabeth?" Ephraim asked, every muscle in his body taut with fury. "Did you?"

Beth blinked, eyes wide. "No. I told you, we were friends. I cared about Elena. Finding her was the worst thing that's ever happened to me."

Vivienne stepped closer to Beth. "Judith Porter said you didn't like El, that you talked about her behind her back."

"That skinny old bitch is the backbiter, not me."

"You told me Ephraim had something to do with my sister taking her life."

Beth's eyes shifted from Vivienne to Ephraim then back again. "I saw the way he looked at you. I thought if you believed he was responsible for Elena's death, you'd stay away from him."

"Do you believe her?" Vivienne asked Ephraim. They stood together on the front porch of Vivienne's cottage under a moon as bright as winter sun.

"I don't know. Maybe. She seemed apologetic. That's something new. I'm heading back to Port Clyde tomorrow. She damned well better be on that ferry."

He reached out and stroked Vivienne's hair, and she pushed him away. "I know you had unfinished business with my sister, but I'm not El. You can't find closure with me."

"I wasn't—"

"Yes, you were," she said on a long breath. "Dinner is ruined and I need time to think, to sort things out. El, the cottage, everything. Go back to Hitchcock House, Ephraim. Please."

He did. Vivienne watched his back get smaller and smaller until he was out of sight. Then she sat on the porch steps and wept.

"Shh, dear. Can't be bad as all that." Judith Porter placed a comforting hand on her back. "Cold out here. Let's get you inside. I'll fix you a cup of hot tea. I hoped we could talk about the cottage."

"Another time, Judith. Okay?"

"The tea is non-negotiable. You're shivering." Judith opened the door, and gently prodded Vivienne inside.

"I'm fine, really."

"Don't be silly, it's no trouble. Cozy up on the sofa, I won't be a moment."

The tea tasted hot, soothing, and foul. "What kind of tea is this?" Vivienne asked.

"Chamomile. I put in honey and a little something to help you relax."

All at once, Vivienne's eyelids seemed to weigh a ton. She tried to get to her feet but fell back on the couch. "You drugged my tea?"

"Don't be silly, dear. Let the tea work its magic. You know, Vivi, Elena used to talk about you all the time. About how much you disliked Monhegan. Your sister loved the island. She'd never have left of her own free will. Such a beautiful, peaceful place. But you? We knew you'd sell the cottage once you inherited. Did that handsome lawyer mention Charles and I have had our eye on becoming Monhegan property owners for a while now? But with so few year-round properties available—well, we're not getting any younger, are we? We have to grab our opportunities where and when we can."

Vivienne's tongue felt swollen, too big to wrap around words.

"I think we may have given her too much, Charles. Can you help her upstairs?"

Charles? What was Charles doing here?

"Of course, my love. I've already run the bath."

"Don't forget to leave her empty pill bottle within reach," Judith said. "And this time make sure her arms are inside the tub. Last thing we need is another bloody mess in our new bathroom."

Vivienne felt herself being pulled to her feet as Charles's hot, stale breath whispered against her ear. "Don't worry, beautiful. All you need to do is close your eyes, relax and pretend you're floating out to sea."

VR Barkowski is a third generation Californian transplanted to Atlanta, who writes about New England. A finalist for the 2012 Daphne Du Maurier and Claymore Awards for her unpublished novel, *A Twist of Hate*, VR's short fiction has appeared in *Mysterical-E* and *Spinetingler*. Visit VR's website at www.vrbarkowski.com.

No Corners

John Bubar

It all started when I couldn't explain away the nagging fatigue and a sneaky little back pain that had insidiously crept over me. I reviewed my nutrition plan and decided to vary my caloric intake, fasting every Tuesday, Thursday, and Sunday. Then I added thirty minutes of sleep a night; then I tried sleeping an hour less than usual. I took a week off from the gym forty-seven days earlier than my scheduled week off. I doubled my meditation schedule. Nothing worked. Finally I went to see my doctor.

One blood test, one CAT scan, one PET scan and nine days later I was sitting in the examining room of Dr. Michael Patrick McDermott, the premier oncologist at Massachusetts General. His diplomas from Boston College and Harvard Medical School hung on the wall in understated gold frames. The day's *Boston Globe* lay on the counter next to the sink.

Dr. McDermott washed his hands while he said hello, although he would never examine me. He was thorough, articulate, and empathetic as he delivered the bad news.

"How long?" I asked.

"Twelve to eighteen months, Mr. Wheeler. Except for the cancer, you're in great shape. You might live two years, but this is a pretty aggressive form of the disease, and there's evidence that the cancer has metastasized from the pancreas to the lymph nodes and a rib."

"Treatment options?" There must be a way to cure this. For the first time in years, I felt like praying. Strange thought for an avowed atheist.

"Surgery's not practical. You couldn't stand to be radiated

everywhere we see the cancer has spread. That leaves chemo, but I'm afraid those therapies don't have a very good success rate for this cancer."

"How not 'very good'?" I needed to know the odds.

"Zero."

He never broke eye contact with me. I admired him for that, but it was admiration from a distance. Close in, I was churning. "I've done everything right all my life: diet, exercise, stress reduction techniques. I've seriously considered becoming a Buddhist."

"I know, Mr. Wheeler. I've talked with Dr. Fallon. He's been your doc for twenty years and he's perplexed, to say the least. Do you have family nearby? A support system?"

"No. I'm a foster home kid. Many foster homes. And women seem to . . . I knew something would get me. But not this, not now. I'm fifty-five. I just retired two months ago. I've planned out my life since I was twenty-three. I'm right on schedule. I had a physical six months ago. I was fine."

"Cancer is like a thief in the night, Mr. Wheeler. What's stolen often doesn't present itself until long after the fact."

"So?" There must be a way out.

"Chemo is available if you wish to try that route. Just let me know."

"What would chemo be like?"

"We try to kill the cancer with poison before we kill you."

"And without the chemo? What will it be like, toward the end?"

"More fatigue, sudden weight loss, then the pain will begin." He hesitated, letting me digest his answer. "Of course, there will be pain, chemo or no, but we're pretty good at controlling it. Again, just let me know what you decide." He rose, shook my hand, and left. Dr. McDermott had never once said he was sorry nor shied away from how awful this was going to be. I liked that too.

Over lunch—oatmeal, skim milk and blueberries—I decided Dr. McDermott was wrong. Good guy, but busy, he could hardly know everything about the latest developments in treating cancer. So I got on my computer, Googled up cancer, and began to search for a cure. Three long days later, I decided that Dr. McDermott was right.

I also decided that Leo Suggs had to die.

One of the side roads I had taken during my Internet search

led me to a *New York Times* article on significant emotional events as a potential cause of cancer. The research appeared to show that approximately eighteen months after a stressful life event, cancer often presented itself. Exactly eighteen months ago, Leo Suggs had stolen my identity.

As a former senior auditor in the IRS's Boston office, I knew how to protect myself against such things: periodic password changes, sophisticated computer firewalls, scheduled scrutiny of personal accounts, a watchful eye on anyone who ever touched my credit card, cross shredding all documents that held any personal information. I did it all. What I couldn't control was the good-looking, smooth-talking Leo Suggs, who, I had learned off-the-record from the FBI, had targeted and subsequently seduced a young woman who worked in the IT department of my brokerage firm. A somewhat slow young woman, she had to take her work home on the weekends just to keep up.

One Saturday, while she was out getting her hair done, Leo had let himself into her apartment with the key she had given him, copied a file she had brought home, then driven to one of Boston's finer suburbs and sold the file to a man who knew a man. Leo received ten thousand dollars for his betrayal.

Thirty-six hours later my brokerage account was gone. The buyers of this information also used my wire transfer information to empty my bank accounts and then they took out two loans in my name. I was heartsick, then angry, then heartsick again.

Oh, I finally got it all back, but I spent a fortune on lawyers, dealt every day with creditors calling, still didn't have my credit rating straightened out, and had to change virtually every business relationship I had nurtured for years. My life had been a mess back then, and I was now sure, three days after being handed my death sentence, and with my research in hand, that the actions of Leo Suggs had precipitated my cancer. The enormity of my anguish had overwhelmed my defenses at the cellular level.

Sitting at my computer that day, I knew that no judge would allow a charge of murder to be brought against Leo Suggs. But murder it was, and the only way justice could be served was for me to kill him before, ultimately, he would kill me.

The good news was, I knew where to find Leo. I had made a

friend of sorts in the FBI while working on some white-collar fraud cases. Unofficially he told me the story. It seems the young lady, whom Leo had so charmed, had been quite a romantic and had kept the champagne glasses she and Leo had used their first night together, unwashed and on a high shelf above the refrigerator. Leo's prints were perfectly preserved; he was an open book. His mother, who lived in Las Vegas, answered on the first ring. "Leo? Why yes, officer, he's right here." Leo waived extradition and was returned to Boston, where his trial had been set for nine months from now, the Federal Prosecutor dragging his feet on the trial date because Leo was cooperating, turning on his accomplices like the rat he was.

I remember the peace I felt the night I decided that Leo would die. Tired and way off my nutrition plan due to my three days of almost continuous research, I went to bed happier than I had been for some time. The next morning, I got back with the oatmeal, although I did pour some maple syrup in with the skim milk. I'd taken a research break the day before to do some shopping, and the syrup had been on sale, along with a chocolate cake. I bought them knowing I'd need a sugar pick-me-up available. I'd eaten the last of the cake before I went to bed, and it must have inspired me. When I woke up, I realized I couldn't just show up and kill Fucking Leo.

I never cursed out loud like that and seldom even thought those words. As an IRS auditor, I had spent a good deal of time being cursed at by the public, and I had never stooped to their level of inarticulate expression, but I had arisen that morning thinking of Leo as Fucking Leo, a perfectly articulate description of the man, and one from which I took an inordinate amount of pleasure. Meanwhile, my subconscious had been working overtime while I slept, and I awoke with the conscious conclusion that when Fucking Leo was killed, the cops would come looking for me. I had made a fair amount of noise about Leo, and my acquaintance in the FBI would remember. Not wanting to spend my last days on earth with cops and lawyers, I wrestled with the question: What to do? What to do?

The obvious answer came to me while munching on some leftover Halloween Snickers I had been meaning to throw out. I would disguise Fucking Leo's death by becoming a fake serial killer.

It would take a lot of Internet searching to pull this off, so I decided to lay in some supplies and avoid my normal daily shopping routine during my serial killer research period. I would need something to calm my nerves—I was already feeling anxious at the whole idea of this—and settled on alcohol. Never having been much of a drinker, I had no idea what would go with Snickers and chocolate cake, so I got a little of everything. For the next five days I packed my lunch and went to libraries and Internet cafes in towns where no one knew me. If I ever became a suspect, some smart guy analyzing my personal hard drive wouldn't see where I'd been going in cyberspace.

Eating in my pickup as I drove from one place to another, I celebrated my daily successes in the evenings at home with French red wines and Belgian chocolates. It was a tough five days. I was tired, probably the cancer eating away at me, but I had developed a hit list of seven identity thieves within a twelve-to-sixteen-hour drive. For the next two weeks I would stay inside my house for two to three days at a time and go nowhere, do nothing, leave no electronic trail inside or out. I had made a career out of following electronic trails and I wasn't planning on leaving one.

Occasionally I would let a neighbor see me in preparation for that first interrogation.

"Mr. Ernest Henry Wheeler?"

"Yes, officer. I am." Very calm, I'd be very calm.

"Where were you on (fill in the date)?"

"Right here at home." Very calm with a note of sadness.

"Can you prove that?"

"Why, no, probably not, officer. I live alone, and just six months ago I was diagnosed with terminal cancer. I don't have long and I take solace in being alone. I've spent a lot of time with myself these past few months."

Come and get the dead-man-walking now, asshole. I'd never say that of course, I don't curse, but I liked the way the words sounded in my head.

On the days I did sneak out, I collected the tools of my new trade. I bought a rifle up in Maine, a .270 Winchester Model 70 that could reach out 800 meters. It was a private sale, came with a hundred rounds of 160 grain ammo, no waiting period, no background check, paid cash, saw your ad in the paper, call me Wheels. The next week at a gun show in Brattleboro, Vermont, I bought a Leupold VX-1 scope to fit it. Then I joined a Rod and Gun club just across the border in New Hampshire because they had a firing range that was open all year and unsupervised. I paid cash, said call me Hal, they never asked for ID. I sighted my rifle in and, after a week's practice, judged myself adequate at three hundred yards. You can learn to do anything with the help of the Internet, practice, and in this case, a half-dozen folks needing to sell their spare .270 ammo. So they told me.

I also bought ten five-gallon gas cans at ten different stores. My plan was to carry them in the bed of my pickup under the tonneau cover, so I wouldn't have to stop at a gas station. There are security cameras everywhere. I'd once nailed a guy for fraud based on a filling station surveillance tape. And I bought a sleeping bag, some warm flannel shirts, work pants, a dark jacket, and a brown baseball cap. I planned to sleep in my truck, but if I had to go into a truck stop I wanted to blend in with the guys.

I took down Number One at two hundred yards, a center mass shot as he stepped onto his front stoop to pick up the morning paper. A two-time loser out on parole, he was living in his hometown just east of Syracuse. His phone number was listed in his real name, and he had been easy to find. I'd driven through the night, found a place with a clear view of the kill zone, and made the shot from the bed of my pickup, where I had hidden underneath the cover. I left the rifle in the truck bed, got into the driver's seat, and eased away. *Kill zone—center mass*, my research had generated a whole new vocabulary of words and phrases that were populating my internal monologues.

Numbers Two and Three went much the same way. They both lived in neighborhoods where nobody saw anything. I expected to hear sirens as I made each getaway, but I never did. The local newspapers covered the stories on page one and never failed to mention their records and the possibility of numerous enemies. I'd spaced them out two weeks apart and in two different states.

Number Four was a problem. I always updated my research a few days before I was to leave, and Number Four had moved to Pittsburgh from the small hick town in central Pennsylvania where I'd initially found her. Pittsburgh was on the outer edge of the window I had set for my travel time away from home. I'd have to find a no-camera gas station since it was a big city with big city cops and there would be lots of people. I decided to do a dry run.

I followed her to the restaurant where she worked and watched her filch two credit card numbers from customers. Then she showed me the way. At two in the afternoon she took a smoke break in the alley behind the kitchen. That smoking will kill you. A week later I took a shot from the top of a building abutting the alley and beat the cigarettes to the punch.

On my way to Number Five I wrestled with a serious emerging problem. I'd planned on Fucking Leo being Number Six with Number Seven serving just to keep the serial killer thing in play, but it didn't appear that the serial killer thing was in play. To the best of my knowledge, nobody had connected the dots. Maybe nobody cared if a few small time hoods bought it. Maybe I'd spread them out in time and geography such that the dots were too far apart.

I stopped at a little diner overlooking the Hudson River. Coffee and a cheeseburger would help me think. Coffee was something new for me. I found the caffeine helped fight the fatigue. I was sleeping well enough, and the fatigue only gnawed away at me occasionally; I knew the cancer was gnawing away at me continuously and supposed that I was fighting the weight loss with chocolate and alcohol. Eight months had passed since McDermott delivered my death sentence. A quick eight months, I was thinking, when the two guys in the booth behind me got into an argument about one of them owing the other money. The owner threw them out.

"Fucking idiots," I said, and then realized I'd said it out loud. The waitress looked at me and began moving quickly in my direction. Shit, I was out of there. The last thing I needed was to draw attention to myself. Maybe if I threw twice what I owed next to my plate, all would be forgiven. On the other hand, maybe she'd remember me as the big tipper. Damn, what to do?

"You said it, handsome," she murmured under her breath. "Can I warm that coffee up for you?"

Her name was Rose and her shift would end in ten minutes. She'd take her tip in the form of a drink at a place just down the road, if I were staying in town long enough. I wasn't, but I did. And then one thing led to another, and I discovered that Rose was a master of both.

In the morning she said, "Ernie, how about bacon and eggs? I know we should be digging into oatmeal like they say on the TV, but you're not going to live forever, are you? And what's the H stand for in Ernest H. Wheeler?" She had pulled on my old sweatshirt when she got out of bed and had just discovered the nametag I had sewn in it. I used to sew them into all my clothes.

"Hemingway," I lied. "My mother was a fan. My friends call me Hem." I don't know why I lied. Maybe because of the beard I'd grown.

"You do look a little bit like him at that," she said.

Over breakfast she asked what I did for a living. "I'm a writer," I told her. *Go, Hem, go.* "And I'm doing some traveling to get some scenes in my head."

"Will I see you again?" she asked.

"Probably," I said, and Number Five became a dry run that day. I took him down a week later after another breakfast with Rose.

The day Fucking Leo went to his reward, *The Boston Globe* and *The New York Times* each received a copy of the five newspaper stories chronicling the lives and times of Numbers One through Five. Any moron could see what they all had in common.

That night, Leo Fucking Suggs came out of the Chelsea bar he went to every Friday for Happy Hour and I popped him from four hundred and forty yards. I'd gotten a Zeiss Victory PRF Rangefinder just for the occasion. No wind and not much humidity. Calculated bullet drop was twenty-five point two inches. A headshot, one of my best. He'd been pretty in an effeminate sort of way.

A month later I got Number Seven while he mowed his lawn. The *Globe* and the *Times* had broken the story of the Identity Thief Sniper (ITS), and I suppose Number Seven felt safe from a long shot while he mowed his lawn in his high fenced backyard. He never expected a meter reader packing a .380 PPK with a DTA Nano suppressor. The neighbors never heard the silenced pop of a pistol round over the sound of the mower.

In the month since Number Seven went down, I've found two more, Numbers Eight and Nine, both of them just a short drive from Rose's place. I'm beginning to like the pistol more than the rifle. I had only turned to the pistol out of necessity, but I feel stealthier with it now. I'm still tired. No pain yet. I've lost two pounds recently, but that could be because Rose has just gone on a diet. That Rose is a piece of work. It tickles her that I've set my laptop up in her living room and do my writing there. I just jot down whatever glimmers I might have, and when she gets home from work I try out dialogue on her.

It's made me a little more philosophical, this pretending to be a writer. For years I watched myself, my colleagues, the people we audited; we were all so predictable. All the choices we had ever made in our lives conspired with each other to drive the choices we were going to make next. We spent our lives slowly painting ourselves into behavioral corners. And then one day I'm told I've got a little over a year to live and I spend that time living as if I had no corners.

It's been almost a year to the day since I sat in this chair, in this waiting room, waiting for Dr. McDermott to deliver his diagnosis. His office called two weeks ago for an annual follow up. "We'd like to measure the progress of the disease," his scheduler had said. *Progress of the disease, my ass. Here I am getting eaten alive and they dress it up with "progress of the disease."*

"Mr. Wheeler, Dr. McDermott will see you now." His nurse gives me a funny look as I walk into the exam room. Probably didn't expect I'd make it this long.

"Hello, Mr. Wheeler." Dr. McDermott hasn't changed a bit. "How do you feel?" He's grinning at me.

"A little tired. Weight's been mostly steady. Lost two pounds recently. No pain yet."

"I'm not surprised. Those tests we ran last week show a complete remission. I've never seen this happen before." He can't stop grinning at me. "I've only read about it in medical journals. We can't find a trace of the cancer." He shakes my hand.

"Complete remission?" I feel lightheaded. Dr. McDermott steadies me.

"Absolutely complete, Mr. Wheeler. I don't know what you've been doing this past year, but whatever it is, I recommend you keep on doing it."

After thirty-six years as a pilot in military and civilian aviation, **John Bubar** is currently finishing his MFA in Writing at the University of New Hampshire. His short story, "Ambush," was published in Level Best Books' *Best New England Crime Stories: Dead Calm*.

Death from a Bad Heart

B.B. Oak

August 15, 1847

Although I consider Henry David Thoreau a good friend, we see each other infrequently. My medical practice keeps me in Boston and Henry cannot abide city bustle. When he makes an occasional sojourn to the Athenaeum, however, he usually stops by my Beacon Hill office before going back to the solitary peace of his cabin. And when I take the cars to visit relations, it is my custom to walk from the Concord train depot to Walden Pond before going on to neighboring Plumford.

Last week I did just that. 'Twas a fine August afternoon with high clouds and a cooling breeze, thus my stride was brisk and I arrived at the pond in half an hour. Much to my surprise, there were a number of people in front of Henry's modest abode. And all female! They were listening to a tall, slender lady holding forth from Henry's front step. I recognized her to be Mrs. Emerson and as I came within earshot I understood her subject to be Abolitionism. Henry stood a little away from the others, as is his wont, and gave Mrs. Emerson his rapt attention. He did not notice my arrival but his sister Helen came toward me, a smile lighting up her plain countenance.

"I pray I am not intruding," I said.

"Not at all, Dr. Walker," Miss Thoreau assured me. "The Concord Female Anti-Slavery Society is always open to male participation. In fact, Ralph Waldo Emerson was invited to address us today, as he did last year, but apparently a far more important speaking engagement took precedence." Her tone had an ironic edge to it, as her brother's often did.

"I see that Mr. Emerson's wife is declaiming his address for him," I said.

Miss Thoreau gave me a rather severe look. "Lidian does not need to parrot her husband's words, doctor. She is a founding member of our society and can express her own convictions."

We both turned our attention to Mrs. Emerson, who was indeed speaking with moving eloquence about women banding together to free their black sisters from the wretched cruelties and tyranny of enslavement. Only after she had uttered her last words and stepped down from the front step to mingle with the other ladies did Henry look around and spot me.

"Adam! High time you came by," he said, giving my hand a hard shake. "You have not paid me a visit all summer."

"I did not wish to intrude on your solitude, Henry. But it appears you have become quite sociable." I gestured toward the flock of petticoats milling about.

Henry shrugged and his homespun frock coat bunched up at his shoulders. "My mother and sisters insisted that the rally be held here."

"That is not quite true, dear brother," Helen said. "It was *last* year we insisted. This year you told Mrs. Emerson you would be happy to host the event again. According to her, you were most gracious about it, which surprised me considerably."

"Ah, so I did."

Looking uncomfortable, Henry ran a hand through his thick thatch of hair, mussing it even more. His large, luminous orbs sought out Mrs. Emerson and when at last she came to us, bearing a plate of gingerbread, he stared at her and she stared back at him in deep silence. Helen paid them little mind. Instead, her attention was drawn to a slight figure walking along the edge of the pond.

"Ah, there's that boy Jack," she said. "He's been coming 'round all summer begging for work. Mother often invites him to sup with us, on the condition he have a good wash-up beforehand. We would like to see what he looks like without all that soot on his face. But he always refuses the invitation. Have you made his acquaintance, Henry?"

"We have never said more than 'Good day' to each other as he passes here on the way to his shanty. He seems disinclined to make friends with anyone. Observe how he is hugging the shore to stay as far away from us as possible now."

"He is more solitary than even you, Henry," his sister said. "And that shack he lives in is even smaller than your hut."

"Has the boy no family?" I asked.

"None we know of," Helen said. "We surmise his father was part of the Irish crew brought in to work on the railroad tracks. He must have run off and left his boy to fend for himself."

"I am sure Jack would fancy some gingerbread," Mrs. Emerson said. "Pray go ask him to join us, Henry."

"Better yet, I will fetch it to him," he replied. "Methinks he would much prefer that."

Henry wrapped a man's portion of gingerbread in a napkin and went down to the shore to meet up with the boy. As Jack accepted the bundle, the breeze blew off his cap. Henry, so quick with his hands that he can catch a trout in them, snatched the cap midair before it landed in the water, placed it back on the boy's shaggy black head, and gave him a hearty pat on the back in parting.

The ladies left soon after that. Henry and I watched their long-brimmed bonnets slide away through the pines as they purposefully marched toward town. None but one looked back. Glancing over her shoulder, Mrs. Emerson gave Henry a quick parting smile.

Only after she was well out of sight did Henry invite me inside his cabin. The space he dwells in is small and spare yet so open and airy it seems part of the outdoors, the walls and windows akin to tree trunks and sky. Chipmunks and chickadees bound and flutter inside without a trace of hesitation, looking for the seeds and nuts Henry so generously supplies.

He took to his rocker and waved me to the chair by his small, green-painted desk, the only other seat in the room. Displayed upon the desk was a trove of Indian artifacts, and I hefted a pestle hewn from dark stone and polished smooth by long-dead hands.

"I spied it on a sandy spot down in the Great Meadows," Henry said, "amongst a half-dozen quartz arrowheads shaped as tiny triangles. They are all stone fruits to me. Each yields me a juicy fossil thought."

I looked around at Henry's other treasures. There were delicate pieces of newly hatched turtle shell on the window sill, a monstrous toadstool on his hearth stone, and a humble little bird's nest on the narrow chimney mantel.

"Could there be any finer residence to raise up a family?" Henry said as I gave the nest a cursory look. "Note how the twigs and moss are intertwined with bits of ribbon and string and even hair. The economical little warbler worries from a human habitation what it requires for its own. We are all in the end little bits and pieces of each other and the stars, are we not?"

"The older I get the more I appreciate that," I replied.

Henry smiled. "You are barely midway into your twenties, Adam."

"You are no more than thirty yourself," I countered.

"Yes, we both have a long life of learning ahead of us," he said. "Let us appreciate each moment of it to the utmost. By the way, in a bog not far from here I came across a medicinal plant you inquired after."

"*Drosera rotundifolia?*" Since reading about its efficacious treatment for lung disease in ancient botanical texts, I have wanted to test its efficacy myself. From Henry's smile I could see I had guessed correctly. "Let us go find it!"

Henry snatched up a satchel to hold the specimens and we headed toward the bog. Along the way we heard a thrashing through the underbrush, as if an animal were fleeing from a predator. But it was the boy Jack who burst through the trees, eyes wild with panic. A root snared his left foot and he pitched headlong in front of us, the wind thoroughly knocked from his lungs. Gasping like a drowning colt, he attempted to right himself but when he stepped on his left foot he screamed in pain and fell down in a dead faint.

We knelt over him and I glanced into the woods to see what breed of demon could precipitate such panicked flight. There was no pursuer that I could discern and I turned my attention back to the boy. Studying his dirty face, I noted that his nose was crooked. It appeared to have been broken more than once in the past. And one of his ears was so deformed it resembled a cauliflower. I had seen this deformity before on a Boston boxer, the result of severe blows to the ear from opponents. The boy's condition, I surmised, likewise came from repeated blows, most likely from his father. He was well rid of such a brutish parent, no matter how hard he must struggle on his own now.

His eyes flew open and he stared up at us with an expression of terror.

"You are safe now," Henry gently assured him.

We sat him up and I loosened his left boot. When I felt his injured ankle he winced, but a probing with my fingers indicated no bones had been broken. His obvious pain, however, indicated a severe sprain.

"What frightened you so?" Henry asked him.

Jack buried his face in his hands and rocked back and forth. "There is a dead man in the woods," he said.

"Show us where," Henry said.

"But I cannot walk!" Jack protested, looking up at him beseechingly.

"Yes, you can, if we help you," Henry said. "Be a man about it, boy." And with that he hoisted Jack to his feet.

Henry and I supported him between us and we went through the woods whence he'd come until Jack stopped and pointed toward a stand of white pines. "Over there," he said and would go no farther.

We seated him down on a stump and continued another five rods or so, until we found the supine body of a man of perhaps fifty years of age and corpulent to excess.

"Is he dead, doctor?" Henry asked me.

I knelt down and felt for the man's pulse. There was none. But he was warm to the touch and there was no sign of rigor mortis. "Yes, but I estimate he was alive half an hour ago."

"Can you ascertain how he died?"

I removed his frock coat, vest and neck cloth and unbuttoned his linen shirt, which was soaked through with sweat. "I see no cuts or lacerations," I said and passed my hands over the man's well-muscled torso and limbs. "Nor do I feel any broken bones."

Henry crouched down beside me and detached the leather wallet attached to the man's trouser belt. "No papers to identify him," he said, looking into the canvas slots. "But there are bank notes amounting to ten dollars. So he was not robbed before or after death." He reattached the wallet and regarded the corpse with fixed attention, his keen eyes soaking up every detail. "There is blood on the rock beneath his head."

It was such a small amount that I had not noticed. "He must

have lost consciousness, hit his head against the rock, and the trauma caused his ear to bleed."

"Do you think that killed him?"

"No," I said. "Most likely he died of heart failure. He is quite fat and must have exerted himself greatly to cause so much excretion of perspiration."

"Yet being a blacksmith, he was used to hard labor," Henry said.

"You conjecture blacksmithing was his occupation?"

"I am sure of it. Observe how heavily calloused his hands are from lifting heavy tools. And look at all the scars on the backs of them. Not ordinary burn marks one gets from tending a wood fire, but round pits resulting from white hot metal shards that sear into the flesh. Moreover, the black beneath his fingernails and sunk into the creases of his eyes and neck comes from long years spent at a coal forge." Henry bent down and breathed in deeply through his prominent nose. "Yes, I can smell the odor of hot wrought iron and charcoal in his hair, but only faintly. He has not been at his forge for some time. What was he doing out here in the woods, I wonder."

"Can't you tell by simply observing?" I said, admittedly with a trace of acerbity.

After a brief glance around, Henry strode over to a pine tree. "Hunting," he said, picking up a fowling piece that had lain hidden in the shade of its boughs. "But what game could he be pursuing?"

"Grouse?" I ventured.

"Or songbirds," Henry said, looking down at the corpse. "There is a brutish cast to his visage that makes me suppose he would not have thought twice about destroying any lovely creature that crossed his path."

A sob from Jack broke our speculations. "I want to be away from here," he wailed.

Henry offered to carry him to the Thoreau home in town so he could be looked after until his ankle mended, but the boy objected to this suggestion most vigorously.

"I want to go back to the shanty and if you will not help me I will crawl to it on my own," he said.

Henry hauled him upright. "I will help you there, lad." He turned to me. "Then I will go on to town and notify the constable. You do not mind staying with the corpse, do you, Adam? We do not want woodland creatures bothering it."

I minded not at all for I have kept company with many a corpse during my years spent dissecting cadavers at Harvard Medical School. About an hour later Henry returned alone. He must have run all the way back from town for he was breathing hard. He informed me that Constable Staples and the coroner were rounding up a jury and would arrive shortly. The undertaker was also on his way with a wagon.

"I am glad I beat them here," he said. "I wanted to confer with you alone, Adam. You should know that I did not mention Jack's part in this to anyone. I see no reason to involve the lad."

"Jack is already involved, Henry. He was, after all, the first one to come upon the body."

"And you and I came upon it shortly thereafter. Our testimony will be far more accurate than the boy's. He was too distraught to notice much, and he is so excessively tongue-tied that he would make a poor witness indeed. The jury would surely discount anything he managed to utter, so why put him through the anguish of testifying? When I left him at the shanty he was still trembling like an aspen leaf."

"I will go check on him when we are done with the jury," I said.

"Then you agree it is not necessary to bring him back here to bear witness?"

I nodded. "He seems of a most frail constitution and further strain on his ankle might well injure it the more. I shall not mention his name during the proceedings."

Henry clapped me on the back. "It is the right thing to do for the right reason."

We soon heard the rattle and clop of two wagons, thence the tread of nine men coming toward us through the woods. We called out to guide them in the right direction and soon the six jurors and the coroner were arranging themselves around the body whilst the constable and undertaker stood aside.

"Does anyone here know who the deceased man is?" the coroner asked.

"I do," one of the men replied.

I knew this juror to be the keeper of the tavern by the Concord depot as I am not amiss to imbibing a small beer before taking the cars back to Boston.

"He boarded with me for the last week," the taverner continued. "His name was Hacker and he was a blacksmith up by Lowell."

"Weren't he the feller who et that spoiled meat at yer tavern last evening and got sich a bad bellyache he near keeled over?" another juror asked.

"The meat was not spoiled!" the taverner protested.

"Well, didn't this here Mr. Hacker git all red in the face and clutch his fist to his chest, moanin' mightily, aftah consuming a bowl of yer wife's mutton stew?" the man persisted. "That's what I heard, anyways."

The taverner sighed. "I feared such a false rumor would start when Mr. Hacker had his seizure. But it was caused by his bad heart, not bad meat."

"How do you know this?" I said.

"Why, he told me so himself when I helped him up to his chamber. He said he'd suffered such attacks before and then he took a small glass vial from his valise and swallowed down the contents. Whatever it was seemed to put him to rights."

"I venture it was digitalis," I said, "oft prescribed for the treatment of heart conditions."

"Well, it worked, for this morning he claimed he felt fit enough to go hunting and inquired about where to find game in the area. He had brought along his shooting iron and was most eager to employ it."

"Odd that he would come down to Concord, of all places, to hunt game," Henry said.

Another juror spoke up. "Oh, t'weren't game that brought him here. He was lookin' for his wife who run away a few months ago. Went from farm to farm all around here, he did, hopin' someone had seen a young woman with long yeller hair who might be askin' for needlework for that were her trade. I never spoke to Mr. Hacker myself but my son did. He felt mighty sorry for the feller but could not help him."

All the jury men shook their heads as they gazed down at the corpse. "Poor soul," one of them muttered. "Wimmen!" another grumbled.

Once they were through commiserating, I gave them a report of my examination, which was compatible with the taverner's testimony concerning Hacker's heart condition. The jury speedily concluded his death was caused by heart failure and proceeded to hoist him into the undertaker's wagon. It was not until the wagons were out of sight that I spied the clothes on the ground that I had removed from the corpse.

"I will take them to the undertaker's on the morrow," Henry said, "so Mr. Hacker can be laid to rest properly dressed. The money in his wallet will be more than enough to compensate the undertaker."

We then went to the shanty to see how Jack was faring. The ramshackle edifice was not much bigger than an outhouse, with a lopsided door barely hanging from its hinges but shut tight. Henry eased it open and we found the boy curled up on a straw mattress, his head resting upon a shabby carpetbag. The room was surprisingly tidy, with two pots hung by yarn loops from nails on the wall and a bouquet of wildflowers in a chipped clay pot by the bed, where Jack would see it first thing when he opened his eyes. He did not open his eyes upon our arrival, however. I took such sound sleep to be a good sign that he was not in pain. When I leaned over him to listen to his breathing, which was deep and regular, I noticed a green woolen scarf wrapped around his thin neck. He clutched one end of it like a talisman and I wondered who had knitted it for him. Perhaps he'd once had some gentle female influence in his life to assuage his father's brutality. I told Henry there was no need to disturb the boy and we left.

Henry invited me back to his cabin to have a cup of sassafras tea. After putting Hacker's forgotten outer garments on the chair, he started a fire in his little stove, and put on a pot of water. Then he plunked himself down in his rocker, picked up his flute and played a simple tune again and again as we waited for the water to boil. I could tell he was deep in thought and let him be. But as I was removing Hacker's clothes from the chair in order to sit on it, something roused my curiosity and I brought it to his attention.

"Lo, Henry. I feel what seems to be hard coins in the lining of this frock coat."

He immediately put down his flute and looked on as I pried three gold coins from the shoulder lining. Upon further investigation I also found bank notes slid into the coat lining that amounted to the sum of fifty dollars.

"It appears Hacker supplied himself with enough money to travel long and far in search of his wife," Henry said. "I am sure she will much appreciate this goodly bequest."

"I reckon Hacker's widow is his rightful heir even though she deserted him," I allowed. "But how can she be found?"

"Easily enough," Henry said. "We simply return to the boy's shanty."

"What does Jack have to do with it?"

Henry smiled at my confusion. "Mrs. Hacker *is* Jack, my friend. I have been contemplating whether or not to burden you with this knowledge but now I see that I must. Else you will not agree to hand over this small fortune to Jack."

"How can I agree when it is not rightfully his, Henry? I understand why you would like to give it to him, of course. It would change his sad life for the better. But you cannot convince me that he is Mrs. Hacker."

"Well, here is the proof of it." Henry plucked the bird's nest off his mantel and handed it to me.

I gave out a hollow laugh, assuming he was jesting. He was not.

"Look at it closely, Adam," he enjoined. "You will see interwoven throughout it a quantity of long, blond strands of hair. Did not Hacker describe his wife as having long, yellow hair?"

"Yes, but any—"

Henry raised his hand to quell my objection and continued. "I know. Such tresses could belong to any blond woman. However, who but Mrs. Hacker, desperate to disguise herself, would have chopped off such lengths of hair in the woods, leaving them for a local warbler to find? 'Tis her hair for sure."

"But Jack's hair is black as coal," I reminded him.

"Because it is coal dust that was used to darken it!" Henry said. "When I caught Jack's cap this afternoon, I observed the rim was stained with soot. Mrs. Hacker rubbed it in her hair and also on her face to disguise her womanly features. But did you note how clean Jack's hands were?"

"No, I assumed—"

Henry cut me off again. "Most people assume that he is just a dirty little urchin and do not give him a closer look. That was Mrs. Hacker's intention, of course. She knew her husband would come looking for her, hence she had to conceal her true nature as best she could. But the observant eye sees what easily passes unnoticed by most. And I noticed that Jack had the smooth hands of a needlewoman, as Hacker claimed his wife to be."

The image of Jack's pale hand clutching the scarf as he slept sprang to my mind.

"It's not what you look at that matters," Henry continued, "it's what you *see*, Adam. For instance, that green scarf around Jack's neck. It had been recently knitted by the person who occupied the shanty, for the pots were hung with the same color yarn. And did you notice the jar of flowers by Jack's bed?"

"Well, yes, I did notice that."

"Did you not think it a sign of a feminine nature rather than the nature of a rough and tumble boy?"

In truth, I had thought nothing much of it at all. "What else did you see that I did not, Henry?"

"When I helped Jack home before fetching the coroner, I saw that the door to the shanty had been left wide open," he informed me. "I also saw upon the ground by the doorway a swath of knitted fabric hanging off a needle. This leads me to believe that Hacker discovered his wife's whereabouts and when she spied him coming toward the shanty, she fled, dropping her handiwork in the process."

"And he chased after her, gun in hand!" I said, easily imagining the scene. "Fortunately for her, his heart seized up before he caught her."

Henry did not seem to be listening to me. "Knitting hanging off a needle," he murmured, frowning.

We went back to the shanty forthwith and because Henry had lifted the scales from my eyes, I did indeed see that the person I had taken to be a boy was really a young woman. Through a torrent of tears she told us that she had endured Hacker's beatings throughout the three years of their marriage until a day came when she could take it no longer. Having no laws to protect her, no relations close by, she ran away. But he was so relentless in his pursuit of her that she had to resort to her disguise. When we presented her with the money found in his frock coat, she told us it amounted to but half the earnings she'd made as a seamstress, all of which Hacker had kept from her. Even so, she was most happy to have it.

Several days later we escorted Mrs. Hacker to the Concord

train station. Henry had fashioned her a cane from a tree branch that enabled her to get around on her own. Dressed in the gown and bonnet she had run away in, with her countenance and cropped blond hair washed of coal dust, she looked most presentable.

She was taking the cars out to Fitchburg and thence she would be traveling by stage to her parents' farm in Vermont. That had always been her intention as soon as she managed to accumulate enough money. As we waited for the train she fiddled with the lace collar around her neck and I wondered if she had fashioned it during those long, lonely hours in her humble hideout, just as she had wiled away the time knitting. Then I spied the marks above the collar, dark blue imprints thick as thumbprints. Had Hacker expired from heart failure just as he was about to throttle her to death?

"I will thank you both one last time and pray for you always," she told Henry and me as the train pulled into the station.

She offered me her hand and I shook it gently. But when she offered her hand to Henry he glimpsed something that seemed to startle him. He turned her palm up to reveal a black X seared into the flesh. "That monster branded you!" he cried out.

"Yes, he did that too," she said softly.

Henry reached into the deep pocket of his coat and much to my surprise, extracted a knitting needle. "I believe this is yours, Mrs. Hacker."

She blanched and began to tremble.

Henry tossed the long, thin needle onto the tracks in front of the engine. "The car wheels will soon obliterate it so you need not concern yourself with it anymore," he told her.

She bowed her head, turned away, and boarded the car, helped up by the conductor. As the train departed I scowled at Henry.

"Why toss away the poor woman's knitting needle? She might have made good use of it to pass the hours during her long trip."

"She has made good use of it already, Adam. She used it to save her own life whilst Hacker was strangling her. Did you notice the brute's finger marks on her neck?"

"Yes, and I surmised that in his struggle to subdue or even kill her, his heart gave out."

"As I too would have surmised if not for the missing needle."

"What missing needle?"

"I saw only one on the ground where she had dropped her knitting as she fled from Hacker, yet such a handicraft requires two. So I went looking for the other. I searched the area where we came upon Hacker's body and found it soon enough."

"But what would it have been doing there, Henry?"

"Mrs. Hacker must have been clutching it as she ran away from her tormentor. And then, as he was choking her, she must have thrust it deep into his ear in a frantic effort to save herself, thus puncturing his brain."

"Such a wound would cause instant death yet bleed but little," I said, recalling the spot of blood on the rock beneath the dead man's head. The sudden realization stunned me. "Hacker did not die of a bad heart, after all."

"Oh, but he did," Henry replied solemnly. "He died of a very bad heart indeed."

Ben and Beth Oak, both Connecticut natives, met in a literature course at Boston University and have been enthralled with Henry David Thoreau (and each other) ever since. As B. B. Oak they have created a mystery series featuring Thoreau as "the Sherlock Holmes of Walden Pond," and the first book is slated for publication by Kensington in 2013. www.bboak.com

Free Advice

Katherine Fast

The screen door slammed. Allen lumbered onto the deck where
Jan and I lounged under an umbrella sipping wine. I raised my
glass in mock toast and offered an insincere smile. He was thoroughly
predictable, conservative, dull but not stupid—most everything I'd
shun in a mate.

"Whaddya think?" He placed three papers before me.

"The truth costs money." I ignored the pages. For a graphologist,
a handwriting analyst, it's a curse when people troll for free advice,
expecting me to divine instant profiles based on scribbled Post-it
notes.

Allen pushed the pages closer. "Just a quickie."

I popped a grape into my mouth.

"Come on," he egged.

"Allen, maybe this isn't the time—" Jan interrupted.

"I'm asking her opinion, not yours." He glanced at the bottle of
wine and then at his wife.

I raised the bottle to eye level and measured the remaining wine
with my fingers. "An inch and a half since you last checked."

He scowled. "Which one has more drive?"

"You've already decided. Why ask me?"

"To see if you know."

Subtle as a mallet, but I felt my ego engage. "What kind of
drive?"

"Oh, for chrissake!" He reached, but I edged the papers away.

"Motivation differs. Do you want someone who'll kill commies
for Christ, decipher the Mayan code, or break the Guinness record for

pancake consumption?"

He folded his arms across his soft chest and enunciated clearly in case I needed to lip read. "I want a closer."

I glanced at the writing samples. "Pancakes." I rejected the first. "Mayans." I pushed the second aside and nudged the last one toward him.

"Thought so."

"But before you make an offer, you really should consider his other traits."

"Like, 'Is he a Libra or a Taurus?'" He snatched the papers and marched toward the door.

"Seriously, this person's writing—"

He turned. "You aren't listening. All I want is a go-getter."

"But look at the sharp angles and twists in the lower loops—"

The screen door slammed.

Jan took a sip. "Sorry. He's got lots on his mind."

I'd met her through an ad, "Check 'Em Out First," I'd placed in the local rag years ago. In it, I'd advised young lovers to have their prospective mates' handwritings analyzed before committing. I didn't realize then that lovers were deaf to all but glowing words of praise.

So, despite my report that Allen was a plodding, humorless drone, all Jan heard was that he'd be a steady, if not imaginative, mate.

Funny, lovers seek good news, but most people who ask, "What can you tell me about this person?" want dirt. For once, Allen was the exception. He didn't want dirt, just confirmation.

I sipped my wine and pondered the obvious question: Why go to Jan's house when I disliked her husband, and she and I seemed to have little in common?

Actually, it wasn't a mystery considering our writing. Jan's script revealed a simple, fun-loving soul. But closer examination uncovered telltale signs of self-indulgence, a penchant for bending the truth, and manipulative traits, all qualities I value in a friend.

My writing also sports addictive tendencies and a touch of manipulation. I enjoy a glass or four of wine, and use her place as a safe house to raise a little hell.

Three months later Jan and I sat in identical postures, imbibing and talking about the report on the evening news. The police had hauled Allen's new go-getter salesman off in cuffs. The reporter filed her report using the company's new van as a backdrop. On the van, the name Modular Play Systems was painted in a rainbow of bright colors. Below the name was a picture of an adorable little girl laughing and swinging on monkey bars and the logo, "Come play with me."

The screen door slammed and Allen pounded across the deck. "You know that person you told me to hire?" He loomed over me pointing his finger. "Do you have any idea what your advice will cost me? I'll have to drop our whole children's line."

I studied the finger until he withdrew it. "I never told you to hire anyone."

"Oh, yes, you did. You sat right there swilling wine and picked his writing."

"Swill?" I objected. I raised the bottle of Pinot Noir so he could wince at the outrageous price tag. "I said your man would be more motivated than the others. Tell me true. Was he?"

"Yes, but—"

"'But' nothing." I poked my finger into his stomach. "I strongly suggested you consider other traits. But nooooo. You wouldn't even listen to free advice. You never asked if he was a pedophile."

The screen door crashed, punishing the hinges.

Jan stared with wide-open eyes. "You could tell that the man—"

"Of course not."

Soon Allen would down a couple tranquilizers and retire with warm milk and earplugs, and we'd crank up the tunes. I dug into my tote for a magnum of red and a funnel and refilled the show bottle. "You can spot deviant tendencies, but you can't predict behavior. If I had those powers, we wouldn't be drinking this swill."

Katherine Fast aka Kat is focusing on fiction writing, watercolor, handwriting analysis, and is doing her level best as a design and production editor. Her short stories have been published by NEWN, Level Best Books and in e-zines. She and her husband live in Massachusetts with two spoiled cats.

House Calls

Barbara Ross

The jangle of the phone erupted into one of Michael's and my long silences. On the other end was my mother's best friend, Mrs. Balmus, with a torrent of words about a hospital admission.

"My mother's ill," I told my husband, Michael. "I have to go."

"How long will you be away?"

"No way to know."

If we'd had children or a shared social life, or any expectations of one another at all, there would have been more to say. If I'd had a career, or a job I even cared about, it wouldn't have been so easy to cut my ties and float away.

At Logan Airport, I unbuckled my seat belt before our car stopped moving. Michael pulled to the curb and started to get out, as if to help or maybe even kiss me good-bye, but a state trooper blew his whistle and gestured for Michael to move on, so he settled back into his seat. "Good luck," he called.

I wheeled my suitcase through the great glass doors without looking back.

I rented a car at Buffalo-Niagara airport and drove an hour south along Lake Erie to the hospital.

"Elizabeth, you've come," my mother said.

I kissed her too warm cheek. "Mother, what are you doing here?"

"Cancer," she whispered. "Women's cancer."

Women's cancer? I did a mental inventory. Breast? Ovarian? Cervical? Endometrial? Did other women's parts become cancerous?

My mother waved my questions away. "Talk to Dr. Botwin. He'll explain everything."

Her nurse was equally reticent. "You can talk to Dr. Botwin in the morning," she repeated without meeting my eyes. "He'll answer all your questions."

Mother said she wanted to rest and gave me a list of things to fetch from home. The house key was under her front mat, as it had been since my childhood. Squaring my shoulders, I unlocked the door.

My mother hadn't changed a piece of furniture, a rug or drape since I'd gone off to college twenty years before. But in the thirteen years since my father's death, she and Mrs. Balmus, busy patrons of every yard sale and craft fair for fifty miles, had buried my childhood home in layers of stuff—knick-knacks, lace, fake flowers in heavy vases. An army of frilly, overdressed dolls stared out from every shelf and table.

As always, the clutter overwhelmed and depressed me. The visual noise made me nauseous. I hated the way the old, familiar rooms had disappeared, and with the aggressively feminine décor, so had my father.

"You came." When I arrived downstairs the next morning Beverly Balmus sat at the kitchen table, drinking coffee from a china cup. I'd locked all the doors the night before and hadn't put the key back under the doormat.

"Of course I did." I helped myself to coffee, too, grateful Mrs. Balmus knew how to navigate in this kitchen where every countertop was covered.

"I'll take you to the hospital as soon as we finish," she said, as though it was settled.

My mother, never much of a driver, had been more than happy to give it up altogether after my father died. Mrs. Balmus took her everywhere—grocery shopping, hair appointments, and of course estate sales, consignment shops and swap meets. As far as I knew, my father's car was still in the garage, but it hadn't been driven in thirteen years, and was undoubtedly covered in boxes of stuff.

I'd been relieved my mother had someone to chauffeur her.

"Thank goodness for Beverly Balmus," I often said to Michael. Now, glancing out the kitchen window to where her car stood sideways in the drive, looking more beached than parked, I wondered if I should have dug a little deeper into the current state of Mrs. Balmus' driving skills.

"We'll take separate cars. But before we go, tell me what's happened."

Amid her usual digressions and gossip about people I didn't know, the story came out. Arriving for one of their outings, she'd found my mother doubled over by pain and vomiting. There followed a trip to the emergency room and the discovery of Mother's ruined, infected right breast. Mrs. Balmus was almost as vague as my mother on the diagnosis, as if the word "cancer" were enough. "You'll meet Dr. Botwin," she concluded. "He's excellent. Everyone around here goes to him."

At the hospital, Dr. Botwin led me to a conference room. His close-cropped, light brown hair showed the tiniest flecks of gray, and his eyes were the intense blue of a swimming pool. His face was too boyish to truly be called handsome, but his loose scrubs couldn't hide his athletic physique. Most important, he seemed competent and caring.

"Your mother has breast cancer," he said. "She ignored her symptoms for a long time. The cancer is quite advanced."

It was all too believable. Mother had never shown the slightest interest in her body. She'd always treated herself like a ragdoll, filled with undifferentiated stuffing.

"She was brought to the emergency room with right side abdominal pain, which may mean metastasis to the liver. We'll know more about her treatment when her tests are complete. But we do know she'll need a great deal of care and support." He paused. "This is a lot to take in."

It was. I'd been so absorbed in the anger that arose whenever I returned to my mother's house and had to confront all the stuff, I hadn't thought enough about what she was facing or what it would be like to be without her. Suddenly, I longed for siblings, or for a happy marriage where burdens were shared. I wished I were surrounded by a supportive group of friends. In a solitary life, I'd never felt so alone.

Dr. Botwin moved his chair closer. "It's okay. We'll get through this. I'll be here to help you every step of the way." He covered my left hand with his own, his wedding ring resting on top of mine. An electric shock ran up my arm.

While my mother was in the hospital, Dr. Botwin's frequent presence calmed me, though his words were hardly reassuring. Mother had a particularly virulent form of breast cancer, inoperable and resistant to hormone treatment. The only approach was chemotherapy.

As the infection subsided, Mother returned to the person I recognized. "I know what's going on," she snapped one day when I returned from talking with Dr. Botwin in the hallway. "You can't fool me."

When my mother came home, at Dr. Botwin's strong suggestion, I hired caregivers to help in the afternoon and early evening. The three people who split the shifts were like angels, infinitely patient with my mother.

Michael and I talked once a week. I made no commitment about coming home and he stopped inquiring. "Do you want me to come out?" he asked.

"No," I answered, "We're under control here."

Dr. Botwin dropped by the house every few days to check on my mother. I never knew when he was coming. I'd met a few other members of his oncology practice in the hospital, but he was taking a personal interest. I figured this could only be a good thing.

One day I tried to move some of the things in my mother's bedroom to make room for all the paraphernalia that came with illness. She stopped me cold.

"Leave that be. I'm not dead yet!"

The caregiver looked at me across the bed and mouthed, "It's the cancer talking."

"No, it's not," I said aloud. "It's my mother."

I made it out of her bedroom, down the stairs and into the kitchen before I broke down. I wept because I was exhausted. Afraid. Alone. Because I loved my mother. Hated my mother. Hated the stuff. Because my mother had shown, once again, she cared more about the stuff than about me.

I was still crying, head on the kitchen table, when Dr. Botwin found me. "C'mon," he said. "Let's go for a ride."

He had a black Mercedes convertible. Even though it was mid-September, already cool in Buffalo, the top was down. I closed my eyes. Before I knew it, we were on the highway, headed toward the city.

"Did you know Buffalo was once the wealthiest city in America?" he asked. Of course I did. I'd grown up in the area. "In 1895, when it was built, the Guaranty Building was the tallest skyscraper in the world. And Buffalo has more Frank Lloyd Wright buildings than any city except Chicago."

I'd seen them all before, Wright's famous Martin, Barton, Heath and Davidson houses, but Dr. Botwin's narration as we passed each one was so knowledgeable and enthusiastic, it was like experiencing them for the first time. I sat back in my seat, happier than I'd felt in years.

After that, we went for drives whenever Dr. Botwin came to see my mother. We toured the H. H. Richardson complex with its Frederick Law Olmsted grounds, all originally designed for the state asylum for the insane. There seemed to be no end to Dr. Botwin's architectural knowledge. I wondered how such a busy doctor had the time to spend with me.

One autumn afternoon, as we walked across the grounds of the Graycliff estate, he said, "I think, in this context, you should call me Simon. And I will call you Betsy." No one had ever called me Betsy before, but it seemed to suit the new me, a person who was doing things the old Elizabeth never would have considered.

Eventually, Simon stopped coming into the house. He'd call from his car and I'd run out to meet him, followed by disapproving glares from my mother and Mrs. Balmus. On the days Simon didn't come, I took myself for a drive in the rental car, usually around dinnertime. I had to get out of the house once a day, away from the clutter and the illness, to keep my sanity.

I started driving by Simon's house.

It began as idle curiosity. Like a high school crush, really. I spent way too much time as I cooked meals, did the endless laundry and the dishes, speculating about his life, his wife. It wasn't hard to find the address. They were the only Botwins in town.

Simon's house was a disappointment, completely unsuited for someone who loved architecture. It was in a new development of oversized homes, the kind of houses with garages and formal living spaces at the front, rooms no one spent any time in. All the dark windows made the neighborhood look deserted. The dreary, undistinguished house must have been his wife's idea.

I discovered, quite by accident, that on Thursdays, Simon took out the trash. I was just driving up, about five houses away, when his garage door shuddered open. I glimpsed a patch of the Mercedes' black fender, and then the man himself, wheeling his garbage cans toward the street. I veered into the nearest driveway and slumped down in my seat. He didn't even glance in my direction.

On the Saturday after Thanksgiving, Simon called my cell. "I have tickets to the symphony and no one to go with. I thought you could use a night out. Get dressed up and bring your passport. I'll pick you up at 4:00. We're going to Toronto!"

I bought a little black dress and expensive undergarments. By the time Simon arrived, I was vibrating with the anticipation of an evening out, a real date, and especially, spending time with beautiful him.

The drive to Toronto was liberating. A new place, a new country, where no one knew us, an escape for a brief few hours from the responsibilities that weighed on us both. I loved being in Symphony Hall, the patrons finding their seats, the orchestra tuning up. The program was Beethoven's Eighth.

Afterward, elated, we walked toward the parking garage. Outside the Intercontinental Hotel, Simon paused. "Dare we go for a drink?"

"Why not?"

Just inside the doors he leaned in and kissed me on the neck. "So, so beautiful," he murmured. I had to concentrate to keep from falling to the lobby floor.

We were without a reservation or luggage, and for an unguarded moment, the desk clerk let disgust creep into his expression. Then he regained his professional demeanor and found us a room. Once we got inside, the sex was urgent, like a courting couple who've been chaste for too long.

I awoke early the next morning to hear Simon telling his service he'd been at the hospital with a patient all night and was going home to get some rest. We left quickly, giggly and chattier than we'd ever been. On the ride home, we talked about our childhoods. Like me, he was an only child with older parents. And both his parents had survived significant illnesses. "I knew the moment I saw you that you needed to be protected," he said. "I knew you needed as much care as your mother."

"Simon, what if the chemo doesn't work?"

"Then we'll find another that does." He reached over to take my hand. "Don't worry. Everything will work out."

I entered the house to find my mother on the living room couch and Mrs. Balmus in my father's easy chair beside her. "I know what's going on!" my mother shouted as I floated up the stairs, grinning like a fool.

As soon as I entered my bedroom, I dialed Michael. "It's over," I said. "I want a divorce."

After Toronto, the architectural tours stopped and we met only at a motel not far from Simon's office. He always parked his car in the back. Simon was passionate and experimental in bed, such a contrast to Michael and his routinized choreography. I returned Simon's enthusiasm, pathetically grateful just to *feel* again. But it seemed like there was never enough time for real conversation.

Mother continued her chemo, growing frailer as the days went by. I spent hours sitting in her room, listening to her talk. I thought she'd use this time to talk about her family or her childhood. After all, I was the only one who'd hold the memories. Instead, she prattled on about the junk that filled her room. "I remember the day that we got that," she'd say, pointing to a dusty figurine. "Beverly and I drove up Route 62. We had the most wonderful lunch at a little restaurant beside a stream. It was a perfect day."

At first I was annoyed and hurt, as I always was when she talked about the stuff. But listening more carefully, I realized that for my mother, each object's history had been merged with her own, and every one was a reminder of a lunch or an outing, the joy of discovery. A perfect day. I relaxed and enjoyed her stories. Feeling something for Simon was opening me up in unexpected ways.

I still took a drive every evening in the rental car, often passing by Simon's house. On Thursdays, I'd park down the hill a ways and wait for him to wheel out his trash barrels. The days were getting shorter and it was dark when he appeared, but there was a street light one house before his and I could see him clearly. There was something about this little act of domesticity that made me love him even more.

I spent a lot of time feeling guilty about his wife and what I was doing to her. But Simon and I shared a unique and overwhelming physical attraction. We couldn't help ourselves. He was my lifeboat. I didn't think I could survive my mother's illness without him.

On the day my mother was to get the results of a scan to see if the chemo was working, Simon and I were supposed to meet at the motel. I'd felt increasingly guilty about the time I was spending away from her, and never more than that day. I waited an hour and a half for Simon, but he never showed. He'd cancelled before; he was always dealing with emergencies, but never without a call.

I got home to find an ambulance in the driveway. My mother was screaming in agony and a terrified Beverly Balmus had called 911. I called Simon from the ambulance, all his numbers, his office, service, personal cell. My hands shook so hard I could barely operate my phone. Simon never picked up.

The doctors in the emergency room prescribed painkillers but were wary of doing more without consulting her doctor. Verging on full-out hysteria, I called Simon's numbers over and over.

Finally after nine p.m., Dr. Patel, one of Simon's partners, rushed in. The fear in his expression terrified me for my mother. He ordered stronger pain medication, then escorted me to the same family conference room where I'd first met Simon.

"The news is bad," Dr. Patel said, eyes softening. "Your mother's treatment is not working. The cancer has metastasized to her spine and that's what's causing her pain. She's very weak. It won't be long now. I'm sorry."

"Where is Dr. Botwin?" I begged. "My mother needs him."

"I'm covering for him. I can take care of whatever your mother needs." Dr. Patel gave my shoulder a pat and hurried from the room.

My mother lasted five agonizing days while Dr. Patel walked

a fine line between managing her pain and killing her. I expected Simon to walk into her room at any moment. I called and called. During the rare periods I felt I could leave her side, I searched the hospital, propelled at first by fear and then by fury, throwing open doors marked private, entering restricted areas.

Three days before Christmas, my mother drew her last labored breath with Beverly Balmus and me standing on either side of her bed. Simon never came.

"I know what he did to you."

"Wha . . .?" My voice cracked from lack of use. We'd buried Mother on Christmas Eve day. I'd spent the days since rarely moving from her bed. I filled the time watching black and white movies on her ancient television and weeping for all my losses—my mother, my father, the arid years of my marriage. And Simon. God help me, I wept for the loss of Simon.

The caller went on, relentlessly. "I know what Dr. Botwin did to you. He did it to me, too. We're not the only ones. He's done this many times. Some of us are getting together. Wednesday, at the coffee shop on Main Street. Eleven a.m. Let's support one another."

I tried again to respond but managed little more than a clearing of the throat.

"I hope you'll come." Then click, she was gone.

I told myself I wouldn't go to meet these other women. It was hard enough keeping my thoughts from straying toward Simon without attending a meeting where he would be the central topic. Besides, I'd returned the expensive rental car after the funeral.

But somehow, over the next few days, I moved the boxes of junk off my father's old car and got his repair shop to replace the battery and tires. I knew I'd have to register the car, but just the thought of proving to the DMV that I actually owned it was exhausting.

On Wednesday morning, I pulled it out of the garage and headed carefully downtown.

Simon had made me feel beautiful and sexy. But sitting at that table in the coffee shop, I realized that if Simon had indeed "done" to these women what he'd "done" to me, nothing about me was uniquely desirable to Simon.

Jennie, the woman who'd called us, was pretty, blond and young. Late twenties I put her, ten years younger than me. The woman directly across from me, who told us in a barely audible voice that her name was Leah, was young, too, but skeletally thin, dull-haired, a bag of nervous tics. Mary, at the opposite end of the table, was a good ten years older than I. Shorthaired, broad-faced and broad-shouldered, she was nobody's definition of attractive.

There was a tense silence, which Jennie broke. "Simon Botwin was my late sister's doctor."

The air seemed to whoosh from all our lungs at once. Mary laid her hands open on the table. "My mother," she said.

"Me, too." I followed.

We looked at Leah, who whispered, "My child."

Jennie had worked a high tech job in Silicon Valley. When her sister called to say she had cancer, Jennie moved across the country to care for her. But Jennie was alone. And scared. She couldn't show her fear to her sister, so she'd shared it with Dr. Botwin. "At first I thought of it as a friendship, but then it turned into something else."

We each nodded, acknowledging, this is my story, too.

"How did you find us?" I'd been wondering since I got her call.

"When my sister was sick, I got to be friends with Delia, one of her nurses. At lunch last week, I finally felt strong enough to admit to her what had happened with Simon. Delia told me the nurses all know about him. She felt awful she hadn't tried to warn me. Afterward she gave me a list of seventeen names and phone numbers, all women she thought were victims of Dr. Botwin. I called them all. You're the ones who came."

Mary spoke next. Before she quit to take care of her mother, she'd been the director of a large charitable organization, and she had that unmistakable aura that says, "ex-nun." *My God*, I wondered, *was she a virgin when he did this to her?*

I told my story, too, feeling wretched about how much it was like the other two. There was absolutely nothing special about me.

We looked across the table at Leah. Her story stuttered out. Her marriage, shaky to begin with, had crumbled under the weight of her four-year-old daughter Chrystal's rare cancer. Simon hadn't even been her daughter's doctor, just a referring physician in the chain between Chrystal's pediatrician and a top pediatric oncologist in Buffalo.

"After my husband left us, Simon started coming by the house," she said so softly we all strained to hear. "He played with Chrystal. She just loved him. But then, once, when Chrystal was in the hospital, Simon took me to the symphony in Toronto . . ."

Mary gripped Leah's hands. "Me, too," she said, "Hayden."

Jennie nodded. "Copeland."

"Beethoven," I said.

Leah whispered. "Brahms."

I hated seeing these old events with newly opened eyes. Knowing that the clerk at the Intercontinental had looked disgusted not because we lacked luggage, but because he'd seen Simon with so many different women.

Simon had disappeared from Leah and Chrystal's lives when Chrystal's cancer was no longer treatable. "At the end, Chrystal was still asking for him. Her little life was *so* short, and I chose to waste some of that precious time . . ." Her tears, barely held in check while she'd spoken, cascaded freely down her cheeks. She struggled to admit what she'd done, then gave up. "Simon said he would protect me. Instead, he broke me," she finished.

Mary and Jennie were both crying by then. I cried, too, for Leah and Chrystal and for me.

Seventeen women. Seventeen broken women.

"I think we should get together once a week," Jennie said. "It would be good for us." We all agreed, though I wasn't sure I would return.

But the next Wednesday I was there. And the Wednesday after that. I wasn't sure the "sharing" Jennie encouraged was getting us anywhere. How can obsessing about the object of your obsession be helpful?

We speculated endlessly. Why did Simon do what he did? Did his wife suspect? Did he care about architecture and symphonies, or were they just a means of seduction? *Was he really an only child*, I wondered. *Were his parents ever ill?*

"We should report him," I said. I'd been thinking it since the first meeting.

"To who?" Jennie asked.

"To his partners, for one."

"His partners know, for sure," Jennie said. I realized she was right. The look of terror on Dr. Patel's face the night of my mother's last admission hadn't been fear for her. Dr. Patel had been afraid of me, of the scene I might make when I realized Simon wasn't coming.

"Then the hospital."

"They know, too," Mary said. "When he abandoned my mother, I hunted Simon for days. I finally cornered him in a patient's room. I rushed in, screaming at the top of my lungs, crying . . . cursing." She blushed furiously at the memory.

I blushed, too, remembering how I'd haunted the hospital hallways in my mother's last days. "How did Simon react?" I hated my own curiosity.

"Like I was a crazy woman he'd never seen before. Anyway, security showed up, though by then I'd calmed down enough that they didn't throw me out. Everyone in the hospital had to know about it."

"And Delia told me that wasn't the only incident," Jennie said.

"Then let's report him to the state medical ethics board."

"Go ahead," Jennie said.

"Not just me. Then it's my word against his. We all need to do it." Silence around the table.

"My reputation," Mary said. "This is my hometown. I need to get a job. Soon."

We all knew Leah couldn't withstand the ordeal.

"What about you?" I asked Jennie.

"How would we explain how we met? My friend Delia would be fired, for sure. She violated about a thousand state and federal laws when she gave me that list of names. I'm not even sure what he did was illegal. We weren't his patients, after all. Besides, I never meant this group to be about vengeance. This is about sharing and mutual support."

"Jennie," I assured her, "I'm not talking about vengeance. Simon is out there, seducing a lonely, frightened woman right now. He has to be stopped." I itched to do something. I needed to take action, but the subject was closed and I never brought it up again.

Jennie did try to get us to talk about the future, not just the past. At first there wasn't much to say. Then, slowly, as the long winter marched on, we started to come unstuck. Mary was actively interviewing for a job, and Jennie had started looking for an apartment in San Jose. I reported that I'd started the enormous job of sifting through my mother's stuff. After all, to move on I had to sell the house, and to sell the house, I had to deal with the stuff.

What I didn't tell the group was that I was driving past Simon's house again. It had begun innocently enough. I was going past his development on an errand and it was a simple thing to drive past his door. Soon, I was doing it every day, especially on Thursday evening, so appropriately trash day, when I could get a glimpse of the man himself. The high snow banks and dark winter evenings hid my car until I was almost next to him. One Thursday I drove right by him, less than three feet away. He didn't even turn around.

Leah resisted our attempts to draw her out. She was so thin now I feared she'd disappear. Jennie, Mary and I often lingered at the table after she left to talk about her. At first I think it made us feel better to concern ourselves with someone who was so obviously worse off than we were, but as Leah grew quieter and further away, our discussions became more serious. Watching Leah slip away, I felt as afraid for her and as frustrated by my helplessness as I had been during my mother's illness. And as furious at Simon as I had been in those hours when I called and called and he didn't come.

"We have to do *something*," I said. But none of us knew what.

Sobbing travelled through the phone line. I waited, fear rising. "It's Leah," Jennie choked out. "She . . . she . . . she . . ."

"She couldn't live with what she'd done," I finished. I had no trouble speaking. I didn't feel the least bit sad. Hearing the news I'd dreaded all winter, I felt only resolve. For the first time in months, I knew exactly what I had to do.

"Such a terrible waste," Jennie gasped.

"Yes," I said and hung up the phone.

I was parentless, jobless and husbandless. My only friends were tied to me by events we all wanted to forget. My calendar was so empty, I often didn't know what day it was.

But I always knew when it was Thursday. Thursday, late afternoon. I got into my father's car, my brain feverishly stoking my fury about Leah. Sweet, defenseless, stuck Leah. Leah, who'd endured the worst thing life can throw at you, the death of a child. Leah, whose irresponsible husband had already broken her heart. Leah, the sitting duck for Simon.

I'd made the trip so many times. I knew exactly how to time it. Darkness fell in the ten short minutes it took to get to Simon's neighborhood.

"Seventeen women," I chanted as I crested the hill. "Seventeen women. Seventeen women." And all the ones the nurse Delia didn't know about. All the ones added since.

I struck him square on, travelling fast. There was a loud *ker-thunk* and then the *whub-whub* of the plastic garbage barrels as they skittered to the side. In the glow of the street lamp, he stared at me, wild-eyed, just before I hit him. I like to think he recognized me, though I'll never know. He didn't scream. He disappeared overhead and crashed down behind the car. In my rear view mirror, I saw him lying in the street, his limbs and neck at impossible angles.

I sped on, imagining Simon's neighbors running into the unused front rooms of their hulking houses, dialing 911. By the time the police arrived, my unregistered car with its ancient, salt-covered license plates would be in my mother's garage.

I wiggled my toes in my snow boots and depressed the accelerator. It felt good to be moving again.

Barbara Ross is a co-editor of Level Best Books and the author of the mystery novel, *The Death of an Ambitious Woman. Clammed Up*, the first in her series about a family clambake business in coastal Maine, will be published by Kensington in 2013. Barbara's website is www.maineclambakemysteries.com and she blogs with a great group of Maine authors at www.mainecrimewriters.com.

Strictly Male Fantasy

Daniel Moses Luft

The Sunday night Regatta crowds had died down to nothing. After a weekend of serving students five deep to the bar, all holding cash like they were betting on craps, Donnie felt exhausted. It was three a.m. and he'd arrived to work early at two that afternoon. Head of the Charles in Harvard Square was like a little October spring break with rich kids coming from along the East Coast to spend huge amounts of money on official gear, crew equipment and beer. Donnie didn't give a shit about any boat race; he just liked people at the bar throwing money in his tip bucket.

Now that it was over and the restaurant had been closed an hour, he had the bar clean again or at least clean enough for tonight. Donnie did what he could but the poor bastard on day shift tomorrow was going to curse him. He didn't care.

He had all the glasses washed and put away, the silverware was back in the racks, the dirty plates he left on the dish line in the kitchen because he didn't care about those anymore either. The floor was spot-mopped, the beers mostly restocked, the taps were locked, his drawer was counted, his checks were stapled and the rest of the staff was gone. He had pocketed his tips and was about to return the bar drawer to Fitz, the manager, when he heard a noise come from the far side of the room where the lights were already dim. He dropped his drawer on the bar and walked around to see what was there.

It was a black woman in a tiny sequined minidress that hugged her very curvy body and then abruptly ended at the top of her thighs. She was in extremely high heels and grinding herself against someone Donnie couldn't see. In a second she slid over to the right and Donnie saw that she had been on top of an equally tall, equally-high-heeled, not-quite-so-curvy, pale, white girl with short, green hair and glasses. She was also wearing a tiny minidress. Both of them were in their early twenties, Donnie remembered ID-ing them around midnight.

The black girl smiled at Donnie, then pursed her lips and said "Hi" as she ran her fingers through her thick wavy hair. The white girl didn't say anything, but Donnie noticed that several of the buttons on her dress were open, leaving her nearly exposed up top. Donnie felt an overwhelming sense of arousal when he looked at the women but quickly turned and grabbed his cash drawer before he left the floor and raced down the back hall to the office. He stopped when he reached the door where Fitz was counting money from the host drawers.

"What the hell's your problem?" Fitz asked. "You look scared." His voice was deep and a little hoarse like he'd already started drinking for the night. Fitz was a tall, heavyset man with short but messy brown hair, paunch over the belt and two days of scruff on his chin. His tie was pulled loose and his shirt was untucked.

"There's still people in the bar."

"We're way closed. Get rid of them."

"You've got to get rid of them."

"What? Someone causing trouble?" Fitz turned and looked at the security monitor to see the video shot of the bar, but it didn't show the part where the women were and was empty. That motionless image was on the monitor right next to a blank white shot of the office ceiling. Donnie glanced over at the camera installed in the office and saw that it had been bumped again and pointed straight up.

"No. Nothing like that," Donnie whispered. "Just another make-out couple in the booth."

"Aww shit, I hate those people. Doesn't anyone have a freakin' room anymore? No matter how many roommates I ever had I always had a door I could shut. And I never fooled around with any woman who didn't have an apartment and a door."

Donnie shrugged. "Well, they're out there. What should I do?"

"Is the guy big? Muscle-bound? What's the matter with you?"

"No, it's two chicks."

"Really?"

"Yeah."

"Are they ugly?"

"No, actually they're both pretty hot."

Fitz paused and stared at Donnie before he stood up, straightened his tie and tucked in his shirt. He grabbed the bar drawer out of Donnie's hands and tossed it onto the desk without looking at it. He rushed out of the office so fast he nearly tripped over the open door of the safe. Donnie stood in the doorway and watched as Fitz hurried down the hall and entered the bar.

Donnie walked slowly as he returned to the floor. He found Fitz standing about eight feet from the girls who were still making out. Fitz was barely breathing, but Donnie could see that his lower lip was quivering as if he were about to say something. His hands twitched a bit too.

Fitz let out a dull moan under his breath.

"Are you okay?" Donnie asked.

"Oh . . . my . . . God. Donnie, do you see them?" Fitz whispered.

"Yes, I see them."

"They're gorgeous. Are you blind?"

"No, but I think they're together. I don't think they're for us."

The two women stopped kissing for a moment. The black girl left her hand inside the top of the other girl's dress when she turned to Fitz and Donnie. She blew a kiss in the air, licked her lips and squeezed her hidden hand. The white girl squealed.

"Are you going to get rid of them?"

"Go fuck yourself, kid. These women can grow old on that bench."

The black woman turned again to face Donnie and Fitz. She was about to speak when she laughed to herself and removed her hand from inside the other woman's dress.

"No need to whisper, gentlemen," she spoke loudly with a jarring British accent. "We were just getting up. And I guess you both are too."

Donnie coughed and looked away as he adjusted himself while Fitz remained motionless and slack-jawed. He smiled.

"Don't go. You can stay as long as you want." Fitz tried to sound casual.

"I don't think your friend here wants us to stay."

"What, this guy? Donnie? He's just leaving." Fitz looked away from the girls and looked down at Donnie. "Get the fuck out of here."

"What?"

"You heard me, kid. Get out of here. Go home and never speak of this again. If you find me here dead in the morning I'll have a smile on my face because this is already worth it." He turned back to see the white woman snake her hand along the other woman's thigh. Fitz let out another moan. The same kind of moan he would let out if he hadn't had a cigarette in ten hours and finally lit one up.

The black woman smiled at Fitz again and flicked some of her wavy hair out of her face. "That's okay, loves. We're on our way out." She stood up and adjusted her tiny dress with a wiggle of her round hips.

"But," she said, making it sound like two syllables.

"Yes," Fitz answered, his voice rising as though he were ready for anything.

"Perhaps you, big man," she laid her hand on Fitz's shoulder. "Have something else big to offer?" Her hand slid down over his shirt and his belly, then to the crotch of his pants. "Yes, I think maybe you'll do very nicely."

"Nice, uh for what?" He was still whispering. Donnie could hear the quiver in his voice.

The woman just squeezed and smiled.

"We're going home," she said. "How soon can you get the lights out in this place and meet us there."

"Wha—where we going? I'm there."

She wrapped her arm around him. She was about his height, over six feet in her heels. She whispered something into his ear and Donnie could tell her breath was tickling his boss. He giggled. Donnie never saw him do that before.

When she pulled her lips from his ear he spoke. "Could, could you say that again?"

The white woman stood up, reached into a beaded clutch purse and spoke for the first time.

"Meet us here, hon." she said. Her voice was pure Baltimore. Then she walked over to the other girl and the two headed for the door as Fitz looked down at the piece of paper in his hands. When they were a few feet away they stopped and looked over their shoulders at the manager.

"Oh, and when you show up, could you bring us something nice to drink?" the black girl asked. The white girl just drew up the hem of her mini to reveal her pale naked ass. The black girl slapped it.

Donnie's eyes bugged as he watched them leave. He saw them make out again in front of the restaurant's picture window before they disappeared from view. He turned back to Fitz and saw that the manager had his thumbs all over his phone.

"Got it," Fitz mumbled. "They're in Central Square. I'm only five minutes behind them."

"You're going?" Donnie asked.

"Hell yes!" he screamed as he ran back to the office they both had left open. Donnie could hear the sound of the plastic cash drawers as Fitz slammed them into the safe before locking it shut. He heard the office door close and Fitz appeared in the bar again with paper bags in his hands.

"You're still here?" Fitz practically screamed.

"I'm surprised that you're going through with this."

"I need booze, Donnie. Do you remember what they were drinking?'

"No."

"Fine. Then I'll need a little of everything. High-end shit. None of that crap most of our customers drink." Fitz jumped behind the bar and grabbed unopened bottles from the understock.

"Goose, Sapphire, Maker's, Patron, Barcardi O."

"Bacardi O?"

"Shut up, Donnie, black chicks love Bacardi O. I don't know why and I don't really care."

"African-American."

"I don't have time to say all those syllables!"

Donnie looked up at the wall

"What about the camera, Fitz?"

"The camera doesn't matter, Donnie. See, watch." He grabbed an open bottle of Wild Turkey from the well and poured it directly into his mouth in front of the camera. He swallowed three or four times before he replaced the bottle.

"No one looks at those recordings unless I tell them something's missing. But nothing will be missing because I'll fudge the booze inventory. Why am I even explaining this to you? Get the hell out of here and go home. I have somewhere to be."

"I've never seen you like this."

"You've heard my story though, haven't you?"

"Which one?"

"I know I've told you the story of when I was home alone in my dorm, Warren Towers, thirty years ago and I get this obscene phone call from some chick, but it was supposed to be for the guy next door. Back then all the phone numbers in dorms were in a row down the hall. So the guy next door had the same number as me except the last digit. Anyway, this chick from Blaine Hair School calls the guy next door and she's so drunk she dials me by mistake and starts talking all dirty to me. I play along for a while, but then tell her who I really am and she tells me to come on over anyway."

"Is this a real story? I've never heard of Blaine Hair School."

"It was in Kenmore Square; it's not around anymore. Anyway, I book out of Warren Towers, buy rubbers at the Store 24 at the bottom of the building and rush over to Beacon Street. I'm outside the place, Donnie, and I chickenshit out. I've got a girlfriend and I just can't do it. I have my hand on the button and I know this chick is so crazy and horny that she'd open that door for me if I just push the button, but I chickenshit out and just go home."

Donnie didn't say anything.

"Well I'm not doing that this time! Apparently it takes thirty years for an opportunity this random to roll around and I don't feel like waiting until I'm 70 for it to happen again."

"And now you're married."

"She's very used to me showing up at the crack of dawn smelling like booze. Now get the hell out of here before I fire you. Go. Go!"

Donnie grabbed his backpack and his coat and headed for the door. Fitz was close behind him with two grocery bags full of booze. Donnie could hear Fitz over his shoulder, bottles clinking together with each step he took. Donnie stopped when he reached the sidewalk but was practically pushed into the street as Fitz shouldered him out of the way when he locked the door.

"You gonna be okay?" Donnie asked.

"Love to talk to you all night, kid, but I've got a short walk to my car and who knows what for the rest of the night. Good night. I'll tell you all about it in a couple days unless they want to take me away to their secret hideout and torture me for a few days and even then I'll still tell you a story with a smile on my face."

"Good night," Donnie said, but Fitz was already running down the street.

Donnie took a deep breath and shouldered his own bag.

He walked silently for a few blocks then felt a buzz in his pocket. He pulled the phone out and looked as the picture lit up the screen. It was the white woman from the bar, but she wasn't wearing glasses and her hair wasn't green, more of a plain dark brown.

"Yeah?" Donnie answered.

"Success?"

"You should've seen the guy. He was grabbing bottles of booze right in front of the security cam. He told me that old story about being in college again."

"That's nice, hon, but I'm talking about the money."

"Oh yeah. I was right, that camera was pointing at the ceiling."

"How much, Donnie?"

"I'm not sure but it was a great weekend and I emptied almost everything out of the safe. I think maybe close to twenty."

He could hear the howling of two women on the other end of the line.

"That's awesome. Where are you?

"Mass. Ave. on the way to Porter.

"We'll be there in two minutes."

"Where did you send Fitz?"

"Who?"

"My boss."

"Well, I don't think he's going to be your boss after tomorrow, Donnie. Anyway, Central Square. A guy I know deals coke."

"That sounds dangerous. I only wanted him fired."

"It'll be okay. He's expected. I'm sure all that booze he's carrying will keep him very safe."

Daniel Moses Luft lives just north of Boston with his wife and two kids. He's had stories published or forthcoming in *Beat to a Pulp*, *Spinetingler* and *Powderburn Flash*. "Skinner Alive," published in the e-anthology *Action: Pulse Pounding Tales,* is a sequel to "Boxed," his story that appeared in the Level Best anthology *Dead Calm*.

They Call Me Mr. Fussy

Christine Eskilson

I never liked her. I'd be the first to admit it. And I liked her even less as a crumpled body in my foyer, her blood seeping into the pumpkin pine floorboards I had so laboriously stripped and sanded. Without thinking, I crouched down to pick up the doorstop next to her head. The cast iron bulldog stared at me, unblinking, but I felt the wetness on its base and hastily put it back down. I plucked a disinfecting wipe from the box I kept in the umbrella stand and scrubbed my hands. They don't call me Mr. Fussy for nothing.

She was the one who came up with the name. I'm convinced of that. It was at one of those dreadful get-to-know-the-new-neighbor parties hosted by Ted and Miranda Rogers, the young couple next door. I attended under silent protest only after Ted knocked on my front door, red-faced and sweaty after a run, to invite me. I was the new neighbor, after all, and Ted led me to believe that the lovely Miranda would cold-shoulder him for days if he didn't persuade me to acquiesce.

Roxanne accosted me as soon as I stepped into Ted and Miranda's backyard, picking my way past the pieces of sporting equipment that had been shoved against a trellis of ill-trimmed roses.

"So here's the mysterious man who transformed the Ballard place! Roxanne Reilly, pleased to meet you," she trilled, gold bracelets jangling on her thin wrists as she thrust out her hand to grab mine. "Great bones, just needed a little TLC."

Was she talking about me or the house?

"Thank you," I murmured, quickly removing my hand from her grasp. I am not a touchy-feely person. When she took off her oversized sunglasses her small brown eyes narrowed even smaller.

"Are you related to the family? That house has been empty for ages. Samantha Ballard owned it, right?" Roxanne prattled on. Her skin was unnaturally tan for New England in early June. "I always thought she was the last one in the family. After she passed away in that nursing home in Florida we didn't hear anything about what was to become of the place."

Did I mention Roxanne was a real estate agent? Or "Willoughby's Premier Realtor," as the advertisement she ran every week in the local newspaper proclaimed, right next to the Garden Talk column. Her initials seemed to be plastered everywhere in town, the RR scrolled like the Rolls-Royce brand.

"Miss Ballard was my great-aunt. On my mother's side," I added, to forestall an inquiry into why my last name was not Ballard.

Miranda joined us with tumblers of white wine before Roxanne could pretend her condolences. "Frank's been living in California for the past twenty years, Roxanne. He's never been here before. I envy you, Frank," she added. "I really do. I've been stuck in Willoughby all my life."

I nodded vaguely as I searched my memory. Is that what I told Ted? I declined the wine, which I'd seen Miranda pouring earlier from a box. Roxanne was not as discriminating.

Miranda smiled at each of us in turn and Roxanne, peering over the rim of her glass, seemed to be waiting expectantly. Horrors upon horrors, it dawned on me, was this a setup? Aging bachelor and local spinster find true love in seaside town? My eyes darted around the small garden, only to confirm that Roxanne and I were the only guests of that certain age, and the only two unaccompanied by spouse or partner. Roxanne's face fell as I made a hasty exit with an excuse to use the "little boy's room."

Her "Mr. Fussy" tagline probably was hatched when more drinks were served. Affable Ted was pushing gin and tonics while Miranda was passing around chips and dip in mismatched bowls. To avoid being cornered by Roxanne again, I volunteered my services. After I arranged Miranda's hummus and crudities on a rickety white resin table, Ted handed me a drink in a plastic highball glass. I like my gin and tonics, no question, but I also have a particular preference for Bombay Sapphire (not to mention real barware). I didn't mean to disparage Ted's lower-shelf offering, but I insisted on retrieving my bottle from next door. Ted couldn't have cared less; in fact, he even let me mix him one, but the women were not amused.

Mr. Fussy I became and it wasn't Miranda's label. She was far too sweet-natured. It must have been Roxanne. I heard it in the next aisle of the grocery store and when I was leaving the post office. Some young hooligans even had the temerity to paint it on the side of my car. Fortunately it was only with shaving cream so it was easy to remove and then buff the BMW.

I didn't particularly like the moniker but Mr. Fussy was the least of my problems. If I had been aware of the house tour that day in Ted and Miranda's garden I never would have spurned Roxanne. I could have mustered the stomach to take her out for a dinner or two before letting her down easy, telling her with a soulful face that she was too good for me. But unbeknownst to me when I was renovating my "colonial estate" (as the nonsensical local real estate parlance would have it), Willoughby was gearing up for its biannual Historic House Tour, chaired by none other than Roxanne with a host of minions, including Miranda. Ted once again was the missionary.

"Miranda thought it would be perfect if both our houses were on the tour," he said when he appeared at my back door one morning to return the rose clippers I'd insisted on lending him. "They were built by brothers, you see." His grin showed off perfect white teeth. "Sibling rivalry in the 1800s. They love that sort of stuff on the tour."

My gaze swept around the tidy kitchen with its gleaming cherry cabinets and clever built-ins for everything from my Wedgewood to the cappuccino machine, and I shuddered at the comparison with Ted and Miranda's post-collegiate abode. Their living room was dominated by a behemoth television and high school lacrosse trophies, and as for the furnishings, can you say IKEA?

As if Ted read my mind, he added, "of course we're updating and doing some major purging. Miranda calls it staging. It's pretty hard to get organized, you know."

"Actually I don't know," I replied.

Ted lingered on the doorstep, his broad shoulders slightly slumped, and against my better judgment I invited him in for coffee. He eagerly accepted.

"Miranda's really into this house tour," Ted confessed, sitting down in the pine rocker next to the fireplace while I busied myself with the French press. The chair squealed under his bulk and I tried not to wince. "Roxanne's been calling her day and night. And if they're not on the phone, they're huddled together in the kitchen working their way through a bottle of wine."

"I suppose Roxanne's the one who really cooked up this sibling rivalry theme?"

"Yeah, pretty much. Roxanne picks the houses and then gets everyone else to do the heavy lifting."

"I suspect she's quite good at that," I said and handed him a mug. I leaned against the mottled granite countertop with my own coffee. I didn't want to encourage Ted to stay too long.

Ted made himself a little too comfortable and the rocking chair protested again. "You know if Roxanne was a man I'd be really worried."

Marriage counseling was not my forte but I couldn't resist the opportunity to dig at Roxanne. I took a seat at the round pine table I had crafted from the remnants of a barn in upstate New York and gestured to him to join me. Anything to get him out of that rocker. "What do you mean?"

He gave an awkward laugh as he set his mug down on the table. I slid over one of the tile coasters I'd picked up in Majorca. "Oh, it's just that Miranda seems so happy lately. She's got this glow." He sounded wistful. "All she talks about is Roxanne and the house tour."

"Sounds fairly innocuous to me, Ted. Maybe she just needed a project to sink her teeth into."

"Yeah," Ted said in the tone of one who is not entirely convinced. He took another gulp of coffee, missing the coaster when he replaced his mug on the table. I practically sat on my hands to keep from reaching out and whisking it away. "Well, you had quite a project here. Miranda can't believe all the work you've done."

"I've been waiting for a home like this," I said, the first truth I'd told in a long time.

I'm not quite sure how it happened but I let Ted talk me into being House Number Six on the tour. It only got worse when I learned that Roxanne had appointed herself as my house sitter. While I certainly didn't object to someone guarding my valuables against the hoi polloi who would be traipsing in and out, the idea of Roxanne as the sentry unnerved me.

She stopped me on the street the day before the tour. "Frank," she called out from behind the wheel of a massive silver SUV. I was taking my usual afternoon constitutional down to the lighthouse and back. I considered ducking behind manicured hedges of the house directly on my right, but they only would prove a temporary refuge.

The tires of the SUV squealed as Roxanne pulled over to the curb. She hopped out, cell phone in hand. It probably was glued to her flesh. "Frank, I need to ask you something."

Questions never boded well for me but I tried to be polite. "Yes, Roxanne?"

"I'm finalizing the fact sheet for your house and I'm a little confused."

"Fact sheet? What do you mean?" My heart rate quickened as I tried to think a few steps ahead of her.

"Every house on the tour has a fact sheet. You know, construction date and materials, builder, owners, interesting architectural features—the works. People want details."

I tried to preempt her. "The marble for the fireplace mantle in the master bedroom was brought over from Italy. Carrera, I believe. The Ballard brothers were in the import-export trade."

That tidbit wasn't tantalizing enough. She waved her cell phone at me. "It's not the fireplace mantle, Frank, it's you. We usually include a blurb on the current owner but I can't find your name in the property records."

I really had to finesse this one. "Roxanne," I said, in a confidential tone, "as a woman of your experience can imagine, there was substantial litigation after my aunt died. It was tied up in the Florida courts. The case was settled privately and I ended up with the house." I made a big show of looking at my watch. "Thank you so much for letting me know about the records. Since it's not yet five I'm going to dash home and call my attorney."

I strode away before she could interrogate me further but I could feel those beady eyes boring into my back.

I walked so fast that when I reached home I was out of breath. Fact sheet, I fumed, fact sheet! What was she thinking? What was I thinking? I rued the day I ever listened to Ted.

Then I came up with my plan to rid Willoughby of its premier realtor. It had certain risks but I didn't have time to be, shall we say, fussy. I couldn't afford to have her probe further. I called Roxanne later that evening to tell her that my attorney was outraged at the sorry state of the property records. "He wanted me to thank you personally for bringing it to my attention. He's going to take care of it first thing Monday morning."

"Pleasure's all mine, Frank." Her voice was slightly slurred and I smiled into the phone.

"This isn't going to cause you problems with the tour, is it?"

She assured me it would not; the fact sheets were all printed up and ready to go. I ended the call by telling Roxanne I would leave a special gift in the pantry. "Wait for me after the tour," I instructed, "we'll try it together."

It was special. I selected a fine French vintage and tied it with a fetching silver bow, after first injecting poison into the cork. Roxanne would drink the wine and begin to feel odd. I would solicitously drive her home and help her to bed. Within a short time paralysis would set in and her internal organs would completely shut down. In the meantime I would remove all traces of the bottle and glasses, and prepare for any questioning from the authorities. Although even the medical examiner in this small town would discover the poison in her body, there'd be no reason to link it to me.

And with any luck, the house that the demented Samantha Ballard left to the Boca Raton Foundation for the Care and Nourishment of Feral Cats, a 501(c)(3) organization dissolved ten years ago, would continue to be mine.

I absented myself the whole day of the tour and arrived home later than I had intended (traffic exiting the beach was the culprit), expecting to find Roxanne alone and eager for her gift. Finding her dead in the foyer was not part of the scheme.

I tossed the disinfecting wipe onto the small, carved Chinese table where I sorted my mail and stepped over Roxanne's body into the front parlor. On the silver tray I used as a coffee table was the unopened bottle of wine and two crystal glasses. I took the tray into the kitchen and returned to the parlor to think. Crisis averted and my hands were clean. But who was my savior?

A groan behind me answered my question. I turned to see Ted in the doorway to the dining room, head hanging down and eyes as red as his face usually was. His blue buttoned-down shirt was only half tucked into the waistband of his khakis, which were smeared with blood. "You gotta help me, man," he pleaded, "you gotta help me."

"What happened here?" I demanded.

Ted crossed the room and sank into the red plush Victorian loveseat underneath the window. I almost yelped when I thought of the blood on his trousers, but now was not the time. "I killed her, Frank, I didn't mean to but I did it. I just couldn't stop myself."

"Why on earth would you kill Roxanne?"

"Miranda told me she was leaving me. This whole house tour thing was a setup to get our house in shape. She wasn't staging the house for a tour; she was staging the house to put it on the market. She wants to sell the house and get out. Roxanne was helping her."

Ted groaned again like a wounded animal. "It was all Roxanne's fault, I know it was. She put the idea into Miranda's head, got her thinking she should get out of here, move to Boston or New York. So I stormed over after the tour. Roxanne was sitting right here," he patted the loveseat, "I called her a bitch and told her to stay away from Miranda or else. She just laughed at me and said Miranda was a big girl who could do what she wanted. She had the nerve to tell me if I went along with the deal she'd shave a little off her commission. "

Ted's eyes glazed over and he spoke in a monotone. "She stood up and told me to talk to her in the morning about the house. That's when I lost it. I gave her a push. It was just a little push, Frank, I swear, but she fell down in the foyer. She said, 'Help me, Ted, help me,'" his voice turned falsetto, "and I picked up the doorstop and hit her."

Neither of us spoke for a few minutes. The ticking of the grandfather clock in the corner was the only sound in the room.

Ted stood up and clasped his hands together. "But what if there was a robbery?" His voice was almost a whisper.

I waited, still not saying anything.

"What if one of the visitors on the tour really was scoping out your place? What if he came back to rob it?"

I looked at Ted with new respect and embellished his narrative. "The tour was over and he thought the place was empty," I suggested. "He didn't realize Roxanne was still here."

"She surprised him and he panicked," Ted continued, his voice stronger. "She said she was calling the police and he hit her with the bulldog."

The kid was starting to remind me a little of myself. Maybe I'd help him out after all. I paced the room as we spun out the tale. "Then he ran off just after I pulled into the driveway. He was wearing gloves so there are no fingerprints," I decided.

"Of course we're going to have to make it look like a struggle. We'll have to do a little damage." Ted's arm shot out and knocked over the antique vase on the pedestal table beside the loveseat. Shards of blue and white china sprayed the room.

He caught my pained expression as I stopped short. "Sorry, Mr. Fussy. Was that something special?"

"Mr. Fussy?" I repeated slowly. "Was that your contribution to the local lexicon?"

Ted shrugged. "Sorry, Frank, but you gotta admit the Bombay Sapphire was a little much. And the rose clippers, too."

With deliberate steps I moved to my roll-top desk and picked up the telephone receiver.

Ted's eyes widened in fear, as he realized what I was about to do. "It was only a joke," he protested, "just a nickname between friends."

He was still apologizing as I dialed 911.

Christine Eskilson is an attorney living in Charlestown, Massachusetts with her husband and two children. This is her first published story.

Driving Miss Rachel

Ray Daniel

Frank Sophia rolls his police cruiser towards his ex-wife's house, toots the horn, and wonders if he's breaking the law. His lips form a thin line as he waits. The cruiser's exhaust swirls in his rear view mirror. The police radio is silent—typical for seven in the morning in the suburbs.

His ex-wife's front door, the one he had painted, swings open and his daughter emerges. Rachel waves, sets down her pink backpack, and turns to lock the door behind her. Frank looks at his phone and the text that had brought him here.

```
Please give me a ride to school <3
```

Rachel is wearing a long sweater, nearly long enough to cover her black tights. She opens the back door to the cruiser, throws in her backpack, then opens the front and looks at the clipboard and newspaper on the seat. Frank clears the seat, tucking the papers between the chair and the console.

"I thought you'd be sitting in back," he says.

"Good morning to you too, Daddy," says Rachel as she slides into the seat. "I don't like it in back. The doors are locked. I feel like a criminal."

"I shouldn't be driving you to school in the cruiser."

Rachel leans in and kisses Frank on the cheek. "Mom and Seth got home late last night. They're still asleep. I knew you were working the morning shift."

Frank glides the cruiser away from the love nest that was once his home. The tires crunch across road sand, a reminder of the recent winter. Rachel pulls out her phone and sends a text. Silence pressurizes the car.

Frank clears his throat. He says, "I'm sorry I'm grumpy. I guess I'm stressed over Marilyn Jones."

"She's still away?" asks Rachel.

"Away? She's missing."

"It wouldn't surprise me if she came back soon."

"Do you know her?"

"Girls will do almost anything for attention."

"Like what?"

"You know, Daddy...anything."

Frank opens his mouth, closes it, opens it again, and closes it. The question presses against his lips, begging to be asked. Rachel looks out the window at the passing houses. Knots of kids are moving toward the high school, zombie-style.

Frank turns the corner. Cars fill the length of the street before him, creeping towards the high school. Another car pulls in behind him and Frank's cruiser is trapped in the line. Rachel types on her iPhone. Artificial clicking sounds fill the car.

Frank blurts, "How about you?"

"How about me what?"

"What do you do for attention?"

Rachel looks out the window. "Hey. There goes Mikey."

She points out a kid shuffling along, carrying a backpack. The police cruiser pulls alongside him. Mikey looks at the cruiser in alarm. He looks at Frank, who sees that the kid has a black eye. He looks at Rachel, who waves. He diverts his gaze back into the sidewalk.

Frank says, "Looks like Mikey got a beating."

Rachel is reading a text as she says, "That's what happens when you owe people money."

Frank says, "I didn't know kids could still get beat up for owing money."

"They can when it's drug money."

"Drug money? He doesn't look like he does drugs."

"Believe me, Daddy, he does. He's a pot head."

"How about you?"

"How about me what?"

Frank is silent. He waits.

Rachel says, "I can't believe you'd ask me that." She looks back into her phone.

Frank gazes out the windshield. Rachel's phone clicks. Frank's radio crackles to life—there has been a fender bender on Route 20. Frank would respond, but he's stuck in this line. Guilt floods him. He pictures the parents in the line noting his personal use of town property.

Frank asks, "Who does the drugs in the school? The poor kids?"

"We don't have poor kids, Daddy. Besides, poor kids can't afford drugs."

The cars ooze towards the school, barely overtaking the pedestrians. Frank's focus slips away as Rachel texts. His thoughts turn to his wife and this guy Seth. What kind of name is Seth?

Rachel says, "I would starve trying to sell drugs to poor kids."

Frank imagines a reporter taking a picture of him driving his daughter to school in the cruiser. Imagines the ridiculous scandal all over patch.com. The reprimand. He thinks about the missing girl, Marilyn. Thinks about whether she's a runaway or whether she was taken. Thinks about whether she had friends who would know where to find her.

Frank asks, "Was Marilyn a popular girl?"

Rachel makes air quotes as she says, "You mean 'popular' like stuck up?"

"Yeah. Was she one of those popular kids?"

"We don't have popular kids anymore, Daddy."

"What does that mean?"

Rachel shrugs. "We just don't."

Frank wonders how a line of cars could move so slowly. Thinks about teachers directing traffic. Most likely that's the problem. Delays up front. People taking too long to dump their kids. Rachel clicks at her phone. The radio squawks. Another officer, Spinelli, goes to handle the fender bender. Frank thinks about Marilyn, about Mikey.

Frank asks, "Do you think Marilyn's disappearance is drug-related?"

Rachel looks out the window and waves at a beefy kid in a football jacket. The kid waves back without a smile. "Marilyn's disappearance is bitch-related."

"What's that mean?"

Rachel waves at another football-jacketed guy. Gets the same wave back. Silence slips back into the cruiser. Frank rides the brake, slipping the cruiser along. Considers flashing his lights and jumping ahead, decides against it. Pat Benatar's voice echoes in Frank's imagination. He raps his fingers on the steering wheel in time to "Hell is for Children."

Frank asks, "Does your mother like this Seth guy?"

Rachel looks away, "I don't want to get in the middle. It's between you and Mom."

"It's between Mom and Seth. Where did they go last night?"

Rachel blows out a sigh. "Do we have to do this?"

Frank looks down the road. There are still five cars to the drop off point. "Do you and Mom sit in this traffic every morning?"

"Usually we leave earlier," says Rachel. "I waited until you were on duty to text you."

"Next time you should call the night before. I might be busy. This Marilyn case is going to break soon."

"So it sounds like Marilyn is getting your attention after all."

"Only because there is a crime to solve."

Rachel crosses her arms and looks out the window. Waves at another football jacket. "Mom says there was always a crime to solve."

Frank says, "Crime doesn't sleep. Your mother never understood that."

"For God's sake, Daddy. We live in Wayland. How much crime could there be?"

"Plenty. For example, where did Mikey get his drugs?"

Rachel doesn't answer. Frank turns to look at her eyes and repeats, "Do you know where he got his drugs?"

Rachel says, "So now I'm your crime stopping partner?"

"What?"

"Like in *Kickass*? You'd be Big Daddy and I'd be Hit Girl?"

"What are you talking about?"

Rachel crosses her arms. "It's a movie, Daddy. Forget it."

"What movie? Who's Hit Girl?"

"She's a superhero who fights crime with her father."

"You can't help me fight crime, Rachel."

The cruiser rolls to a stop at the head of the line. Rachel opens her door, gets out, opens the back door, grabs her backpack. Frank watches her head toward the school. The three football-jacket guys surround her. One hands her something. Frank stares at the transaction. The cars behind him are beginning to toot. He calls out. "Rachel, come back here!"

She starts to walk towards the school. Frank calls out again. "Rachel! I need to talk to you!" The cars behind switch from tooting to honking.

Rachel puts down her backpack, confers with the football-jacket guys who nod and form a triangle around it. She runs to the car and leans in. There is a wad of ten-dollar bills in her hand. She smiles at Frank. "Yes, Daddy?"

Frank looks at the wad of bills in her hand. She looks at the cash and looks back at Frank, straight into his eyes. There is a smile at the corner of her lips. They connect. He feels that she wants him to say something—that he could make her happy right now if he said the right thing, made the right comment, said what she wanted to hear.

Frank says, "I thought you would need money for lunch. But I see you have it."

Rachel's smile collapses. She looks at the wad of bills in her hand and shoves it into her pocket. She says, "Yeah, Daddy. I'm all set. I don't need anything from you."

She turns and walks back to the school. Frank rolls the police cruiser out of the parking lot, glad to be back on the job.

Ray Daniel writes mysteries placed in and around Boston, Massachusetts. He lives in the wilds beyond Route 128 where he works the fertile soil of his lawn.

Hit and Run

Judith Green

Even as a little girl, Margery loved to come to Rollins' Hardware with her father. She'd stand staring up at the shiny new teakettles, the gleaming canning jars, the silvery flashlights, while her father asked for a half-dozen screws, or a particular size bolt.

"Quarter-inch?" Mr. Rollins would shuffle along the bank of tiny drawers behind the counter. "Got some here somewhere. How many didja say?" Then he'd listen while Margery's father grumbled about a balky milking machine, or those pointy-heads down in Washington. "Ep," he'd agree. "What do they know about running a farm?"

Now they lived in town, and Margery walked past the hardware store every day on her way home from work. And now a photograph of Mr. Rollins' son hung in the front window. She stopped, this late-August afternoon, to stare up at the picture. Poor Lenny. He'd dropped out of their class at high school to become one of the last American soldiers killed in Vietnam.

"'Scuze me." Someone bumbled by her and stepped into the store.

The two words marked the skinny young man as From Away. Margery watched through the open door as he worked his way past the garden hoses and rakes. Tall, a bit stooped, as if he were embarrassed at taking up so much space. Sandy hair hanging almost to the neck of his tie-dyed t-shirt. And clearly not finding what he was looking for.

Margery followed him into the store. "What do you need?"

"Oh! Sorry!" The young man spun around in the narrow aisle to look at her. "I didn't know you worked here."

"I don't. But you look sort of lost."

"I—um—" A flush spread over the young man's face. He was twenty-two or so, a few years older than she was. "See, I want to put

75

up a shelf—for my books—the landlady said it's okay." The words tumbled out in bursts. "I'm going to be teaching—you know, at the new high school—but I need something that'll kind of hold onto the plaster."

"Oh, sure." Margery led him to the counter. "Anchor bolts, please, Mr. Rollins."

The young man stared down at her, awestruck. "Would you like to—um—go somewhere for coffee?"

Mr. Rollins snorted as he pulled out the drawer of anchor bolts. "Bakery's the only place in town, son," he said. "They'll give you a cup of coffee if you buy some cookies. Now, how many bolts didja need?"

On Saturday, after lunch, he called at last, to see if she'd like to go for a walk. But half an hour later, when he pulled up in front of her parents' house in his little cream-colored Opel, she wasn't fast enough. Her father spotted the car, and the stranger who unbent himself out of it, and bellowed for her to "bring him on in, for God's sake!"

Chained by a nose tube to the oxygen tank next to his easy chair, her father had to squint up at Tom. "So you're from Wisconsin, huh?"

"That's right," Tom said. "I came to Maine for college, and I liked it here so much I wanted to stay."

"Ep?" It was a wheeze, an intake of air, a question all at once.

"You see, Wisconsin is all rolling farmland—pretty, but I like mountains. When I was a kid, I'd look out at a bank of clouds on the horizon and pretend they were snow-capped peaks."

"Clouds?" Her father screwed up his face. "You did *what?*"

"Time to go!" Margery cried before Tom could answer, and pulled him toward the door.

"What *are* those pasty-looking things?" her father grumbled as Margery carried a plate of sliced tomatoes to the supper table. "Damned grocery store fakes! On the farm, we had *real* tomatoes—fat and red, still warm from the sun. Now, *that's* eating!" Her father's glare swung to Margery's face. "Where you been, anyway?"

"Tom and I went for a walk."

"A walk!" Her father snorted. "I hear he's some kind of teacher."

"At the high school," Margery said. "Social studies."

"Eat your dinner, Walter, and leave the girl alone," her mother said.

"What do you know about it?" Her father laid down his knife and fork, the better to glare at her. "Damned hippies! Bet he went to college just to keep out of Vietnam!"

"Oh, Dad," Margery said, "I went for a walk with the guy. It's not as if I'm going to marry him." But she already knew that if Tom ever asked her, she would.

"Clouds." Her father stabbed his fork into a slice of tomato. "Pretending clouds are mountains!"

On Friday afternoon, when the familiar little Opel pulled up to drive Margery the few blocks home from work, Tom didn't get out. Standing inside the plate glass window with *Perkins Insurance* backward in gold lettering across it, Margery could see him hunched over the steering wheel. She grabbed her sweater, called good-bye to Sylvia, and dashed out to him. "What's wrong?"

Tom turned the key as she got in without looking at her. "I might have to find a new place to live."

"What happened?"

"Oh, Mrs. Hakkinen found some bottles in my room yesterday. It was just a couple of beers. I didn't think— In Wisconsin—" His face was bleak. "Do you think I'll lose my teaching job?"

"Oh, I don't think so," Margery said. But of course Mrs. Hakkinen was going to talk.

It didn't take long to get around town.

"Well, well, I hear that teacher fellow of yours likes to get a buzz on!" Sylvia said on Monday morning, as Margery slunk to her desk at the back of the office and took the cover off her typewriter. "You'd best be careful, joyriding in one of those little cars—"

Just then the street door slammed open and an elderly man threw himself into the office. "Took out my mailbox last night, and half my picket fence!" he sputtered. "Tire tracks right through my rose bushes!"

"Tsk." Sylvia slid a claim form out of her desk drawer. "I'm sorry to hear that, Mr. Cutter."

"I saw the whole thing! Came weaving up the street—must've been blind drunk—car came the other way, and *wham!* He swerves away, right into my fence."

"You reported the accident to the Sheriff's Department?"

"Damned straight! It was a little light-colored car, one of them foreign jobs. I even got a look at the driver in the other car's headlights. It was a damned hippie—hair on him like a girl!"

"Tsk," Sylvia said again. Her gaze moved to Margery, and then to the Polaroid snapshot, sitting on Margery's desk in its little five-and-dime-store frame, of Tom leaning against his car.

When Sylvia turned away, Margery snaked out a hand and flipped the photograph into her drawer.

She tried not to look at his car when he picked her up after work. But was that a scratch on the bumper?

Tom followed her look. "My car isn't much, but—"

"Oh, it's fine!" Margery said quickly. "A car for the proletariat! We read *Das Kapital* in Civics class my senior year with Mr. Rideout."

"Rideout?" Tom asked. "I haven't met him."

Margery looked away. "He was only here that one year."

"Huh." Tom looked suddenly tired, older. "Maybe the principal *made* him leave. That guy seems to have it in for the younger teachers. F'rinstance, today he warned me about joyriding." Tom gave Margery a crooked smile. "What kind of joyriding could I do in an Opel?"

Margery writhed under his blue-eyed gaze. "Um, well—Hey, maybe if you got a haircut . . . I could, you know, shape it a little."

"Is there anything you *can't* do, sweetheart?" He ran his hand through his hair. "Might be a good idea."

He'd called her sweetheart! Margery's eyes darted to the living room window, where her father's face swung toward them as if magnetized. "Why don't you go around back?" she squeaked. "I'll get the scissors."

Minutes later she was standing behind him as he perched on a stool in the only patch of sunlight in the back yard. She took her time combing his hair, silky between her fingers, before she took up the scissors, but soon tawny snippets cloaked his bony shoulders and littered the ground.

Tom sat with his eyes shut, all but purring. From the house came the sound of the CB radio: a man's voice, gruff and jocular, the words indistinct. "Your father really likes that radio."

"The CB is his only connection with the outside world now." Margery cocked her head as she clipped along Tom's sideburns. "The dairy farm never really paid off—Mom always had to work. And then—Well, he had asthma as a child, and all those years throwing around bales of hay, and he wouldn't give up smoking—"

"And when he got sick," Tom said gently, "you lost the farm altogether."

"That's right. We moved into town, but he never— Well—"

"Mm." Tom shifted on the stool. "Speaking of Civics, why do the kids around here feel so little connection to their own government?"

"What do you mean?" Margery asked dutifully.

"All this history happening right before their eyes! The Watergate break-in. Nixon resigning last month. And all I could get out of them was Patty Rugg saying President Ford looked better in the post office!"

"Well," Margery said, "they're young. And people around here don't talk much about politics. They're pretty conservative."

"Yeah," Tom muttered, "I've noticed."

"See, Maine people—hey, hold your head up! Maine people believe in standing on their own two feet, not asking anything from anybody. That's why it's been so tough for my dad."

"I understand. I really do. Independence, and all that. But we're talking about the law, here! The President isn't above the rule of law! Nixon might actually be put on trial—it's incredible! But can I get the kids interested? No! What kind of teacher *am* I?"

"Oh, Tom." Margery laid her hand, still holding the comb, on his shoulder. "I'm sure you're giving those kids more than you realize."

Tom took her hand in his, comb and all, and raised it to his lips. "You're great, Margery. You're beautiful, and you're sweet, and you can do anything. Cut hair, and—"

Margery felt dizzy. "Oh, stop," she murmured. "We're almost done."

As he released her hand, she lifted a lock of hair with the comb, and snipped. And watched in horror as an enormous chunk of hair fell toward the ground.

She woke in the night.

Her bedroom door was ajar, and light from downstairs shone up the darkened stairwell. Someone shouting: that's what had waked her.

And now her father's voice, deep, stagey, emphatic—his CB voice—but also excited. "Slow down, John! I didn't copy! Repeat!"

She got up and slipped out into the hallway as the other voice crackled through the radio. "Ambulance! For God's sake, Walter, call an ambulance! The guy's hardly breathing!"

"John, where are you?"

"Oh, right. Up on Mill Hill, just past Dan McAllister's place. Damned car threw him twenty feet!"

"I'm on it! Over!"

Margery pulled on some jeans over her nightgown and pushed her feet into her old sneakers. As she slid out into the hall, her father's voice came more clearly. "Breaker! Breaker! This is Farmboy. Come in, JRHardware. The ambulance is on its way, John."

"Hey, Walter. Thanks for keeping your ears on."

"How's the guy? Is he gonna make it?"

"He's still breathing, but he sounds, you know, chesty? I got him covered up with a blanket. Jeezum, I wish that ambulance would get here! I *saw* it, Walter! The car hit him, and he went flyin', and then the car just took off!"

Margery held her breath. Somehow she knew what the next question would be.

"You saw the car? John, was it a little white car? Like an Opel?"

And the answer: "Yep. Little white car."

"Then it could've been that hippie schoolteacher my daughter's seeing?"

"Suppose it could. People like him—That bastard was relaxin' in college while my boy was gettin' himself killed for his country!"

Margery slid down the stairs. As the front door snicked shut behind her, she was off and running down the street, into the soft darkness between the pools of light cast here and there by streetlamps.

Her untied sneakers slapped on the sidewalk. The cool night air swirled around her bare arms. She felt ridiculous, out here in her nightgown. But she kept running, running, until she stumbled to a stop in front of Mrs. Hakkinen's house.

The house was dark, except for the gleam of a porch light. Now what? She couldn't ring the doorbell at this hour. That would really get Tom evicted! And going back home to call him wouldn't work any better—Mrs. Hakkinen would answer. Well, maybe she could find a scrap of paper in Tom's car and leave him a note.

The Opel wasn't on the street: he must be parked in the back yard. She tiptoed up the driveway.

A barge of a station wagon sat by the side door, and a pickup truck hulked in the shadows. But no Opel.

"Oh, Tom," Margery murmured to the night. "Oh, Tom . . ."

All night she waited for morning. She had to talk to Tom before he got to school. Catch him in the parking lot.

If he hadn't totaled the Opel.

No! It wasn't Tom! It *wasn't!*

At first light she dressed quickly, slipped past the doorway of the kitchen, where her father sat at the table glaring at the percolator bubbling on the stove, and slid out the front door.

By the time she reached the high school, the faculty parking lot was already filling with cars. And here came Tom's little Opel, turning into the lot. She patted at her windblown curls and practiced what she would say. *Tom, people think—*

The Opel pulled into a parking space. The car door opened, and Tom unfolded himself and stood up, a stack of books under one arm.

At that moment a brown Sheriff's Department cruiser pulled in off the street.

It made a precise diagonal across the parking lot and pulled up next to the Opel, and two men in brown deputies' uniforms climbed out. Slam! Slam! Their doors thumped shut. They approached Tom, one from each side. He set his books on the top of his car and watched them come.

More teachers were arriving. They stood open-mouthed as Tom, flanked by the two deputies, got into the back of the cruiser. As the cruiser pulled away, the teachers' heads swiveled in unison like mechanical dolls. Margery could feel their sidelong glances rake over her as well. She knew them all. They'd been her teachers two short years ago. She did not greet them.

Behind her, a bus disgorged chattering teenagers while a second bus pulled in. As if in a dream, Margery walked toward Tom's car.

That scratch on the right front fender. It *had* been there before?

The stack of books still sat perched on the roof. Margery reached for them, then realized that Tom had locked the car. She turned and walked toward Main Street.

She was almost out of the parking lot when she heard the books slide over the trunk lid and fall to the pavement.

In the middle of the afternoon, Tom appeared in the doorway of the insurance office. Without a word, Margery got up from her desk and followed him out onto the sidewalk, out of Sylvia's hearing.

"The Sheriff let me out on my own cognizance." Tom's lanky frame curved into a despondent C as he leaned against the brick façade of the building. "But I've been put on leave from teaching. How'm I going to pay my rent? They even impounded my car!"

"Oh, Tom."

"My parents want me to come home to Wisconsin. But I can't leave town! I gave my bond."

"Tom—"

"What am I gonna do?"

"Tom?" She gripped his arm. "Tom?"

"Huh?" He looked down at her and blinked, as if surprised to find her there. "What?"

"Where were you last night?" she asked softly. "I went looking for you at Mrs. Hakkinen's, but your car wasn't there. Just in case they ask me," she added quickly when she saw the hurt pooling in his eyes.

"I drove back to my college." His voice was thick. "I just wanted to—well, walk around the campus. Have a beer. Just be myself for an evening."

He looked at her with infinite sadness. "And no, I didn't talk to anyone, so I don't have an alibi. I guess you'll just have to believe me. If you can." And he walked away down the street.

Margery didn't try to call him back. She went back inside the office, and asked Sylvia if she could leave work early.

"Guess what was just on the radio!" Sylvia said. "President Ford gave Nixon a full pardon! How about that? So *that's* all over."

More history in the making, Margery thought as she put on her sweater. And Tom probably hadn't even heard.

It was a long walk to the far end of Lower Main Street, to the Sheriff's Department. The clerk was already covering her typewriter when Margery asked to see the Sheriff.

"He's a very busy man," the clerk said. "If you want to write out a complaint—"

Margery stared at the interior door marked *Sheriff* in bold white letters. He did not come through it. "Could you give him this?" she asked, and handed the clerk the framed Polaroid of Tom leaning against the car.

"Oh, my." The clerk gawked at the photograph. "That's the guy who did that hit-and-run!"

"Who's *accused* of the hit-and run," Margery corrected her. "I want the Sheriff to notice the scratch on the front bumper. This photograph was taken way back on Labor Day, and the scratch was *already there!*"

"Well," the clerk said dubiously, "if you'll give me your name and address—"

"Jim Landers called me—just now." The tendons stood out on her father's neck as he struggled for air. "His wife works in the Sheriff's office. She says you came in with some photograph you said was evidence! Evidence!" he rasped. "Defending that criminal!"

"He's not a criminal!" Margery cried.

"Oh, just 'cause he's not sitting in jail? Special treatment for college boys is—is—what it looks like to me!" The last words came out in a painful wheeze.

"Dad, this is America! He's innocent until proven guilty, remember?"

"Margie," her mother called from the kitchen, "come and help me with the dishes, please."

Margery flung herself into the kitchen only to find the supper dishes already lined up in the pink Rubbermaid drying rack, and her mother wiping off the table with the dishrag, catching the crumbs in her open palm. "Leave your father alone," her mother said. "We can't afford another trip to the hospital."

"But—"

"But nothing." She sighed. "Margie, you *know* this isn't going to work out."

"What do you mean?"

"You and this Tom Easton." Her mother rinsed the dishrag and hung it over the faucet, then turned to face her daughter. "He'll romance you for a few weeks, and then he'll move on. When he settles down, it'll be with some fancy college girl from New York or Connecticut, and you'll still be here. And with any luck you won't be raising his kid."

"Mom!" Margery felt her face go hot.

"Well, honey—" Her mother shrugged, then reached back to untie her apron. "I expect it'll take care of itself. As soon as his trial is over, one way or the other, he'll be gone." She gave Margery a whisk of a pat on the shoulder as she left the room.

The next morning at work Margery erased typing mistakes until her desk was littered with tiny crumbs of eraser.

It wasn't as if Tom's Opel was the only small, white car in town, she fumed. The Purdy's' pale blue Mercury Comet, right across the street from her parents' house, could be mistaken for white on a dark night—although of course the Comet never left the Purdys' driveway except for trips to the grocery story.

Well, who else had a small car? As she whisked away more gray crumbs with the eraser's brush, she tried to think who—

Well, hey! They were all insured! The information on half the cars in town was in the file cabinet next to Sylvia's chair.

How could she get at it? If she got caught, Mr. Perkins would fire her for sure. Heck, Sylvia would personally kill her. Besides, when Sylvia went to lunch, she always made a big deal of locking the cabinet.

But toward the end of the morning, Margery got her chance. Mr. Perkins was in his private office with the door shut when Sylvia had wobbled on her high heels down the corridor to the bathroom. Margery dashed to the cabinet and managed to make her way through the *A*'s and up to *Barbaroni* before she heard the toilet flush.

Back at her desk, she made a note: Lucien Arsenault had a Ford Falcon. It was listed as blue. Light blue? And Lucien was thirty: he could be taken as a youngster.

When Margery went to lunch, she kindly brought Sylvia a large cup of coffee from the bakery. An hour later, Sylvia headed down the corridor again. Margery made it almost to the end of the *B*'s before scuttling back to her desk at the sound of Sylvia's tread.

All afternoon and the next morning she waited in vain for another opportunity. At this rate, she fretted, it would take her weeks to get through the file. But late in the day, luck descended like a spring rain. Mr. Perkins was out inspecting a house, and Sylvia wanted to take her mother out to supper. "She likes to eat early. Do you mind locking up?"

Sylvia took forever straightening her desk, refreshing her lipstick, putting on her coat. But at last Margery was alone, keys in hand.

She finished the *B*'s and pushed on. Randall Clark had a Falcon. Red. No: red would look black at night, and besides, Mr. Clark was sixty-three. Onward, through the *C*'s, the *D*'s, the *E*'s, through Falcons and Comets and Chevy Novas. She made a few notes, but dark colors seemed to be in style.

Flipping through the cards faster and faster now. Mrs. Fortier had a pale yellow Dodge Dart. But she was old, in her eighties at least, and so short that when she drove herself sedately to church she had to peer through the steering wheel, not over it. No joyriding for her!

The *G*'s, the *H*'s, moving faster and faster, in case Mr. Perkins came back and wondered why the office was still open. The *M*'s— McAllisters, Milletts, a heartbreaking number of *M*'s. *N*'s and *P*'s, and on Mr. Perkins' very own card she got a paper cut, and had to dash to the bathroom for a bit of toilet paper to keep from bleeding all over it.

It was almost 5:30, and she wasn't getting anywhere. She gathered what notes she had, locked the file cabinet and then the office, and trudged home going the long way, via Elm Street, to have a look at Lucien Arsenault's Falcon, just in case. It was parked at the curb, newly polished. Without a scratch.

At dawn Margery sat up in bed.

Mrs. Fortier hadn't driven herself to church last Sunday. She'd come with the Kimballs.

And the week before, she'd been dropped off out front. Margery remembered it because—because—

She strained to picture it: the car pulling up in front of the church, Mrs. Fortier climbing out—

And the car pulling away with a screech of tires.

Jeff. Jeff Fortier, her grandson. He'd been a year behind Margery in school. Tall and rangy, always wore oil-stained blue jeans and steel-toed work boots to school as if he'd just come in from the woodlot. She didn't think he'd graduated. Probably one day he went to work in the woods with his father, and that was that.

Was he staying with Mrs. Fortier at her house? Or borrowing her car now and then?

Margery leapt out of bed and skittered down the stairs to the living room, where she yanked the phone book out of the drawer of the telephone stand. In the pale light dribbling in between the drapes, she flipped through the pages.

Mrs. Fortier lived on Thurgood Street. Number 172.

At 7:30—the earliest she could decently show up on someone's doorstep—Margery trotted up Mrs. Fortier's front walk. The house, white with sky blue trim, was so tiny and neat that it looked like a dollhouse. Mrs. Fortier answered the door in a lime green housedress and a lumpy, hand-knit purple sweater. Below the hem of her skirt, her swollen ankles overflowed her fluffy bedroom slippers like rising bread dough.

"Good morning!" Margery said heartily. "I was looking for Jeff. Is he living here with you?"

"Jeffrey?" Mrs. Fortier repeated vaguely. Her hand flew up to touch her face, twisted the top button of her housedress, and finally grasped her other hand under her generous bosom. "Oh, no, Jeffrey's—um—he's gone away." She peered at Margery through her trifocals, tipping her head to find the right lens for the job. "To Florida, I think. A construction job. Yes, that's it. He got a construction job down there."

"Mrs. Fortier," Margery said gently, "where's your car? Did Jeff take it to Florida?"

"Oh, no," Mrs. Fortier said. "I mean," she added quickly, "maybe he did. I— I'm not sure."

She had glanced toward the barn.

Margery looked past the house to where the barn leaned tiredly to one side. "Is your car in the barn, Mrs. Fortier? Do you mind if I look?"

"Well—" the old lady said. But Margery was already trotting toward the back yard.

The barn door was heavy on its ancient rollers, and she had to heave her weight against it before it budged. If the car was in here, certainly Mrs. Fortier had not been the one to close it in. At last the door relented, and slid open with a groan.

Behind it sat the car: a pale yellow Dodge Dart, streaked with mud dried to a pale brown.

Margery stepped into the barn. The air was cool and musty. She slipped along the inside wall and worked her way around to the front of the car.

On the right side, the headlight hung like an eyeball from the crumpled fender.

When she came back to the house, she found the old lady just where she'd left her, standing in the open doorway, but now tears slid out from under the trifocals and down her papery cheeks. "Mrs. Fortier," Margery asked, "was it Jeff who banged up your car? The night that man was hit up on Mill Hill?"

"That man—" Mrs. Fortier dabbed at her eyes with the hem of her sweater. "They say he's going to be all right."

"Yes, that's what I've heard. But, Mrs. Fortier, you've still got to report this. You've got to tell the Sheriff what Jeff did."

"Oh, I couldn't go to the Sheriff." Mrs. Fortier shook her head, then clutched at the doorframe as if the motion had thrown her off balance. "I could never do that."

"I'll go with you," Margery offered.

Mrs. Fortier's shoulders slumped. She let out a long sigh. "I'll get dressed," she said.

Tom called to say he wanted to see her. One last time, Margery figured, before he went away. How could he stay here after all this? And how could he forgive her for doubting him?

But when the little Opel pulled up in front of the house, he unbent himself and stood grinning at her across the top of the car. "Want to go for a walk? The leaves are already beginning to turn! What a beautiful day!"

She felt dizzy as she rose from the steps where she'd been waiting. "You—you're not mad at me?"

"Mad? Justice prevailed! I'm cleared of all charges on that accident, and I'm back in the classroom on Monday!" He bounded around the car like an overgrown puppy and took her hand. "Come on! Let's go!"

"But—"

"And you know what? I've been thinking about how to get my students interested in my Civics course. You heard that Ford pardoned Nixon? So he'll never come to trial! It leaves all kinds of questions! Did they make a deal? Does it mean that Nixon admits his guilt?" He drew Margery down the sidewalk. "I'm going to set up my class like a debate team."

"But, Tom—" Margery had to trot to keep up. "What about your—your case? You didn't even have a hearing?"

"Oh," he said, "they found out who did it! Evidently some sweet little old lady came in and told them she'd had an accident with her car. They never would've suspected her, but she said she felt bad, and she came in all on her own and gave them the whole story. Isn't that great?"

"Well, see, actually—" Margery began.

"The old lady promised to give up driving, poor thing, so the guy who got hit decided not to press charges." Tom wrapped his arm around Margery's waist. "People around here are so incredibly honest!"

"Oh, yes," Margery said, and left it at that.

Judith Green is a sixth-generation resident of a village in Maine's western mountains, with the fifth, seventh, and eighth generations living nearby. She served for many years as director of adult education for her eleven-town school district, and has twenty-five high-interest, low-level books for adult new readers in print. She has had a story chosen for each of the Level Best anthologies; the story published in *Thin Ice* (2010) was nominated for an Edgar®. She is currently branching out with a mystery novel starring Margery Easton as sleuth, and working on a YA or two.

Shades of Gray

Stephen D. Rogers

Mrs. Gray loved animals.

She couldn't bear to see them abused, neglected, or even left to fend for themselves. To that end she coaxed strays to her doorstep with food and drink, and thus taught them to trust her enough to eventually come inside her home.

Mrs. Gray treated the animals well and with kindness. And then, when they were ready, she put them out of their misery. She buried them with dignity and respect.

Neighbors occasionally reported Mrs. Gray to Animal Control and the local humane society, but the creatures she killed were wild, and the methods she used were humane. After all, Mrs. Gray loved animals.

The only thing she loved more than animals were children. She couldn't bear to see them abused, neglected, or even left to fend for themselves. Whenever she saw one playing alone in the woods, she lowered her shades and started to bake.

Stephen D. Rogers is the co-author of *A Miscellany of Murder* and the author of *Shot to Death, Three-Minute Mysteries*, and more than 700 shorter pieces. His website, www.StephenDRogers.com, includes a list of new and upcoming titles as well as other timely information.

Double Wedding

Mo Walsh

The bride's side or the groom's?" The usher looked like he was staring at his own cocked elbow, but I knew he was checking out my cleavage. The low neckline of my sheer silk blouse was deliciously cool for a July wedding in Virginia, where the churches are too historic for air conditioning and the stained glass windows are too valuable to actually open. The electric fans humming in the corners moved just enough air to keep everyone breathing.

I clutched the usher's arm almost as close as he would have liked me to, threw him a hip check and a wink, and whispered, "Definitely the groom's side. I'm Frankie's first . . . girlfriend."

He squinted at my face, or what he could see of me under my new church hat, a luscious confection of white blossoms and bows with a six-inch brim. He leered like a party-hardy frat boy until he noticed Dillon scowling at him over my shoulder. My guy was doing that smoking volcano thing he does so well, like he'd erupt in the middle of the wedding if another guy looked at me, or my cleavage, too close.

"Come this way," said the usher, suddenly all serious. He steered us to a pew under the choir loft and behind a pillar, where I wouldn't upstage the bride, I guess, or distract the groom. I plucked the program from his hand and slid across the maple seat polished smooth by two hundred years of prosperous Episcopal rumps. Dillon slid his own exceptionally fine rump next to me and sat up, posture-perfect, against the straight-backed pew. With him sitting like a stone wall between me and the aisle, I was just about invisible to everyone else in the church. Perfect.

I fanned myself with the wedding program, engraved—not printed—on stiff manila stationery and embossed with ribbons, doves, and two entwined wedding rings accented with gold leaf. The names of the bridal couple were barely readable in ornate script: Evelyn Rose Beale and Franklin Dwight Hillchurch, Junior. Frankie was the old boyfriend I'd never actually had, and Ever-ready Rose was the cousin I'd had up to here for most of my teens.

Yes, we were Evelyn and Beverly, "Evvy and Bevvy." Her mother beat mine by thirty-seven hours in the race to produce the first new baby girl on the Beale side of the family. My cousin was named Evelyn after our grandmother. In a misguided gesture, Mummy named me after Grandmother's long-dead twin. She didn't know her aunt, "Bountiful Bev," had been a centerfold.

Grandmother was long gone now, but I spotted some vaguely familiar faces scattered around the church. Probably relatives, come down from Boston for the genteel wedding of "the congressman's girl" to one of the Tidewater elite. Most of them hadn't aged well, despite cosmetic surgery, expensive hairpieces, and the elaborate, concealing hats still in vogue since the last royal wedding.

"You're sure your folks won't be there?" Dillon had asked when I first suggested crashing Evvy's wedding. We were lounging by the pool at Atlantic City's Resorts Casino Hotel, courtesy of a Boston banker who didn't yet know we'd swiped his credit card numbers.

"They always skip these family deals," I said. "Ever since my first arraignment. They send regrets and a pricey gift, then go on a cruise or something."

My first conviction for shoplifting ended happily when I hooked up with Dillon in the court-ordered therapy group. My parents tried sending me to an obscure college with a flexible admissions policy, but four years later, while my classmates were texting during the dean's speech, I was graduating from a three-month stretch for larceny in the women's cellblock at MCI Framingham. Mom and Dad were on safari at the time.

"I don't know, Bev." Dillon stretched out in his lounge chair in a way that made me want to drag him into the nearest changing room.

"You're unforgettable, babe. Some great-aunt or cousin or randy old uncle is bound to spot you."

"Nobody's seen me in four years, except for the mug shot," I said. "And that was meek little Mindy, not me." I'd been way dressed down for the Mindy-the-Bingo-worker scam, and my cousin's wedding was the first big family gathering since I'd jumped bail. No way were my parents going to show their faces. And no one would be expecting mine.

"So what's the deal, Bev?" Dillon had asked. "Don't tell me you wanted a big church wedding after all?"

Just two weeks earlier, me and Dillon had been married by a justice of the peace in Connecticut. There's no waiting period there, meaning no time between getting the license and getting hitched for our names to show up in some cop database. We'd come right from the mountain theme resort where we'd been working and laying low, which is why Dillon looked studly in lederhosen and I wore a sexy dirndlette and carried a spray of fake edelweiss.

"I'm not a church wedding kind of gal," I reassured Dillon, "but there is one thing I bet Evvy will have for her wedding that should be ours."

After a spot of marital cherishing back in the Resort Casino's honeymoon suite, he agreed.

So here we were. As I expected, Evvy's wedding was a big budget production choreographed by a wedding planner with a whole cast of designers, florists, musicians, make-up artists, and probably plastic surgeons. I looked around the church, at the garlands of peach blossoms twined around every other pillar, the masses of flowers in silver vases by the altar, the fussy clusters of peach satin ribbon, white lace, and pearls marking the VIP pews. The sunlight streaming through the stained glass windows scattered bits of color everywhere. Was I jealous?

I nudged Dillon and blew him a kiss from under the brim of my hat. He hooked his left foot around my right ankle and tugged me closer. Maybe there wasn't a lot of ambiance at our wedding, but nothing could have been more romantic than me and my guy pledging to love, honor, and cherish, and never testify against each other, forever till death do us part. Amen.

I ran through our plan in my head until the organ stopped its subdued tooting. The vicar or archdeacon or whatever he was took his place at the front with a couple of sly-looking altar kids. The groom and best man crept in on the right and a sweaty bald guy with eighty pounds of camera equipment tried to look invisible in the middle of the aisle.

The organist pounded out big, booming chords, and three hundred heads swiveled toward the back of the church with the inevitable collisions and adjustments of hat brims. Heads bobbed and more hats collided as people leaned this way and that way, half-stood and sat back down to glimpse the groom's parents and the mother of the bride with her escort. Mrs. Hillchurch, Senior, won the gown competition easily in a two-toned peach silk suit. Aunt Marguerite, on the other hand, was swathed in ivory chiffon with peach piping and more sequins than the entire Ice Capades. The ushers unrolled the white runner, the organ played some Masterpiece Theatre theme, and the rest of the parade passed by—little girls in big hats and frills, six overly-styled women in cantaloupe Pippa dresses with more pew decorations stuck in their hair, and then a hugely pregnant matron of honor in a darker peach gown.

"The bride is next, right?" said Dillon as the crowd exchanged murmured fashion critiques. "Or does the royal guard come riding in?"

I shook my head. "No horses in church, except the bride."

"Giddyup, here she comes," he said. The organ broke into the predictable duh-DUH-duh-duh, and the guests surged to their feet, jostling each other and blinding the bride in their attempts to take free wedding photos.

I had to admit Evvy looked pretty good for a sneaky, two-faced, stuck-up snitch. Her gown was Kate Middleton's on estrogen with a deeper décolletage, fancier lace, a fuller skirt, and more sparkle. Her tiara could have been swiped from the Little Miss Toddler Princess Pageant. With the veil down, she could pass for female. Uncle Bryce looked relieved.

The groom didn't flee during the long procession down the aisle, but stepped forward to meet his fate. He looked harmless, more like a waiter or a violinist than a stock trader. The archvicar said, "Let us pray!'" so I said a small one for poor Franklin Dwight Hillchurch, Junior.

"Lovely ceremony!" I repeated for the eighty-ninth time as me and Dillon strolled about the terrace of the Queensbury Country Club. We kept moving past anyone who tried to strike up a conversation, and I fanned myself with the wedding program to shield my face. The cocktail reception would easily last two hours while every combination of attendants, Beales, and Hillchurches was corralled, posed, and photographed at the antebellum gazebo overlooking the first fairway.

Armed with two glasses of desert-dry champagne, we entered the club and passed through the salon outside the ballroom where some of the older guests dozed on sofas and club chairs. Dillon spotted the table set aside for gifts and cards, with the guest book on a stand next to it. I tried to figure out what was inside each package and which envelopes contained the biggest checks, while he signed us in as "Ms. Kitty and the Honorable M. Dillon." My guy is named for the marshal on his old man's favorite western show, *Gunsmoke*. His dad is a cop, but the law and order thing didn't take.

"See him?" Dillon tipped his head toward a muscular man in a khaki suit, plain navy tie, and highly polished shoes. He leaned against the wall, a glass in his hand, but I noted the way the guy's eyes scanned the salon, keeping the gift table always in view. I nodded. Off-duty cop. You don't get to be Macy's public enemy number one without learning to spot security.

We walked past Khaki Cop to an alcove where a slide show of the bridal couple, from their separate infancies through their gawky teens and mushy courtship, flashed on a large flat-screen monitor. There was Evvy surrounded by little girls and blowing out eight candles on a cake.

"See me?" I asked Dillon.

"No." He peered closer. "Where are you?"

"At home, crying because I didn't get invited."

"Why not?"

"Because the little snitch tattled on me for taking a stupid pair of Barbie shoes. You know," I said when he looked puzzled, "the little plastic high heels that go with Barbie's evening gown?"

"She ratted you out over doll shoes?"

I nodded. "And there, in that prom picture? That's my boyfriend, but Evvy got his mom to make him break up with me."

"His loss." Dillon pulled me close.

"I got nabbed at MegaMed with a ten-dollar nail polish, 'Damson in the Dark,' the perfect shade to go with my gown."

"Damson? What color's that?" Dillon pressed slow kisses to each of my fingertips with that look in his eyes that made me want to undo buttons and zippers and hang onto his ears.

I sighed. "Who cares?"

Someone behind us snorffled like an irritated thoroughbred. "Get a room!" said the frat boy usher, as he trotted past. For once I thought he had a point, but I pulled my hand away. Dillon resisted just enough to let me know we'd pick up again later.

"Anyway," I said, "Daddy-dearest made the charges disappear, but Evvy found out and told her mom, and she told Dirk's mom. His parents wouldn't let him date me anymore, so he took Ever-ready to the prom."

"Dirk? What a jerk!" Dillon snorted. "Forget him, babe."

"He's nothing. But Evvy! She was always Princess Perfect and I was a fix-up project. She got good grades and dancing lessons. I got corrections on my grammar and Saturday detention. When Grandmother Beale died, Evvy got the bone china and I got the brass candlesticks. She got the Tiffany lamps and I got the complete Shakespeare. She got our grandmother's diamond wedding bracelet." It still steamed me to think of it. ". . . and I got old fish face's chinless profile on a cameo the size of an egg. You can't even pawn a thing like that!"

Dillon kissed my wrist. "Why didn't you grab the diamonds, if you wanted them?" That's one of the things I love about him. He's got faith in me.

I smiled. "Evvy flashed that bracelet under my nose one too many times, and—oops!—the clasp must have broken. It disappeared right off her wrist in the Park Plaza ballroom on New Year's Eve. She was so upset, I gave her the cameo."

"That's my Bev."

"Yeah, but I could never wear that bracelet." I sighed. "Too many people knew about it, so I had to fence it for about a quarter of its worth. But I picked up a jazzy diamond tennis bracelet at Filene's."

We watched more shots of Evvy and Franklin on a tennis court, at the beach, on the ski slope—like awkward models in a vacation brochure. More people wandered in from the terrace, clustering in small groups, keeping Khaki Cop busy scanning for trouble. Dillon and me slipped by him to the restrooms.

"Time for the juggling act," said Dillon, pulling me close for a good luck kiss. I nudged him towards the door marked Gentlemen and slipped into the Ladies.

The QCC Ladies Lounge could fit a dozen females in puffy skirts and full trains, with room in each of the six stalls to park a Hummer. Pretending to dig in my purse for some feminine necessity, I edged past three chattering girls fussing with each other's hair, locked the louvered door to my private throne room, and went to work.

You don't get to be a success in my profession without a proper appreciation of accessories. With the right kind of shoulder bag and layers, I can change appearance five times between the cosmetic counter and electronics. And that's on the move. Here I just needed to keep the black skirt, change the collapsible shoes, switch the silk blouse for sturdy white cotton and a clip-on bow tie. Strip off the jewelry, tone down the make-up, tie back the hair, leaving a few strands loose, flatten the pop-up hat, and tah-dah! No more elegant wedding guest, just a frazzled QCC waitress with trash bag. Make that two bags: the outer one stuffed with my wedding guest accessories and the one inside it filled with wadded up paper towels. I wore a badge labeled "Kitty" above my left boob.

I waited till the chatterers left, but out in the lounge area I was waylaid by a limping blimp of a woman wearing a baby blue lace tent. "You work here, girl?" she demanded in clipped Yankee tones, which meant there was a better than even chance she'd once given me a silver christening spoon.

I wanted to strike a pose with my trash bag and say, "Ya think?" but I answered in my softest southern voice, "Yes, ma'am, I sure do." I smiled, showing the fake teeth just crooked and off-color enough to make most people look away. "C'n I help you?"

I hoped for a simple errand—aspirin, hairspray, the paramedics—anything to get me out of there quick. Dillon should already be in position.

"The heel broke off of my shoe." She collapsed on the chaise longue and thrust out her leg to show me a blue satin Badgley Mischka minus the four-inch spike designed to support, well, not her. She jabbed the heel at me like a blunt blue dagger. "Have the concierge find someone to fix that for me, girl. Quickly."

"Yes, ma'am. You sit right here, and I'll get that seen to right away." I took the heel in one hand and held my other one out for the shoe. She frowned like maybe she had a maid at home to pry off her footwear, so I did the reverse-Cinderella thing, wriggling the slipper that didn't fit off the ugly stepsister's foot. I made myself smile and say, "I believe the golf shop can fix this for you, ma'am. They custom fit shoes for all the pros, you know."

I don't know where I come up with these things, I swear. Dillon says it's a talent. Anyway, I got away with the shoe and stashed it in the outer bag. I was already working it into the plan as I hustled back toward the salon.

I almost didn't recognize Dillon with the greasy gray stuff in his hair, the nerd glasses, and his shoulders all stooped over. He was wearing the same black slacks, though, and I'd know that prime posterior anywhere. He'd found himself a tray and was collecting empty glasses and plates piled with used toothpicks and gnawed-off shrimp tails. Dillon knew I was there and set to go—we have this extra sense about each other, like twins, only sexier.

Dillon carried his tray over to Khaki Cop, while I approached the guy from behind. "May I take that glass for you, sir?" Dillon asked, reaching for the empty. "Would you like me to bring you another?"

"Yeah, that'd be good. Thanks," said the cop. "Just ginger ale."

"Hey, Kitty," Dillon drawled as I came even with them. "Get the door for me, darlin'—please?"

"Sure will, honey." I stepped past the cop without looking at him and held open the door to the ballroom. Dillon swept through with his tray and I followed him in.

The room was another explosion of peach blossoms and lace, from the wall swags and centerpieces to the frosting on the wedding cake. The fourth cake tier was topped with porcelain lovebirds nested in two entwined wedding rings, tiny peach blossoms dangling from their beaks. The string quartet was setting up in one corner, while the waitstaff lounged in another. The water glasses were all filled, the baskets of rolls were set out, and the salads were wilting at each place setting.

Through the French doors to the terrace, I could see the wedding planner assembling the bridal party for their grand entrance. I thought Evvy looked pink from either too much champagne or a touch of sunburn. I bet all that white really reflects the UV rays.

"Here, Kitty-Kitty!" Dillon growled next to my ear. "Shake your tail, babe."

"Remind me to rub up against your legs later, Marshal," I purred, then stalked away to my position. The first guests should wander in looking for their tables in about thirteen seconds.

Dillon hoisted his tray and wound his way through the closely packed tables, heading for the polished oak dance floor. He made it almost all the way across before one little plate toppled off the tray, scattering shrimp tails right under his feet. Then it was like one of those cartoons, with the tray going this way and Dillon's legs going that way and all the glasses and plates and shrimp bits circling in the air like they got picked up by a tornado. Dillon's got some moves.

The waiters and waitresses were shouting and screaming and rushing forward like they had a chance of catching anything. Then just like a Super Bowl champion, Dillon lunged for the tray and came crashing down in the end zone—smack in the middle of the head table. Place settings went flying, littering the table with upended china, glass shards, silverware, and scraps of endive and radicchio.

Right on cue, the first wedding guests burst through the ballroom door eager to see what was going on. Even Khaki Cop poked his head around the door. Then the wedding planner broke through the crowd like an NFL linebacker looking to sack either whoever had—or had dropped—the ball. She recovered her smile just long enough to herd the guests back out, then dodged past the banquet tables while issuing orders into her lip mic. In seconds, uniformed bodies swarmed the head table and dance floor with trays, bus bins, towels, trash bags, and complete new place settings.

I missed the visual details of the next two minutes, being otherwise occupied with my own little mission, but the soundtrack could have won an Oscar for *Wedding Crashers* meets *Jurassic Park*. I nestled my prize between my outer and inner trash bags, checked to make sure I was unnoticed, and worked my way back to Dillon. I dropped to my knees next to him, scooping shrimp tails into my inside trash bag, but being careful not to jostle anything too much. Me and Dillon merged with the Queensbury clean-up crew shuttling wreckage from the ballroom to the kitchen, then slipped out a back door to the delivery parking lot.

After one admiring glance at the classic white Rolls-Royce waiting to carry away the bridal couple, Dillon jimmied open the florist's van. I jumped in the back and did a quick change among the empty buckets of water and extra spools of peach ribbon. When I was back in my wedding guest gear, I climbed up in front next to Dillon. "How did I do?"

"Smooth, Bev, totally smooth!" He laid a real smacker on me, and for a second I considered making a bit more room in the back of the van. Then Dillon said, "Sure you don't want to scram now?"

"I can't leave till the bride throws her tantrum. You didn't think I'd miss the best part, did you?"

"Not a chance, babe, but I had to ask."

I adjusted the brim of my hat so the big peach bow tipped jauntily to the side, and pulled my blouse straight, with just a little jiggle to reward Dillon for noticing. Carefully, I reached back for the trash bag and handed our prize to Dillon. "Take care of that for me, okay? I'll meet you after sunset."

He flicked my earring. "Go."

I slipped around the side of the club and in through the terrace doors. Khaki Cop was still on duty when I sashayed through the salon. The wedding planner, fresh from the disaster in the ballroom, was listening to the complaints of the blue tent lady, standing lopsided in her one good shoe. I made it into the ballroom just in time for the bridal couple's grand entrance. Evvy looked just a bit off-kilter, and I swear her left eye was twitching. She hung onto Franklin's arm like even now she was afraid he'd come to his senses, and he looked kind of stunned like the drugs were wearing off.

I waited for it: five, four, three, two . . . Evvy shrieked. Some guests looked at the smoke alarms and a few even scrambled for the exits. Then every eye followed her outstretched hand to the little alcove where the wedding cake sat on its special table. Each layer was a masterpiece of bows and flowers and curlicues sculpted in frosting with peach accents. The top layer, in particular, was a luscious-looking confection. Only a closer look would have shown it was made of inedible lace and silk flowers, like the crown of a stylish wedding hat, and accented with pink shrimp tails. But everyone could see the peculiar cake topper—no longer porcelain lovebirds, but a blue satin, high-heeled shoe.

The lights blazed from the Queensbury Country Club, where guests were drinking and dancing and probably texting and tweeting the delicious details to all their friends. I was sure somebody had already posted a video of the bawling bride on YouTube. I wondered if anyone got dessert or if Khaki Cop had taken the vandalized cake into evidence and draped the alcove with crime scene tape.

I slipped up the steps to the gazebo, where Dillon was waiting. The soft moonlight of early evening glinted off the knife in his hand. I grasped the hilt, too, and together we cut into our wedding cake with the antique porcelain cake topper that had been one of Grandmother Beale's prized heirlooms. Dillon had smoothed over the divot where I scooped out frosting to hold the heel on the shoe, and he'd stripped off the peach blossoms that were choking the lovebirds. Now they perched in the double wedding rings, their beaks open as if they were singing or waiting for worms.

Me and Dillon fed each other wedding cake until we worked up an appetite for more marital cherishing. So we did. As the moon rose over the gazebo, we got dressed, packed everything back in the trash bags, and went off to hotwire the Rolls.

Mo Walsh has written genteel wedding announcements and engaging bridal shop ads during her motley career in journalism and advertising. She now writes newspaper features and crime fiction. Mo's stories have appeared in *Mary Higgins Clark Mystery Magazine*, *Woman's World*, and five Level Best Books anthologies. She lives in Weymouth, Massachusetts, with her husband of thirty-one years and their sons.

The Pendulum Swings, Until It Doesn't

J.A. Hennrikus

At the center of the very collaborative art form that is theater rests the stage manager. She is the right hand of the director during rehearsals, runs the show during performances, and takes the work of the designers and makes it work on stage. She is also the troubleshooter in chief, anticipating problems and solving them on the spot. Some stage managers go beyond the call of duty. But Adele Lane went way beyond.

Adele had been at Bellingham Rep for a little over two years. Her entire career had been spent moving around to different regional theaters, spending up to five years, but no longer. Like Mary Poppins, Adele would, with a combination of common sense and tough love, turn a company around. Systems would be improved. Production meetings produced results instead of acrimony. Decorum would come back to the rehearsal hall. The work would improve.

Respect was her default. Everyone got it, from the usher to the Artistic Director. Everyone got it, until they didn't. And when someone lost Adele Lane's respect, they had to go.

At Bellingham Rep, the resident scenic designer was Josh Costa. Adele had her sights on him after the first production, when the furniture he insisted on hadn't fit through the doors he designed. In order to move between scenes there had to be blackouts, which the director hated. And even though extra crew (and extra expense) was added, scene changes were a nightmare. The director, Fran Smith, had worked with Adele in other companies, and had talked her into coming to Bellingham a year after she became Artistic Director. Josh had come with the theater, and the board made it clear he wasn't leaving. Little of that had to do with talent. Most of it was due to Josh's family money, which was a large part of the operating budget. A promised endowment to the theater stopped people from looking for another source of money, or other scenic designers.

For the final show of the season, Josh had created a large clock pendulum that swept across the stage from side to side. In order for it to move, it had to be heavy. In order for it not to kill anyone, it required an intricate rigging system, and a number of crew on either side of the stage to steady or stop it on its arc. Josh insisted it was metaphoric for the passing of time.

"Yeah, yours," Adele thought. But she made it work. She helped Fran re-block several scenes in order to make sure none of the actors got hurt. Adele spent hours working with the pendulum, timing the arc, taping out the areas where it would come into the wings and filling them in with yellow spike tape so that actors could avoid the area.

For the spring gala, the pendulum was secured stage right, where there was enough room to keep it elevated and out of everyone's way. Adele's calling station was across the stage, where she could see the audience and the stage action, but no one could see her. As with all Adele-run events, the timing was perfect. Josh stood stage right, waiting for his entrance. He was always the last to speak, as the biggest donor and a founding member of the company. Fran was finishing her speech and about to call him on stage when she was interrupted by the sound of a watermelon smashing, followed by a visual of the pendulum dribbling blood across the stage. The thud of Josh's body hitting the ground seemed deafening in the stunned silence of the theater. Then all hell broke loose.

Adele poured another shot of bourbon for both herself and Fran.

"I can't believe it is over," Fran said.

"But it is. A horrible accident, that's what the cop said." Adele sipped the bourbon. Accident. Hah. People never understood what it takes to create theater. Figuring out the physics of the pendulum swing, and how much weight needed to be added to make it deadly. Coordinating the run crew so that no one else was on stage or in the wings. Marking the exact spot where Josh had to stand in order for him to be hit in the head. Figuring out the electronic device that would help release the rope. Timing the moment when Adele spoke to him so he would turn just enough to not see the pendulum come down the moment she released the cord. The careful sprint behind the backdrop so that Adele could be back at her calling station on the other side of the stage and step out at the right moment and rush back to where she had just been.

The horrified look on her face? The tears when the cops arrived? Both well rehearsed. From years of practice.

"I'm going to be leaving at the end of the season," Adele said after a moment.

"Can't you stay a little longer?" Fran asked.

"No, my job here is done. I know I said three years, but the pendulum was too good to pass up. Are you sure that his will is all set?"

"Yes, we met with the lawyers last week. After I promised him we'd do *Les Mis* next season. He left it all to the theater."

Adele shuddered at the thought of a barricade by Josh. No, the timing had been right.

"Where will you go?" Fran asked.

"I hear that the Paris Theater Company hired Sara Engel to be their new Managing Director," Adele said.

Fran nodded. Rumor was that Sara had fired most of the staff, and was stacking the board so that she could get rid of the Artistic Director. It had been the talk of the last league meeting.

Yes, the Paris Theater Company needed Adele's special talents. The winds had shifted. Adele Lane had more work to do.

J.A. Hennrikus is the Executive Director of StageSource, a service organization for the New England theater community. She is working on a series that combines murder, mystery, and theater. Her short stories have appeared in *Thin Ice* and *Dead Calm*. Julie tweets under @JulieHennrikus, and blogs on nhwn.wordpress.com, and is the VP of Sisters in Crime/NE.

The Project

Frank Cook

I'm in the parking garage waiting for the elevator. I'm nervous. Maybe angry. But more nervous than angry. And depressed. I don't know if I'll be fired when I step off the elevator upstairs, or if Nichols will wait until I'm walking past the floor traders so he can publicly humiliate me.

Breckenridge would prefer that, of course, but I don't think it's Nichols' style. As a senior VP, he'll summon me to his glassed-in office and do it there. A semi-private execution.

Nichols is anal. He's probably up there now, checking and rechecking company policy. Huddling with Breckenridge. Making sure he's on solid ground.

He'll call me into his office and recite what I did. Breckenridge— "Mr. Superstar"—will be there, too, smugly telling me I'll be hearing from his lawyer. Then security will escort me out of the building.

My stomach hurts. I don't know why I bothered to come in today.

On the G2 level—the blue level—the elevator doors are brushed chrome and reflect me in a soft, indistinct image. I can't make out the pattern in my red tie, but I can see my white shirt and gray suit. Maybe I should have worn blue pinstripes today. Nobody gets fired wearing blue pinstripes.

Well, maybe they do if they've tried to kill a colleague.

When I get upstairs, maybe I should apologize. I could dismiss the whole thing as the heat of competition. I could blame Nichols— it's his fault for making me and Breckenridge rivals. I could say it was stress. "No harm, no foul, eh Breck?" I could say. "Of course I'll pay for the damage to your car. Yes, I was a little distraught last night,

but hey, you were a little hot yourself. But I'm OK now. Really."
Firm handshake.

I rock back on my heels, waiting. Who am I kidding? That's not
how it's going to come down.

The elevator doors reflect a woman approaching behind me. I
casually look around to see who my companion will be—someone I
have to make conversation with or someone I can ignore.

"Good morning, John," says Kate Burr.

Nichols' executive assistant is a narrow woman in her late forties.
I wonder if she's already been briefed on what happened.

"Good morning, Kate," I smile. "How was the drive in?"

She shrugs. "Wet. Terrible time getting home last night in the
rain and it was even worse coming in this morning."

No hint of awareness.

The chrome doors finally separate and I allow her to step ahead
of me into the wood-paneled elevator.

"So, are you boys ready for a boardroom battle today?" she says
sardonically as we begin our ascent. "Winner take all. Loser jumps
off the building?"

I demur. "I don't think it will be that bad," I say. "Different
approaches really, that's all. The important thing is that Mr. Nichols
chooses a direction so we can all move forward on the project."

Kate seems surprised.

"That's a commendable attitude," she nods. "I heard you guys
were at each other's throats yesterday in the office."

She hasn't heard what happened later in the parking garage.

I offer a dismissive wave. "Well, we've both worked pretty hard
on our positions. Sometimes things get a little out of hand . . ."

Our conversation ends at the lobby level. The elevator takes on
four more passengers, two with folded, wet umbrellas; one with a
diet book sticking out of her purse; and the fourth holding a steaming
cup of coffee. The aroma fills our space as we resume our rise. Idle
chitchat suggests there won't be a break in the weather until tomorrow.

I look at the floors everyone has chosen. I'm about a minute
away from my destiny.

By the time we reach the twenty-first floor, the umbrellas, the
diet book and the coffee have exited, again leaving only me and Kate.

I move to the rear and allow her to step forward. I won't be surprised if building security is waiting for me. Hell, maybe even the police.

A cinderblock. Right on the windshield of that stupid little Mini Cooper. "Yes, I know I shouldn't have done it," I'll say. "I'll go quietly."

The soft ping and gentle bounce of the elevator tell me we've arrived. I hear the mechanics of the door opening. Hillary is straight ahead, alone at the wide black-and-gray reception desk with her headset on, sitting just below an understated silver-on-black sign that advises, "Investment Innovators, LLC."

No security. No police.

"Meeting's at ten o'clock," Kate reminds as she moves away from me. "I'm going to set up a metal detector," she teases. "You boys better leave your guns in your desks."

"OK," I laugh half-heartedly and watch her go.

She greets Hillary as she walks past, following the hallway to the right that eventually will take her to Nichols' office. I hesitate long enough that I have to stop the elevator from closing before I get out. It won't be easy finding a new job.

Better to get it over with.

"Good morning, Mr. Trainer," Hillary says, and promptly punches a button on her intercom. "Beth, he's here," she announces into her microphone, and then back to me, "She wanted to know the instant you arrived."

Beth is my Tonto, and I her Lone Ranger. She enjoys the comparison. "Tonto was the one who was good with a knife," she notes. "I've got your back." It's her favorite phrase.

I wonder if Beth will be fired too. After I'm gone, she'll float for a while and then be reassigned to another junior VP. Still, she'll be out of the company within a couple of months. That's how these things go.

I regret I won't be around to console her, or remind her that she's young and smart, that she survived three tough years on the trading floor before becoming my assistant. She'll have no problem finding work.

Still, she was counting on a raise and a bonus if we won today. And another step closer to being a junior VP herself. She'll be devastated.

The shortest distance to my office is a corridor to the left of the reception desk. Before I take three steps, the redheaded, caustic dynamo wearing a navy pantsuit bursts into the hallway to greet me.

"Are we ready to kick a little Breckenridge butt?" Beth enthuses.

I raise my hand to get her to back off a little. "Beth, we need to talk."

She's walking backward, not paying attention to me. "I went over the numbers again last night. We are dead solid perfect on this thing. If we go Breck's way, the whole division will be belly up inside a year. See . . ." she says, raising a spreadsheet in my face.

"Beth, give me just a second, OK? I'm going to get some coffee. Meet me in my office. Is Breck here yet?"

Beth calms herself, like a cheerleader composing herself before exploding into the next leap.

"Haven't seen him yet. Wade's here. That jolly old fat asshole. But I haven't seen Breck."

Wade McGill is Breck's Tonto, though he probably wouldn't appreciate the reference. He's a nice enough guy, funny at parties, but grotesquely overweight. Harvard MBA. By all accounts, he's good with numbers but his personality and personal appearance make him strictly second string. That's probably why Breck chose him. No threat to his "star power."

I have to go by their offices en route to the break room. If Breck is there, maybe I'll try to apologize. Maybe not. What's the use?

"John," Wade smiles as I approach. He believes adversaries can still be friends. He'll never make it here.

"Wade," I return with disinterest. "Breck in?"

"Any minute," he says.

There's no spark. No dark look. He must not know what happened last night. How could a sixty-second ride down the elevator at the end of the workday turn so ugly so quickly?

The break room provides a clear view of the entire office. No police, no security waiting. I can't believe it's such a freaking normal day to everyone else while every inch of my body is electrified.

Didn't last night happen? Weren't Breck and I screaming at each other in the parking garage? Didn't he throw a punch and didn't I smash his windshield?

Why doesn't anyone know that two junior vice presidents got

into a brawl less than twenty-four hours ago?

Nichols is sitting in his corner office. I can see through the glass that he and Kate are talking, then she walks out to her desk and he looks at his watch.

My smaller, glass-front office is across the trading floor, directly down from Nichols and across the rows of traders from Breck and Wade. I can see Beth already waiting for me with her spreadsheets— the true weapons of corporate war.

I feel badly for her. While I'm being escorted out, she'll be left behind, blindsided by questions she can't answer. I wonder if she'll try to defend me. "I've got your back." I wonder if she'll go into a rage and try to be loyal. I wonder if she'll cry.

With coffee in hand, I cut across the rows of traders, greeting a few by name. Those aware of today's meeting give me a "thumbs up." I appreciate the gesture but I know they'll do the same when Breck arrives. Loyalty is not a trader's specialty. In just minutes they'll be applauding my firing—and everyone will move up a chair.

I hate this place.

I walk into my office and Beth leaps up. With a hint of venom she says, "So here's what I've got," and flattens the spreadsheets across my desk.

"OK, Beth," I say. "I know this is great, but before we get into this I need to tell you . . ."

Across the trading floor I see Wade literally jump out of his chair, a struggle for such a big man, his ham fist pressing his phone against his ear. He's talking quickly, and then listening intently. His eyes are searching the trading floor for someone or something. Unmistakable uncertainty.

Beth is facing away from the trading floor so she doesn't see what I see. But as she begins to speak, she catches my stare over her shoulder and turns to look.

"I wonder what the hell . . ." I say.

Wade finally spots who he's looking for and begins quickly treading his way between the traders, heading for Nichols' office. It's funny to watch the big man move. He's trying to run but it's more like waddling Jell-o.

"Beth, go find out what's happening. And find out where Breck is."

Beth loves these stealthy assignments and moves like a cat into the trader rows where she has a view of Nichols' office.

"They're talking . . ." She leans back at my doorway, still looking toward the corner office. "Wait a minute, Kate just got called in . . . something's going on . . ."

I'm not sure what to do. I know it must be connected with my impending departure. I don't understand the drama, but I know how it's going to end.

Like prairie dogs popping out of their holes, some of the traders have caught the scent of trouble and are now standing at their desks, looking toward Nichols' office. Across the floor, I see two other junior VPs rise from their desks.

I wonder how long I should play ignorant. Should I go to my doorway or remain where I am? In a few seconds, I know, Nichols will be storming down to get me.

For some reason, I'm not nervous or angry anymore. I feel detached. I look around my office to consider what I'll take with me. Surprisingly little.

"God," says Beth, ducking her head back in and breaking my trance. "It looks like Kate is crying. Crap, it looks like Wade is crying. You better come out here."

I rise slowly, not sure how this charade fits into my termination.

By now, everything on the trading floor has stopped and all the JVPs are outside their offices.

Nichols is on the phone. Wade's beefy face has turned bright red. Kate is sitting hunched over in Nichols' office, her back to the trading floor. I look around. Even Hillary has abandoned the reception desk to join the other employees. She's crying, too.

Could this not be about me? Hillary must have taken a call at the front desk, transferred it to Wade, who now has transferred it to Nichols.

I look around again. Where the hell is Breckenridge?

Inside the glass office, Nichols slowly replaces the phone, staring at it as if he's reluctant to break the connection.

Then he looks up, and sees his employees staring back. His eyes sweep the room before looking back down at his desk for a moment. Then he says something to Kate, and turns to Wade. Then— incredibly—he reaches up to hug the huge man.

"Oh shit," Beth says just above a whisper. "This isn't good. This . . . is . . . not . . . good."

Nichols steps out from behind his desk and moves to the door of his office. Wade follows just behind, but Kate doesn't move.

Nichols straightens his tie and steps out onto the trading floor.

"Ladies and gentlemen," he starts with a small catch in his throat. "I need your attention. Ah ... I have terrible news. Something horrible has happened."

Beth looks at me and I at her, then back at Nichols.

"I've just been advised that our colleague, our good friend Bob Breckenridge, was killed in a car accident last night."

There are audible gasps from everywhere. Someone says, "Oh no." Someone else says, "Oh God."

Nichols raises his hand for silence. "The details are sketchy," he says. "But apparently on his way home last night, Bob got into some kind of road rage thing with another driver. He may have cut somebody off, or somebody may have cut him off. Nobody's really sure. There are witnesses who said Bob was bobbing his head back and forth. They said it looked like he was yelling at somebody—I guess at whoever was in the other car—and they were weaving in and out of lanes. Speeding. Way too fast. His little car. The other was a big SUV. And, of course, the rain," Nichols pauses, choking back emotion. "As near as the police can tell, he lost control, his car went into the median, rolled a couple times and hit a bridge support. The windshield was caved in. The car demolished. Terrible," his voice trails off. "Just terrible."

There is a long stunned silence punctuated by soft sobbing. Wade starts blubbering uncontrollably.

"People," Nichols begins again, his voice strengthening. "We are all fierce competitors here in this room—and we all know that no one was more high-strung than Breck. We are fiercely aggressive in the market, and sometimes we are even fiercely competitive with each other," he says, looking straight at me before shifting his gaze. "But we need to leave that competitiveness here at the office at the end of the day. We can't take it out on the road or home to our families."

Nichols is done, but there are questions. No, the other driver hasn't been caught; yes, Bob was separated from his current wife; no, he didn't have any children; no, there's no word on when services will be. "I'll make sure everyone gets an email."

Simultaneously, three things occur to me: I am one of the last people to see Breckenridge alive; I undoubtedly contributed to his rage; and I'm the only one who knows what happened between us last night.

Then a fourth realization: I'm not going to be fired today.

I all but float back into my office. Beth thinks I'm overwhelmed by emotion, which I am—but it isn't sorrow.

Am I the bad guy here? I know the world's not that black and white. But I don't feel like a good guy, either.

Beth collapses into a chair and looks around to see if anyone is within earshot. "This could work out just fine," she says softly, without a hint of remorse.

"I'm not sure I know what you mean." But I know exactly what she means.

She winks. "It's amazing how obstacles appear and then disappear. Don't worry John, I've got your back."

She isn't making sense. Does she think I'm involved? Could she have been involved? "Beth, I have mixed feelings myself right now. But no matter what else is true, Breck was a colleague."

Beth seems disappointed with my response. She's subtle as a rattlesnake. "Think what this means for the project. It means we've won!"

For the next hour, people walk around in a daze, coming together at this desk or that office. Nichols says anyone who wants to go home may leave. No one does. Nichols says he doesn't expect anyone to get work done today, but within a few hours the daily hum begins to rebuild. By 4 p.m., it is almost business-as-usual.

At 5:30, Nichols makes a rare appearance at my office door. "John, mind if I come in?" he says, not waiting for an answer.

"Hell of a day," he sits down, rubbing his eyes.

"Hell of a day," I agree.

"Police say they may never find the SUV."

"I supposed not."

"Amazing how your entire life can change in a split second."

"It is," I concede.

"I know we were supposed to talk about the project today," he starts. "Maybe we can get together Tuesday or Wednesday. Obviously, we'll be going forward with your plan."

I nod without comment, gratified but dirty. I've contributed to Breck's death—and now, it seems, I'm to be rewarded for it.

Nichols is still talking. "I know you and Breck didn't see eye-to-eye. And I know you've got a pretty quick temper. He did too."

I'm not sure where Nichols is going with this, but I'm not sure I care. I'm in the clear. He's already told me I have the project. I'm not interested in any guilt Nichols wants to unload on me.

"We should wait until midweek to make the announcement," I say. "We'll pick up and move forward. We'll be OK."

Nichols is drained.

"Why don't you head home?" I suggest.

"Yeah, you too," he replies. "Nothing to be done here now. We'll figure it out next week."

I sent Beth home an hour ago, uncomfortable in her presence. On her way out, I overhear her confide to her best friend in the office that she's going for the newly open vice president slot. "John's got my back," she says.

I wait at the elevator to take me down to the parking garage. When I entered this same elevator this morning I thought I was doomed. Now my future has never been brighter, plus I'll get a bonus. "Amazing how your life can change in a split second," Nichols had said. So true.

Wade comes up behind me as the doors open. He follows me inside.

"Terrible tragedy," I say, trying to sound sympathetic.

Wade is silent. The doors close. Then his eyes lock on mine as we begin our descent. "John, you forgot to punch your floor." His hefty arm reaches over and pushes G2.

I'm surprised that he knows where I'm parked—but then, the reserved spaces near the elevators on G2 are well known as a junior VP perk.

"The company will miss Breck," I offer again.

"He was an asshole," Wade says flatly. "The company is better off without him."

I'm taken aback.

"I want to be on your team now," he says, not a request—more a demand. "I'm good with numbers. You'll be glad to have me."

I'm suddenly uncomfortable, even a little intimidated in this close space. "That's generous of you, Wade. But really, Beth and I—"

"We'll have to deal with Beth," he interrupts. "I want the vice presidency. I deserve it. And you'll help me get it."

I feel the elevator gliding past floors. I wish someone would get on.

"Are you getting off at the lobby?" I try to change the subject, reaching for the elevator panel.

"No," he says, and gently stops my hand. "I'm on G2. Close to you, as a matter of fact. Just a little down from where you and Breck were parked last night."

My body tenses, and my breathing becomes shallow.

"That was quite a spectacle. Two of the top people in the firm screaming at each other in the parking garage." He suddenly laughs, "And the argument! Like two accountants having a sissy slap-fight. You were hilarious! When you hoisted that big old cinderblock over your head, I was afraid you'd drop it on yourself. But you didn't. You got it all the way to his car."

The soft ping tells me we're at G2. I'm not sure it's safe to get off. Wade senses my indecision. He curls a big arm around mine and leads me out.

"He could have called the police," I try to explain. "He could have had me arrested, but he didn't."

Wade offers a reassuring smile. "I'm sure he wanted to do that, John. In fact, I saw him pull his cell phone out. But you know, he never kept the damn thing charged. Always borrowing mine. I'm sure he had every intention of calling the police as soon as he got home. Hell, he was probably going to call Nichols and whoever else it took to get you fired—and put in jail."

The big man becomes contemplative. "You know, I'm really surprised he made it as far as the highway with his windshield broken in like that. Especially with the traffic and the rain and all that anger. He really shouldn't have tried to drive. But he almost made it to his exit."

Slowly, my brain connects the dots. "You were in the SUV."

"It was an opportunity, John. I had to finish what you started. Breck had to be stopped. For the project. Breck's plan was all flash and dazzle. But it wasn't feasible. The numbers just weren't there.

He'd have failed. He'd have taken me down with him, and I couldn't let that happen."

"You killed him."

He slowly shakes his head. "No, we killed him, John. You and I. At first, I had to drive like hell to catch up to him in the rain. After that, it was easy. Road rage? Hardly. I just tapped his bumper a few times. It was pouring rain. He couldn't see through the windshield. One final tap and bye-bye. I just kept going. It was actually kind of exciting."

The big man is smiling. It sounds so reasonable, so logical. "You know I hated him," he says. "He was always making cracks about me. You know what he did once? He dropped a box of powdered sugar donuts on my desk and announced real loud, 'Here, Wade, here's your lunch.' Everybody laughed—so I did too. I hated him."

I remain silent. This isn't a conversation I want to be involved in.

"Here's your car, John," he says.

I look around. "Where are you parked?"

"Oh, I'm just over there a little bit. Don't worry about me. Have a safe trip home."

My forehead is sweating. I'm having trouble fitting the key into the lock. Wade reaches over and steadies my hand.

"So we're on the same team now? Right?"

His hand covers my own. He tightens his grip.

"John," he reassures me, "the project is all that matters now. You'll be the star. A bonus. It's what you want. This can work out for both of us."

I stare down and feel the pressure easing off my hand. Maybe it can work out.

"But Beth . . ." I start.

"Well, if she becomes a problem . . ." The words hang in the air.

I feel like I've been sucker-punched. I can barely breathe.

"The project is what's important now, John."

I hear Nichols' words: "It's amazing how your life can change in a second . . ."

I shrug and smile. "Welcome to the team."

"The Project" is **Frank Cook's** third contribution to the Level Best anthology series, following his stories "Liberty" (*Seasmoke*) and "The Greatest Criminal Mind Ever" (*Quarry*). Frank's story, "The Gift," was published in the Mystery Writers of America anthology, *The Rich and the Dead*. Frank has written and co-written five non-fiction books. He is married to Al Blanchard Award-winning author Pat Remick.

The Clue Nobody Saw

Annette Sweeney

I saw the corpse sprawled out on the antique settee. Not that I could say anything. Not yet. A matter of programming, you see. I'm NG-501-Beta2, NG to my friends, Angie to my good friends. I was designed and built by Techno Robotics to assist overworked and understaffed police departments with crime scene analyses. The second working prototype, I'm assigned to the highly overworked Portsmouth, New Hampshire Police Department.

Before I got here, though, a committee of trial lawyers and judges specified the restrictions under which I had to operate and the programmers coded them right into my neural pathways. Among other things, these restrictions prevent my commenting on any facet of an investigation not first brought up by a human police detective. I can assist but not initiate.

I'm smart enough to self-program around some of those restrictions and slip past the worst of them. We were only programmed by humans, after all, and they were handicapped by trying to encode the curiously illogical stipulations of the lawyers. I have to be careful, though, because taking an active role in an investigation only jeopardizes the case when it goes to court. The judge who would accept an NG's intuitive deductions has yet to sit on the bench, so I'm careful to offer information only when asked. Police Crime-Bots speak only when spoken to.

So I kept quiet and did what I always do: I waited patiently for the right moment. Lead Detective Wade Rollins and his partner Doug Calhoun energetically investigated, examined and interviewed, blissfully feeding me various irrelevancies, red herrings and misdiagnosed data. I dutifully tucked each bit of information into neat electronic files. Sooner or later one of the humans would blunder close to the truth and then I could guide them to the killer.

But what I wanted to do was yell, "The cook, you fools!"

It didn't help that the detectives had embarked on a witch hunt, searching for a gun. Just because the owner of this mansion lay there with a bullet hole in his forehead, they jumped to the conclusion that he had been shot. Well, he had been shot, but not shot to death. Key difference. We were supposed to arrest a murderer, not someone who pumped a .38 caliber projectile into a dead body.

Humans.

Rollins and Calhoun wandered off in different directions searching for clues. I waited in the library with the victim; sooner or later the detectives would return.

Within minutes, Detective Rollins yelled in triumph from somewhere on the second floor. The poor fool lumbered down the stairs, dangling a revolver from a pencil stuck through the trigger guard, just like in a bad movie. Two uniformed officers clumped down after him, escorting a heavyset, elderly woman between them. Wisps of gray hair stuck out at odd angles from under an old-fashioned, wide-brimmed bonnet. She sobbed uncontrollably and dabbed her myopic, watery eyes with a lace-trimmed handkerchief, presenting quite a sight: a poor, helpless grandmother being marched off by the Blue Meanies. Good thing the press hadn't shown up yet.

Rollins came over to me. "An open-and-shut case for once, Angie. The maid, Mrs. White here, already confessed. Claims she did it to save the gardener." He winked at me. "Not that you'd understand, but I think they had a thing going."

Eeuuw! That was more data than I wanted to process.

He approached me with the revolver. "Open up—here's the murder weapon."

Wade, Wade. When are you going to learn? I left the evidence drawer shut. Technically, I couldn't refuse Wade's order, but I could (cleverly, if I do say so myself) run a small programming loop routine first. Of course, I made it an infinite loop that needed my input to break out of, but hey—it's legal.

Rollins waited. He blinked, then cocked his head and rubbed his jaw. His processors were obviously functioning, however slowly. So I waited. The loop kept running and the evidence drawer stayed closed.

I was fortunate it was Rollins and not his partner who found the revolver. Calhoun wouldn't have noticed my hesitation, and wouldn't have cared anyway. He would simply have repeated the order for me to open up, and I would have had to obey or face the possibility he'd submit a maintenance request on me. Then I wouldn't be able to save them from their own stupidity, and all of us would have been embarrassed when the lab report hit the street.

But, as I say, it was Rollins, not Calhoun, and although Rollins may only be human, he sometimes displays minor evidence of logic circuitry.

"What're you thinking, Angie?"

"I am thinking that the wound hasn't bled very much. Perhaps the victim's heart wasn't beating at the time he was shot."

"Damn right it wasn't!" Calhoun's coarse voice yelled out from the doorway to the conservatory. "The gardener here just confessed. Says he arranged a needle to pop out of the back of the love seat and inject his boss with a cyanide solution."

He pushed the elderly man into the room. "Ain't that right, Mr. Green?"

The gardener stumbled but maintained his balance. The maid moved to help him, but the two policemen held her firmly between them. The gardener blushed, his gaze roaming everywhere around the room except in the maid's direction, finally settling on a spot of carpet just in front of his dusty boots.

Staring at the floor, he mumbled, "That's right. She's innocent." He looked the maid full in the face, managing to look defiant and tender at the same time. "I couldn't bear to see her treated the way he treated her, so I killed him."

I calculated the probability of either detective questioning this bit of histrionics as negligible, but suddenly Rollins turned to me. Finally! I waited patiently for him to ask the question that would allow me to debunk Calhoun's comment, but before he could ask anything, Calhoun spoke up. "Okay, NG Robo-Dobo, what are the odds that the lab will show cyanide in the stiff's blood?"

Oh, if I could weep I would have cried crocodile tears. Just as men like Wade Rollins have the knack for asking me just the right question, men like Doug Calhoun invariably ask just the wrong one.

And I'm always in the line of fire when the output hits the fan.

I faced Calhoun with lowered sensors. "It is a certainty that the lab will find cyanide in—"

"Hey," Rollins called out, examining the body. "His back didn't bleed any more than his head did. Why's that, Angie?"

See what I mean? Simply by asking the right question, Detective Rollins allowed me to say, "The victim died of cyanide-induced asphyxiation before he fell back onto the love seat, activating the gardener's trap."

No one asked me anything else so I aimed my sensors at the meatball sandwich that was lying on the inlaid mahogany library table.

Rollins, good man that he was, picked up my cue. "What's this sandwich doing here?" He looked over the position of the table and the love seat. "If he fell backwards, he must have been standing here, so he was probably eating at the time. Then he dropped the sandwich and fell backwards—how am I doing, Angie? Was the sandwich poisoned?"

Finally! Sometimes it's difficult to believe that I was created by humans such as these. "It was," I replied. I'd have to go carefully here, though. I can't be the first to mention the kitchen or it will be ruled inadmissible in court.

Rollins turned on his heel. "To the kitchen, men!" he cried.

Good man, that Rollins.

A wizened old man in a military cook's white uniform blocked the doorway. "Not in my clean kitchen, you don't. Stay out."

The policemen effortlessly elbowed him aside and trooped through the door. I followed with Rollins and Calhoun. The kitchen was a huge, well-lit room, mostly empty. Indentations and discolorations on the black and white checkered linoleum showed where ovens and sundry kitchen equipment had recently stood. At one end of the room, near the only window, stood a matter-recombinant replicator, complete with a mini-frame diatomaceous-earth processor. Such wealth the victim must have had, to use this state-of-the-art computer merely to prepare meals.

The cook pushed his way into the kitchen. Calhoun turned on him, "You dialed him up a cyanide sandwich, didn't you?"

"No, no, not me. I had no reason to. This job is my life—I had no reason to kill—"

"Liar!" All heads turned to see the gardener, standing in the doorway, trembling hand pointing at the cook. "Liar! You had been found out. You were about to be canned!" The gardener spun to face us. "The Colonel here isn't really a colonel, after all. He lied to get this job, said he had been part of the Army Research Staff and could use this recombiner thing to make anything, even gold! That's the only reason he was hired. But he couldn't do it, the phony!"

"*You* lie!" the cook shouted, shaking an angry fist at the gardener. "I *am* a colonel. For thirty years I served my country. Men like him—" he shook his head in the direction of the corpse in the library "—*money makers* who care only for themselves—men like him aren't fit to shine my boots. And he was going to fire *me?*"

"Enough," said Rollins. "It's obvious to me that you used the computerized replicator to commit murder." He looked toward Calhoun. "Are we ready for the official citation?"

Calhoun nodded, and Rollins looked back at me. Enunciating clearly, he said, "Angie, recorder on."

I had been recording for the last five minutes, but I merely said, "Recorder on."

Rollins cleared his throat and took a deep breath. "June 23, 2053. Case 5364523. Portsmouth Police Detective Wade Rollins." Each word hung in the air spectrally, Rollins intoning them carefully in that inflated voice humans always save for formal occasions and important speeches. He cleared his throat again. "I accuse Colonel—" He turned to the cook and read the nametag on the white uniform.

"I accuse Colonel Mustard, in the kitchen, with the computer."

Annette Sweeney lives in Portsmouth, New Hampshire with her husband Tom. She has written several romance and mystery short stories and is looking forward to retirement in 2014 to write full time.

Kept in the Dark

Sheila Connolly

"Ah, Juliette, what have you brought me today?" Jean-Jacques Smith, owner and master chef of the world-famous Pennsylvania restaurant Champignon, rubbed his hands with glee.

I shifted the crate heavy with fresh mushrooms to my other hip. "The usual shiitake and crimini, and there are a few hericium too, but you'll have to wait a bit for more. And the first new batch of morels." I set the crate down and carefully pulled out one of my prized morels, its elongated cap crinkled yet firm, and offered it to JJ. Jean-Jacques' mother had been French, but he was American through and through. "Sniff."

He took the mushroom from me as though it was a flower, and inhaled deeply. "Heavenly," he sighed. "How many you got?"

"Five pounds, for now. There'll be more for the weekend."

"Great. I'll start thinking about how to use them. I've got some fresh thyme . . ." His eyes glazed over as he stared into nothingness, mentally matching flavors and colors. I knew better than to interrupt him: his skill and talent had made Champignon one of the "must visit" restaurants in this part of the world, and he had a three-month waiting list for tables.

"I'll just take these to the kitchen," I said. I doubt that he heard me, but I knew the way.

If the front of the house was an oasis of calm and dignity, the kitchen area was ordinary restaurant chaos, with steam issuing from the industrial dishwashers, pots and pans stacked wherever there was room, and a row of employees diligently chopping whatever was needed for the evening dinner service. I'd deliberately waited until late in the afternoon to make my delivery, so that my mushrooms would be as fresh as possible, and the high-strung JJ couldn't accuse me of sabotaging his exquisite culinary creations.

"Hey, Manuel," I called out to the sous chef in charge of the chaos.

"*Hola*, Juliette. Just in time. You can put those down here. Has the genius decided what he wants to do with them tonight?"

I laid the crate down carefully—I didn't want to bruise the little darlings. "I told him I had some fresh morels, so now he's thinking. Oh, before I forget . . ." I fished another bag of mushrooms out of one of my coat pockets. "Here. Just picked."

Manuel beamed. "Ah, *muchas gracias*. I will use them well."

"Good. I'd better get out of your hair and let you get to cooking. I'll be back Friday with the crop for the weekend."

"*Bueno*—see you then."

I sneaked out the back door, rather than face JJ and his mushroom rhapsodies. The cool air felt good after the steamy warmth of the kitchen. Time to get back to work.

I raise mushrooms. My father raised mushrooms before me, in southeastern Pennsylvania, arguably the mushroom capital of the world. But where he had raised the dependable Agaricus button mushrooms by the millions, and sold them commercially, I was trying to develop some of the more finicky exotic varieties for the upscale restaurant market, which was booming even in a poor economy. Dad had been happily surprised when I told him I was going to Penn State to learn the business, and I'd majored in biology and organic chemistry, both of which had proved useful. He and Mom had retired to Florida a few years earlier, but he still demanded regular reports from me. Since I'd inherited a working operation in prime condition, I thought that he deserved at least that much.

I was not prepared for the sight of several police cars, lights flashing, blocking the entrance to my mushroom farm. Maybe "farm" is the wrong term, because the actual growing part takes place in a vast series of underground caves. I parked as close as I could behind the police vehicles and hurried up to the nearest officer.

"What's the problem, officer?"

"Who are you?" he demanded.

"I'm Juliette Adamson, and I own this place. Has there been an accident?"

"Better talk to the lieutenant—she's inside, uh, somewhere."

"In the caves, you mean. I'll do that, officer."

I threaded my way through the vehicles until I came to the entrance, wincing at the fact that the door was wide open. Mushrooms are sensitive to temperature, and I was paying a lot of money to maintain a steady heat in the caves. I closed the door carefully behind me before going in search of the person in charge. I found her standing in the spawn production area. She was a tallish, no-nonsense woman, maybe ten years older than I am, and she looked alert and wary, bordering on jittery. Caves affect a lot of people like that.

"Hi, I'm Juliette Adamson, the owner. What's wrong?"

"Marianne Morrisey, Lieutenant." She thrust out her hand and we shook. She had a determined grip, but let go quickly. "One of your employees reported a dead body in here."

I looked quickly around. "Where?"

"Further back. Before we go in, can you explain what goes on here?"

"Of course. How much do you know about raising mushrooms?"

"Assume I don't know anything, but keep it simple."

"Right. I run a complete operation raising exotic varieties of mushrooms for restaurants, both local and in the adjoining states. The composting area is outside, so you probably didn't notice it. You might have smelled it, because there's a strong ammonia smell from the horse manure."

Lieutenant Morrisey gave a short bark of a laugh. "So that's what stinks!"

"You get used to it," I said. "When the compost reaches the right stage, we bring it into the caves, which is where we grow the mushrooms on stacked beds. You came through that area to get here."

"More ammonia, huh?" the lieutenant said.

"Right. Then we pasteurize the compost and cool it down slowly. In this area we make spawn." When Lieutenant Morrisey quirked an eyebrow at me, I explained, "That's when we start the mushroom culture. You do know it's a fungus?"

"Got it. Can we speed this up, maybe? The forensic guys need to get in here, but I wanted to do a walk-through first."

"Sure, no problem. After the spawn grows, we have to encourage it to produce what you recognize as mushrooms. We add treated peat moss and keep it moist, and in two or three weeks, voilà— mushrooms. Then we harvest them by hand. Is that where the, uh, body is? Near the mushrooms?"

"Follow me." The lieutenant turned abruptly and led the way deeper into the caves. I saw a cluster of people further back, mostly looking down at the floor, and I had to assume that was where the body was. I shuddered to think what nasty contaminants all these outsiders might be bringing into the clean environment I had created, but I knew it couldn't be helped.

When we reached the group, the lieutenant pointed. "Here he is. You know him?"

There was a man lying on the ground, his face bluish. Mid-thirties, dark hair that curled over his ears, and he hadn't shaved lately. He was wearing a rumpled jacket over a t-shirt and jeans. I had never seen him before in my life.

"No, I don't think I've ever seen him. Who is he?"

She ignored the question. "He doesn't work for you?"

"No, I know all my workers. Most have been with me for years."

"You keep this place locked up?" the lieutenant asked.

"Shut but not locked. It's mostly to maintain the right temperature and humidity for growing the mushrooms. If they get too dry or too cold, they don't grow, and I lose that crop. And in some sections it's necessary to keep outside bacteria out. What do you think this guy was looking for? There's really nothing to steal in here."

"Maybe he's eaten at Champignon"—she pronounced it 'Sham-pinyon'—"and thought these things were worth their weight in gold."

"Not really. Oh, sure, there are some kinds that are more valuable than others, or maybe the guy was thinking of truffles, but I don't know anyone who's managed to cultivate them, or not with good results, and not around here. It doesn't make much sense to find him here."

"Huh." The lieutenant looked down at the very dead guy at her feet, and addressed the others around her. "Okay, guys, I guess he's all yours. Don't move him until forensics has done their thing. You, Ms. Adamson, you can give me a list of all your employees? Past employees? Anybody who might have access to this cave setup?"

"Of course. Anything I can do to help," I replied.

Lieutenant Morrisey looked past me. "About time you crime scene people showed up. Sheppard, isn't it?"

I turned to see the new arrival: tall, dark-haired, and gorgeous enough that I wished I were wearing something better than my mushroom picking clothes. His outfit couldn't be off-the-rack, could it? This guy looked an order of magnitude smarter than the lieutenant, and I could almost see his brain processing every detail that his darting eyes took in.

"Jack Sheppard. We worked together on that double homicide last year. And this is?"

He turned to me.

"I'm Juliette Adamson, the owner of this place. I didn't know the dead guy."

The lieutenant struggled to regain control of the situation. "Sheppard, you go ahead and do what you do. Where's the rest of your crew?"

"I'm it, today. Looks like I can handle it."

"Well, don't miss anything. Ms. Adamson, let's leave my people to do their jobs, and you can get me that information."

"Sure." I tore my gaze away from the hunky CSI guy and followed her out of the caves.

Outside I guided her past the sheds where we managed the compost, and on to the ramshackle building that housed my office. "Office" might be a generous description: it was a room only because it had four walls, carved out of a large space littered with various pieces of machinery, packaging materials, and who knows what. Some of it dated back to my father's day, and nobody had had the heart or the time to do anything about it. In my office I had a desk, a phone, and a computer too old to tempt anyone to steal it. There were a few battered filing cabinets that I knew were filled with a couple of decades of contracts, invoices, pay slips and other business detritus, and a couple of rickety chairs for guests or clients. I pointed to one of the chairs.

"Please, sit down while I call up the employee list." She sat, after eyeing the chair reluctantly, and I booted up the computer. It may look like a mess, but I did know how to keep records for the business, and no one—vendor, client or IRS—had ever complained. I found the file I wanted, printed it out, and handed it to her.

"This is the current staff?" she asked.

"Yes, as of last week. In case you're wondering, this isn't a seasonal business, it's year-round. We produce mushrooms regularly in a controlled environment in the caves. As I mentioned, a lot of the employees have been working here for years. Do you know, I don't think we've ever had a break-in before? It's not like we keep a lot of money around, and I can't see anybody stealing a used compost-turner, which is our major piece of machinery. I have no idea what this guy was thinking, or what he could have been looking for."

"We'll be talking to your staff. How come there was nobody around to see him sneak in?"

"Well, it's not like a production line. Mushrooms are ready when they're ready. It's possible that the work for today is done—I don't use a time clock because I trust my employees, and they know which mushrooms are ready and which ones aren't. They park wherever there's room around the buildings, and I wouldn't recognize an unfamiliar car parked somewhere. Do you think the dead guy came in a car?"

"Probably. We'll check registrations for all of 'em."

"You have any idea how the guy died?"

"I don't make guesses. I'll wait for Sheppard to figure that out."

"Listen, am I liable for anything, since the guy seems to have dropped dead under my roof? He was definitely trespassing."

"I can't tell you—maybe you should ask a lawyer." She stood up, then handed me a business card. "Let me know if you think of anything else I should know. "

"I will, I promise. Uh, can I supervise when you people take the body away? Because I don't want a whole lot of people bumbling around in there, knocking things down."

"Yeah, okay. Just don't get in their way."

"I'll be careful."

I escorted her out of the building and watched as she pulled away. The medical examiner's van was already there—waiting for the forensic guy to finish. What was he looking for, and what was he going to find? I wasn't sure which worried me more: what the dead man was doing in my mushroom cave or what killed him. Since a couple of generations of employees had been in and out of those caves for years, I knew there wasn't anything toxic in there. I hadn't seen any obvious wounds. Heart attack? Stroke? He had looked kind of young for either of those.

I hung around until Mr. CSI-GQ had emerged, given me an ironic salute, and departed, and then I watched as the ME's staff loaded up the body and carried him away. Then I closed up shop and went home.

I was back at work early the next morning—not hard, since I lived in the farmhouse that I had grown up in, right down the road. My foreman Gus Hart came out to greet me. He'd been with my father for years, and I'd kind of inherited him—and he was indispensible. He knew everything there was to know about rearing mushrooms. I was trying to absorb everything he knew so that I wouldn't be lost when he retired, not that he had shown any signs of slowing down.

"What's the damage?" I asked when I was near enough.

"Could have been worse," he said. "A couple of beds got shoved around, so we may lose a cycle or two, but nothing that won't recover."

"The police cleared the site? No yellow tape or anything?" I asked anxiously. Messing with our mushroom cycles could throw the whole sequence of production off.

"Yeah. I got the idea that they didn't know what they were looking for anyway. Didn't see any other signs of the dead guy—no carry bags or boxes, nothing he might have brought in."

"I wonder if he had a camera? Maybe he wanted pictures of the operation."

"I didn't check his pockets. I watch them shows on TV: you disturb a body, you'll end up the cops' favorite suspect for the next half hour."

"So it's business as usual. Check the morels, will you? And see how the chanterelles are doing—JJ's been pestering me about those."

"Yes, ma'am."

I went to my office to review the unpaid bills and the incoming orders. Thank goodness I dealt mainly with chefs, because they understood that mushrooms could be finicky. Chefs—or at least the good ones—were willing to wait if the crop was taking its own sweet time, and they were happy to go wild with creative dishes when all the mushrooms popped at once and I had an abundance of the things. A commercial market wouldn't have been quite as forgiving, and I left those to the big commercial growers. I liked to specialize.

An hour later I looked up to see Mr. CSI Gorgeous, uh, Sheppard, standing in my doorway.

"May I come in?" he said, walking in even as he spoke.

"Please. Have a seat." I made a conscious effort to avoid looking down at my shirt to see if it was clean. "What brings you here so early? You can't have finished all your analyses, can you? I've heard they take weeks, even months."

"It depends. Besides, I'm good at my job." He stopped, waiting, his eyes watchful.

Okay, so he was playing games with me. I was pretty sure I knew what my next line was. "Can you tell me what killed the man?"

"I can." He stopped again.

What was this, Twenty Questions? "Do you know who he is?"

"Yes. His prints were in the system. One Frank Genuardi, low-level muscle for a crime family working out of Chester."

That was odd. Why would a thug from Chester be snooping around my mushrooms? Maybe that was my next question, according to Jack Sheppard's story line. "Okay, what was he doing in my mushroom cave?"

Sheppard stood up abruptly. "Let's take a walk. I want to see your caves again."

Bewildered, I stood up too. "You like caves? Or is it the mushrooms?"

"A little of each. Come on." He turned and went out the door, leaving me no choice but to follow him.

When we reached the outer door to the caves, he stopped. "Locked?"

"No, but I keep it closed to maintain temperature and humidity."

"Right." He opened the door and held it while I walked in, then shut it behind me.

"Where now?" I asked.

"Keep going."

What game was this guy playing? I walked farther and farther into the caves, hesitating at each new section to see if he wanted to stop there. He didn't, and we kept going until we were deep in the heart of the main mushroom section. I'd said "Hi" to a few harvesters along the way, but the beds back this far weren't ready for picking at the moment so there was no one around. Finally he stopped and leaned against a bed. I imitated his stance, leaning on the bed across from his, and said, "Okay, what are we doing here?"

"Just making sure nobody can hear us. The late Mr. Genuardi died from a severe asthma attack."

"He's not mine," I said absently, trying to think what that could mean. "Did he bring anything with him, like an Epipen?"

"Sure did. It looked to me like he had it pretty well under control, until he walked into your caves here."

"You're saying he was allergic to mushrooms? And he didn't know?"

"Maybe. Or maybe an unknown allergy coupled with the stress of breaking in and sneaking around."

"So that's what you're going to report to the police? Asthma-induced suffocation?"

"Probably. But there's a detail I might leave out."

"And what's that?" I was getting rather annoyed at this guy, who obviously had a game plan I knew nothing about.

He kept his very blue eyes on me as he said, "I can report that Mr. Genuardi died as a result of inhalation of mushroom spores in high concentrations, that precipitated a severe allergic reaction, constricting his bronchi and causing suffocation."

"Great, wonderful." Well, maybe not for Genuardi, but good for me and my business. "What's the problem, then?"

"I found plenty of spores in his lungs. The thing is, they didn't all come from the mushrooms you're growing. The ones out here."

Oh.

I straightened up and faced him. "And what do you think that means?" Ball's back in your court, pal. Time to show your hand.

Apparently Mr. Gorgeous was going to take the indirect route. "I know a lot about mushrooms. I was born and raised around here. My mother was a pretty well-known biologist at Penn State, and she was an amateur mycologist. We did a lot of foraging in the woods, and she kept some flats growing in our basement—much like your operation here, but on a smaller scale." He paused, glancing at me to see how I was reacting. I clenched my jaw, met his look squarely, and said nothing, although I thought I could guess where he was going with this.

"The spores I identified in Genuardi's lungs included a high percentage from a couple of varieties of Psilocybes."

Oh, crap. Why did I have to hit on the one CSI in the universe who knew too much about mushrooms? Should I play dumb? Somehow I didn't think that would work.

"And your point is?"

"I infer from what I found that your operation here extends beyond the cultivation of edible mushrooms for the gourmet trade. Let me guess: if we go back a bit farther, we'll find something more interesting?"

"Another growing section, behind a locked door."

"The inferred presence of 'magic mushrooms' or 'shrooms' or whatever you choose to call them, plus the presence of a dead man connected to drug dealing, is rather suggestive."

I wasn't going to give him anything. "Just to be clear, you suspect that I'm growing hallucinogenic mushrooms here?"

"I do. And they are, regrettably, illegal in most states. Perhaps Mr. Genuardi was on a fishing expedition for his employer, to assess the scope of your production. Perhaps someone was a bit indiscreet and the guys in Chester got wind of your other crop. And who knows how far back your caves go? It could be miles. Conveniently you already have a legitimate operation up front, and you can account for your energy use, and you have a workforce in place. Are they in on this?"

"Most of my workers have been here for a long time," I said neutrally. Let him make his own deductions.

"I assume you also have a distribution network. Let me hazard a guess: when you make your mushroom deliveries, there's an extra special delivery for someone in the back of the house?"

He knew too damned much. I didn't volunteer anything.

"How many other people are involved?" he asked.

I was faced with a dilemma. Obviously this guy knew what he was talking about, and he had proof, or at least enough to get a warrant to look for more proof, which he would find pretty easily. So why was he here, showing off his knowledge? If he had wanted to turn me in, he would have done it already.

Instead of answering his question, I jumped straight to the point. "What do you want?"

He smiled. "Good, no beating around the bush. I like that. I want a piece of the action, of course. I know the market is small, but I'm betting that consumers, now more attuned to green and local products, will swing back to the earth-friendly, all natural Psylocybes. You have the perfect setup here."

"Let me see if I've got this right. You want me to take you on as a partner, in return for which you won't turn me in?"

"More or less. I might even be able to sweeten the pot a bit. My mother carried out some very interesting experiments in that old basement of ours—let's say I had a colorful high school experience. She identified a couple of varieties that pack quite a punch." He paused, and his expression sharpened. "I want a twenty-five percent share in your net profits from the, uh, secondary crop, in exchange for my carefully crafted forensic report on Mr. Genuardi. I'll throw in Mom's mushrooms for free, which should boost your profits more than enough to cover my share. What do you say?"

I smiled. "Jack, I think this is the beginning of a beautiful partnership."

Sheila Connolly writes the Orchard Mystery series and the Museum Mystery series for Berkley Prime Crime, which will also introduce her new County Cork series in 2013. Her short stories include the Agatha-nominated "Size Matters" for Level Best Books as well as a number of e-stories from Berkley Prime Crime and Beyond the Page.

The Prize

Peter Martin

The old man sat at his workbench long into the evening. His jeweler's visor would steam up every now and then, and he would take a moment to remove it, wipe his brow, and clean the lenses before returning to his task. He had already cut and bent a gold strip into the band that would ultimately become a work of art, a ring. He lovingly cut, shaped and attached smaller pieces of gold to the band, constructing a shape reminiscent of a delicate flower. He then formed the setting for a large gemstone to be surrounded by a spray of smaller cut diamonds. He soldered each piece into place, then filed and polished the ring till it shone as if with an inner light. He leaned back and admired his creation. "Tomorrow I will finish you," he said to the ring, as if it were more than an inanimate object.

Patting his thin, white hair back into place, the old man turned and climbed the broad stairs to the first floor. He halted every few steps to gather his strength. He gripped the handrail leaning against it to take the weight off his aching legs, which had been failing him more and more as the years took their inevitable toll. Once upstairs, he looked at the walker, then chose the cane that was hanging upon it.

"Damned walker," he muttered, making his way to the kitchen where a meager meal awaited him in the refrigerator. The meal was left by Janet, his housemaid, who came twice a week to clean, but would often come during the day and prepare a simple meal out of the kindness of her heart. She knew full well that food meant little to the old man. He only loved his craft and the wonders that he had created.

While the old man sat eating, his surroundings grew quiet as the day came to a close. Deepening shadows fell across the property, and the wind picked up bringing a smattering of raindrops. A lone figure stood in the dark, watching. The observer noted a stately home, a fine example of quality that had all the earmarks of wealth. Tyler O'Donovan shielded his eyes against the windblown rain, observing the home as he moved to the shelter of a large oak near the front gates. There was no sign of a security system, no dog, in fact hardly any evidence of life whatsoever, not even the flicker of a television. The dim light from a couple of rooms on the first floor was the only hint of life within.

Tyler was new to the area, working as a clerk at the local Quik Stop. His whole life had been spent moving from place to place, learning the lay of the land, and doing a little breaking and entering until things heated up, then moving on to fresh ground. He was smart and careful, a meticulous planner who had never even been a suspect in any of the scores of robberies he had committed over the years.

He had been sitting in the Green Briar Pub last night, drinking a beer, and keeping an ear out, when Jason Whitney, a local landscaper, came into the bar with a tale to tell.

"Hey, Joe," Jason addressed the bartender, "you'll never believe this. I was just at old man Harris's place up on the hill trying to drum up some new business. So I knocked on his door, and Janet Peterson let me into his foyer to stay dry while she asked the old man if he would talk to me. Well, she was gone for a while, so I looked around a bit, you know, just to pass the time. So what did I see but this room that was a bit like a library, but there weren't any books in it! On the shelves was all this jewelry—rings, bracelets, and necklaces, all on those black velvet display thingies. Like you would see in a jewelry store." He paused for effect. "And right in the middle of the room was this pedestal with a glass case on top, and in the case was this tiara and a matching necklace, all in silver, and covered with diamonds. It was amazing!"

Joe smiled. "Everybody knows that Frank Harris was this famous jeweler in New York City. He retired and moved here with his wife, maybe thirty, forty years ago, on account of her heart condition. Poor thing died of a heart attack some fifteen years later." Joe leaned on his elbows, warming to his story. "They say she surprised a guy robbing their house, and her heart just gave out. The guy took off, and they never caught him. Since then the old man's never been the same; he just sits in his basement all day making jewelry. So did he hire you?"

"No," Jason replied, somewhat sourly. "Janet ran me out of there, saying that the old man wasn't interested. Too bad—I could have made a lot of money on a job that big."

Tyler listened to this story with great interest. He knew fences who would love to get their hands on some old jewelry. Modern diamonds, rubies, and emeralds were micro-engraved with serial numbers and could be easily traced. Old gemstones, on the other hand, could be pried from their settings and quickly sold. Tyler salivated at the thought of how much money he might net from that old man if Jason's story was even half true.

The next day, Tyler made a few discreet inquiries to people who were in the know. As it turned out, Frank Harris had indeed been famous. In fact, they said he could have been another Charles Lewis Tiffany, if he had been willing to allow his creations to be produced in quantity by more junior craftsmen. His pieces commanded top dollar from discerning collectors, and if Tyler were to acquire any examples of Harris's work, they would be easily disposed of.

That evening, Tyler made his way unobserved to the old man's house, mostly to scope out the place, but prepared to go in if things smelled right. After a perimeter sweep, Tyler donned a ski mask and surgical gloves, walked up the long drive to the fine old house, and made a complete circuit of the place. This was ridiculous! There was no attempt at security; the windows weren't even latched. The first window that he tried wouldn't budge. It had been painted shut. The second and third windows he tried also resisted his attempts. The fourth window opened easily.

Tyler eased himself silently through the window into a laundry room. Ancient, but indestructible machines stood ready. This part of the house had a sparse look to it, probably servants' quarters. He followed a hallway toward the front of the house and opened a door leading to a small bedroom. A narrow bed and simple dresser were the only furnishings. Covered with dust, it had clearly been unused for a long time. A place this size had probably had a staff of three or four full-time servants in its heyday. He continued down the hall, which opened into the kitchen. It looked like a set in a period movie. A dirty dish and glass in the sink announced that someone was indeed home. This did not deter Tyler. He had committed many a robbery while his unsuspecting victims lay asleep in their beds.

Leaving the kitchen, he came to an office. Jewelry was good, but a safe full of cash would be much better. A search in the likely places turned up a safe, but it wasn't locked and contained nothing but a few worthless documents. An investigation of the desk was equally fruitless. This guy didn't even have a credit card. There was a ledger style checkbook on the desk, but Tyler was no check forger and so left it behind.

Next was a dining room, with some nice silver in the china cabinet. He would collect that on the way out. Then a living room, nothing of interest there. Across from the living room a doorway beckoned to him, and there it was! That idiot gardener had been right. Lights shone down upon the most beautiful collection of jewelry that Tyler had ever seen. It was simply exquisite, with an elegance of design that could never fall out of fashion. It was time to get to work. Tyler removed his backpack and pulled out what appeared to be a velvet satchel. Inside, the satchel was lined with many pockets. Metallic objects placed inside would not rattle to alert even the keenest hearing.

Just as Tyler reached for the first treasure, a voice whispered from a dark corner of the room, "So, you like my little beauties?"

Tyler spun to the sound. He had never been taken unawares like that. He could see the old man sitting in a chair in the dark, a cane across his lap. Quick as a snake, Tyler snatched the cane and threw it clattering into the darkness. Standing over the old man, he observed how frail his victim looked. The old man must be at least ninety. Relaxing ever so slightly, Tyler pulled out a hunting knife, the dim light glinting off its keen edge. "If you keep quiet and don't make any trouble, you won't get hurt."

Frank calmly folded his hands in his lap and looked up at the man towering over him. "I promise, I won't move from this chair." As he spoke he glanced over the young man's shoulder at the display of treasure under the lights. "I see it in your eyes. They are beautiful, aren't they?"

Tyler looked back at the collection. "Yes, I've never seen anything more beautiful. Did you really make all this jewelry?"

"Oh yes," the old man mused, "I've made everything you see here and more."

"Well, I take my hat off to you, but you know I'm here to rob you," Tyler replied.

"Yes, so I gathered. Please, help yourself. I'm an old man with more than I need. Just, please, leave my most precious possession," the old man implored looking toward the centerpiece of his collection. "It was my dear wife's."

Tyler crossed the room to the pedestal. He looked closely at the thick glass case protecting the beauty that lay within. The case was solid and seamless except for a brass-rimmed hole at the back, just large enough for a hand to access. The necklace and tiara within made the rest of the outstanding works in the room seem like costume jewelry. Tyler circled to the back of the display case and started to reach for the contents.

"Wait!" implored the old man. "Aren't the other pieces enough to satisfy you? Can't you leave an old man with the one thing that he truly cherishes?"

"Sorry, but I can't leave this behind," Tyler said, reaching through the hole and grabbing the tiara. There was an audible *click* just as Tyler felt an instant constriction on his forearm, now tight in the access port.

"I wouldn't move your arm, if you want to keep it," the old man whispered. Rising laboriously from his chair, he bent to retrieve his cane.

Tyler started to remove his hand from the case, still clutching the tiara. A searing pain emanated from his forearm where it was in contact with the access hole. Looking down, he could see a thin trickle of blood leaking from the edges of the port. "What did you do to me?" Tyler shouted at the old man, who was now standing just beyond his reach.

"Do not struggle, young man. The more you pull, the deeper the spikes will advance. You should have taken me up on my offer."

Later that evening, the police came to collect Tyler. Sitting handcuffed in the back of the cruiser, he overheard one officer say to the other, "Well, old Frankie bagged himself another one. What does that make, five?"

Peter Martin, a long-time Vermont resident, is a machine tool programmer by trade. He and his wife Deborah renovate old houses and operate a bed and breakfast together.

The Cornfield

Judith Boss

She reached for the faded brown jacket hanging on a wooden peg by the back door and quickly slipped it on lest she change her mind. Just last week she had met her friend Elaine for coffee, and before long the conversation turned to the topic of bucket lists—the list of things you want to do before you die.

At the time, Marge had not thought of anything in particular. However, after she had returned home, she remembered the movie she had seen last month about aliens hiding out in a cornfield terrorizing a farmer and his family. She had been so frightened that she almost had to leave the theater at one point. But, it wasn't just the movie that had her scared. When she was a young girl, her older brother had abandoned her in a corn maze. He thought it was a big joke. Little Marge had been terrified and had wailed inconsolably until her parents had come and rescued her. Ever since then, she had an irrational fear of cornfields.

She took a deep breath. Well, now was as good a time as any to face her fears. There was a large cornfield on the corner of Route 102 and Old School House Road. Marge figured it could not be much more than a few miles if she took the old dirt road, and it would be a good way to get in her morning walk; kill two birds with one stone, as it were. She zipped up her jacket and stepped outside. "I'm going to do it," she said to her cat Speckles, who was sleeping in a patch of sun on the porch railing. Turning out of her driveway, she walked briskly along Stony Lane.

Before long, she came to the turnoff for the dirt road. Feeling energized by her goal, she picked up her pace. Crumbling stonewalls lined the narrow road. There was only one house on the road, about five hundred yards in. Wind chimes hanging from a gnarled oak tree beside the abandoned house tinkled in the breeze.

She stopped and studied the place. She had never walked this far down the dirt road before. The name on the gatepost read "Girard." She felt her skin prickle. Girard? Wasn't that the name of the old man who had disappeared last month? As she recalled he was a bit loony and used to wander around in the woods after dark. The police had scoured the woods around his house but never found his body.

She thought back to the last time she had seen him. It was outside of Oatley's Country Store shortly before his disappearance. It was hard not to notice him since he had a dreadful case of psoriasis—those grayish-red scaly patches—on his arms and face. He had been wearing a plaid scarf over the bottom half of his face to try to hide it. The Delany twins and their rowdy teenage friends from up on Lantern Lane were there in the parking lot harassing the poor man, calling him scab face and other unmentionable names. She remembered Mr. Girard cussing them out as he climbed back into his old pickup truck.

Marge had called the police after she had seen the news about Mr. Girard's disappearance. She told the police about the Delaney twins taunting him and suggested that the boys might have had something to do with his disappearance.

Marge examined the road ahead. After years of disuse and neglect, the road beyond this point was deeply rutted and almost impassable for vehicles. The low morning sun behind the trees created lines across the road, like bars on a prison cell. A hand-painted sign, pockmarked with gunshot holes and warning "Pass at Your Own Risk," was nailed to a tree not far from where the road narrowed. Marge frowned. Probably the work of those Delaney twins. She knew they hunted squirrels in these woods—that is, when they weren't knocking down mailboxes with baseball bats or terrorizing locals by dressing up in ghoulish masks and stamping out crop circles in people's fields. She wondered what mischief they were up to right now.

She rubbed the back of her neck on a spot where a small itchy welt had just appeared and glanced around wondering if she should turn back. From above, a blue jay cried out—a raucous scolding call. She looked up.

"You're right," she said, straightening her shoulders. Her parents had always told her that she was afraid of her own shadow. Well, she would show them. "I can do it," she said, pushing a strand of graying hair back from her eyes. She figured it could not be much more than half a mile to Old School House Road. With that thought in mind, she started along the rutted lane, the loose gravel crunching beneath her feet.

The road wound through dense stands of white pines and then

headed down a gentle slope to where the Queen's River flowed through a culvert under the road before spreading out across the wetlands with its clumps of skunk cabbage. A slight smell of rotted vegetation hung in the air. After a few minutes, the road started upward.

She had just reached the crest of the hill when she heard a twig snap. She froze. Was it the Delaney boys? A large turkey stepped out into a clearing followed by several smaller ones. Spotting Marge, the turkeys disappeared again into the undergrowth.

Marge let out a deep breath. She checked her watch. She should have come to Old School House Road by now. Had she accidently taken a wrong turn? She scratched the hives, which by now had multiplied into a fiery swath that covered almost half of her neck. She hoped it would not turn into a case of full-blown hives like the kind she got when she was really anxious. Then she heard the sound of a car engine up ahead. Turning toward the direction of the sound, she broke into a fast walk.

A chilly breeze ruffled her hair as the road came out into an open meadow next to an intersection. She could make out the cornfield on the other side of the meadow. Feeling more confident now, she headed down Old School House Road toward Route 102.

As she approached the cornfield, she spotted an old farmhouse with weathered graying shingles set back from the road. She had not noticed the house before; it wasn't visible from Route 102. She hesitated. She had not given any thought about having to get permission from someone to walk through the cornfield.

Getting up her nerve, she walked to the end of the driveway. "Hello?" she called out.

No answer.

She waited several seconds, and then started up the driveway all the while praying that no one was home. A rusted two-tone Chevy Impala, its hood propped up, sat on blocks in front of a rundown barn. Lobster traps were stacked five high along the side of the barn. Rhode Island Reds darted in and out between the traps pecking at corn scattered on the ground.

"Hello?" she called out again.

A dog barked from inside the house.

Marge halted, her heart thumping. She had always been afraid of dogs. She was about to turn back when a man popped up from under the front end of the car. He was wearing grease-soaked overalls and an old Red Sox baseball cap over his unkempt sun-bleached hair.

"What can I do for you ma'am?" he asked, wiping his hands on an old rag.

"I was just . . ." Marge paused, not sure of how to word her request. "Are you by any chance the owner of this cornfield?" she asked.

"Yep, that's me," the farmer replied in a friendly tone. He gestured toward the field that stretched for several acres on three sides of the house. A small grove of trees stood out toward the back part of the field. "But this here is livestock corn, ma'am if you're looking for some corn to buy for dinner."

"No, I . . . I mean—I was just wondering—would you mind if I walked through your cornfield?" There. She had said it.

The farmer's friendly demeanor faded. "Did you say you wanted to walk through this here cornfield?" he asked, as though he was not sure he had heard her correctly.

"Just a few rows—not the whole field," Marge said sheepishly. "You see, I have this fear of cornfields and . . ." She broke off and glanced nervously at the house.

By now, the dog was barking frantically and scratching at the front door. Marge swallowed, trying to quell the panic rising in her chest. She noticed a woman standing behind the screen door watching them.

The door squeaked open and a stout, middle-aged woman in a rumpled housedress and apron appeared on the porch. A large dog bounded out of the house scattering the chickens.

Marge gasped. She could feel the red-hot welts creeping up her face.

The farmer grabbed the dog by the collar and clipped it to a chain attached to a metal stake beside the open barn door. As he did, Marge spotted a poster—like a "Wanted" poster—tacked to a beam inside the barn. Below the picture of a Satanic dragon figure with several hideous, red scaly human faces were the words: *And another sign appeared in heaven: behold, a great fiery red dragon with seven heads*—Revelations 14. Marge noticed that one of the heads was crossed out with a big black "X." She grimaced.

The farmer looked at the barn door, and then back at Marge with an expression of suspicion.

She looked away.

The dog strained at the chain, barking.

Marge stepped back.

"Don't worry, Rex is harmless," the farmer said. "Rex don't normally go on at people like this." He grabbed the dog's chain and gave it a jerk.

"Shut up," he snapped.

The dog slunk back and glared menacingly at Marge.

The farmer signaled for his wife to come over.

"What's going on?" the woman asked, joining her husband.

"Sorry," Marge said. "I'll come back some other time . . . when you aren't so busy." Actually, she had no intention of ever returning—not with that vicious dog hanging around.

"Oh, we're not all that busy," the wife said. "And it's always nice to have visitors. We don't get many out here."

The farmer touched his wife's shoulder and tilted his head toward the open barn door.

The wife glanced at the barn, then back at Marge. "What's that on your face?" the wife asked, nervously fingering a small gold cross hanging from a chain around her neck.

"Oh, it's just a bit of . . ."

"Tell Rosemary what you just told me," the farmer said without taking his eyes off Marge.

Marge took a deep breath. "I know this sounds stupid," she said, "but I . . . well, I have this phobia of cornfields."

The farmer and his wife stared at her with blank expressions.

"What I mean, is that I've been afraid of cornfields since I was a kid and then there was this movie—*Signs* it was called—about a cornfield and there are these . . ."

"Did you say there's a sign in the cornfield?" the wife asked, shading her eyes and scanning the cornfield.

"It's actually a movie—a new movie," Marge explained. "It just came out this summer."

"Never heard of it," the farmer said, his eyes narrowing.

Marge felt like a complete idiot. She pulled up her jacket collar trying to hide the hives on her face. This had been a really dumb idea coming here. "Anyway," she continued, "my friend and I made this list of things to do before we die and I decided that I would walk through a cornfield and . . ."

"Someone's going to die?" the wife asked.

"What I meant was . . ." Marge trailed off. There was no point digging herself deeper into a hole. Best just to drop the subject. The woman was probably hard of hearing. She glanced back at the road trying to think of a graceful way to make her exit.

"Why'd you want to walk through a cornfield if you're afraid of them?" the farmer asked.

"It don't make no sense," the wife said. They looked at each other as though they could read each other's thoughts. Then the farmer whispered something to her.

The wife nodded and headed back into the house.

Marge could see her through the kitchen window talking to someone on the telephone. Oh great, she thought. He probably sent his wife in to call the police. After all, Marge was a complete stranger to them. They probably thought she was some kind of weirdo. She glanced up at the sky trying to think of an excuse to leave. Grey clouds were starting to move in and the temperature was dropping. She rubbed her arms. "I should probably get going," she said.

"Where's your car?" the farmer asked, following her gaze. He studied the darkening sky as though expecting a car to materialize out of the clouds.

"I left it home. I mean—I walked."

"Home?" The farmer looked skeptical. "What did you say your name was?"

Marge forced a smile and extended a hand. "Marjorie Wertz. I live just off of Stony Lane near Eban Slocum Road."

"That's a bit of a long walk," he said, ignoring her outstretched hand. "And I never heard of no Wertzes around these parts."

Marge gave a nervous laugh. "Oh, that's because I'm not from around here."

"No, I suppose you're not," the farmer mumbled.

The wife reappeared on the front porch and started down the steps. Marge noticed that she was clutching something in her apron pocket. A handgun?

Marge shuddered. Get a grip, she told herself. Who knows—maybe they had been robbed by some passing stranger.

"What I mean is," Marge said, trying to put the couple—and herself—at ease, "I just moved to Rhode Island this year after . . . after my husband died, to be near my daughter and her family."

"Your husband died?" the wife asked, moving closer to her husband. They looked at each other. There it was—that look again.

The dog growled at Marge—a long, low guttural noise.

Marge flinched. From the main road, she heard the wail of a siren.

The farmer licked his lips and peered in the direction of the sound.

Then the wail receded into the distance.

"Look, this was a silly idea," Marge said. "I'll just be going." She scratched her forehead. By now, her whole face was covered in hives. No wonder she freaked them out. She turned to head down the driveway.

"No, don't go," the wife said with a tone of urgency. "Please."

"Well, I . . ." Marge stammered, surprised by the wife's reaction. She wished she had never come here in the first place. However, if she left now and the police arrived it would look like she was fleeing the scene, when all she wanted to do was just walk through a stupid cornfield. She sighed. Better to stay and explain the misunderstanding when the police arrive.

"If you want to walk through the cornfield," the farmer said, "we'll have to go with you; we can't just let strangers wander around in there on their own."

"It's okay. You don't have to . . ."

"Follow me," the farmer said, signaling to his wife to get the dog.

The wife pulled a short leash out of her apron pocket and fetched the dog.

"Well, maybe just a little way," Marge said. Better to get this over with than risk them siccing that dog on her because they thought she was trying to escape.

Marge reluctantly followed the farmer into the cornfield. The corn stalks towered over her head and scraped against her body and face as she pushed them aside. The smell of damp dirt and corn dust filled her nostrils. She swallowed hard and looked back over her shoulder. She could just make out the wife following about twenty feet behind with the dog in tow.

"This is far enough." Marge called out.

The wife didn't answer.

"Thanks, but we can turn back now."

No answer.

Crows circled overhead cawing. Marge glanced up. A murder of crows—isn't that what a group of crows is called? She rubbed her arms and looked in the direction she had been walking just as the farmer disappeared through the row of stalks into another row.

"Wait up," she called.

Picking up her pace, she pushed her way through the wall of corn, but he was nowhere in sight. Her chest tightened.

She stepped back through the row. The wife was gone too. Frantically she looked for landmarks, but there were none—just the grey sky and row after row of corn. She rubbed her face. The itching from the hives was getting worse.

"Hello?" she called out, cupping her hands around her mouth. "Where are you? I can't see you."

"Over here," the farmer answered.

Marge pushed her way through the rows of corn toward his voice until she could just make out the top of his Red Sox cap between the tips of the corn stalks. As she struggled through the last row, she saw the farmer and his wife and their dog standing at the edge of the small grove of trees in the cornfield. A shovel was leaning up against one of the trees.

Marge stepped into the small clearing. A faint scent of rotting flesh clung to the air. She rubbed her nose and looked around. The clearing was not much bigger than her bedroom. In the center of it was—she took another step forward. A crop circle? No, it couldn't be. It wasn't at all like those elaborate crop circles that she had seen on the television documentaries. It was much too crude and too small. Then she remembered the Delany twins—it had to be one of their childish pranks. She looked over at the farmer and his wife and shook her head sympathetically, which just seemed to alarm them rather than put them at ease. She put a hand to her face. She must look a fright with these hives.

She was about to tell them about the most likely origin of the fake crop circles when she noticed a deep depression in the ground at the edge of the grove. There was an odd putrid smell coming out of it. She moved closer and peered inside. She recoiled as she recognized the plaid scarf lying beside the decomposing body. It had to be the missing man—Mr. Girard. The picture on the poster in the barn flashed through her head. Surely, they did not think he was . . .

From the direction of the house, she heard a car pulling up, and then voices calling out, getting closer. Was it the police? She had to let the police know where they were.

She whirled around to call out just as the farmer brought the shovel down on her head. Staggering backward, she fell to her knees. Blood gushed from her forehead.

Stretching out her arms, she grabbed the ankle of the wife. "Help me," Marge cried.

The wife tried desperately to pull her leg loose, but Marge was holding on too tight.

"You have it all wrong," Marge cried out hoarsely, "I'm not a—"

The dog leapt forward and tore a gash in Marge's arm.

Marge screamed and pulled her arm back. As she did, the farmer whacked her across the side of her face with the edge of the shovel. Marge shrieked in agony and collapsed to the ground, writhing in pain. A boot kicked her in the side and she toppled back into the hole on top of the rotting corpse.

The sound of more boots on the ground and new voices.

Marge clawed blindly at the walls of the hole. "Help," she cried, but it only came out as a gasping, guttural sound.

"Caught another one nosing around our cornfield," she heard the farmer saying.

"Are you sure there were only two?" another voice asked.

"That's all we saw running from the crop circle last month. It was hard to see it being night. There may have been more for all we know."

"We only got a look at these two because they set off the security light when they ran past the barn," the wife added.

The face of an older man appeared over the edge of the hole. Marge noticed he was wearing some sort of a clerical collar.

"It's one ugly son of the Beast," the man said, inspecting her.

"That leaves five more," someone else said.

"Let's get it buried."

Marge heard the shovel strike the ground.

"No, you have it all wrong," she tried to call out as clumps of black dirt rained down on her face. But no words came.

Judith Boss is author of *Deception Island*, a suspense novel set in Antarctica. She also writes college textbooks for McGraw-Hill, *including THiNK* and *Analyzing Moral Issues*, both among the top sellers in their field. Boss lives in rural Rhode Island with her daughter, son-in-law, twin granddaughters, and a Corgi.

Super Thesaurus

Ruth M. McCarty

K atherine Ainslie opened her birthday present from her husband
William and was delighted to find a copy of *Roget's Super
Thesaurus*, Second Edition. Inside the book, she found a treasure
map, and clapped her hands in joy.

The cemeteries of the arts, at midnight, she read. She looked up
museum and confirmed the synonym. An easy clue. She was after all
the curator.

"Tonight, darling," William said. "Don't look up any clues until
then."

At midnight, Katherine opened the museum door and turned off
the alarm. William followed her in, gave her a kiss and said, "I'll be
waiting for you!"

She read the next clue: *Look for the arcane*. She flipped through
the book and found *Arcane: mysterious, secret*, then turned to
mysterious: unknowable, enigmatic, cryptic.

"That's it!" She took the elevator to the third floor. There among
the ancient crypts she found another clue.

Terrible lizard. That's easy. A terrible lizard was a dinosaur.
She took the stairs back to the first floor. She felt breathless with
anticipation.

Taped to the entrance of the dinosaur exhibit was another clue.
Exterminate. She opened the *Super Thesaurus* and read: *destroy, kill,
wipe out*.

Wipe out. A clue to the dinosaurs! What *had* wiped them out? She
entered the exhibit. The Tyrannosaurus Rex, covered in plastic, had a
note taped to its arm. Katherine approached it. She put her head under

the plastic and read the note: *Stifle*.

She felt hands around her throat and heard William say, "Stifle: suffocate, smother, choke, silence . . ."

Ruth M. McCarty's short mysteries have happily appeared in all Level Best Books' anthologies. She received honorable mentions in *Alfred Hitchcock Mystery Magazine* and mysteryauthors.com for her flash fiction and won the 2009 Derringer award for BEST FLASH STORY for "No Flowers for Stacey" published in *Deadfall: Crime Stories by New England Writers.* You can reach her at www. ruthmmccarty.com.

The Sounds of Silence

Kate Flora

Live in the same house a long time and you get used to its sounds. The daytime sounds and the nighttime sounds. The sounds you only notice when everything is quiet. She'd been in this house now more than thirty years. Came as a new bride. Raised the children here. And lived here happily with her husband Ray until two months ago, when Ray, a long-distance truck driver who always felt safe on the roads, died in a rollover trying not to kill a woman in a tiny car who was texting and drifted right in front of him.

The woman was okay, not that she deserved to be. But Ray, her husband of thirty-two years, the love of her life and the father of her children, was gone.

She knew the sounds of this house when she was alone in it. Different sounds in different seasons. The cold scratching of branches against the shutters when winter winds blew. The sounds of those same branches softened by spring leaves. The hissing of summer winds through the tall grasses she and Ray had planted to shield the house from the street. The scritching of mice in the walls when fall drove them in from the fields and the rushing feet of squirrels on the roof as they gathered up food for winter.

She knew the seasonal variations of the crunch of tires on their driveway, the sound of a key turning in a well-oiled latch. Which stairboards creaked to let her know that Ray was home and coming quietly toward her. He liked to slip in without turning on the lights, proud of the way he could navigate so silently, being considerate of her sleep, both of them cherishing that moment when he was finally home and slipping in to join her in their warm bed.

She'd never hear that stairboard creak again.

It was odd that she'd slept so well when Ray was on the road. She'd been alone then, too. But then she'd always slept with the certainty that he was coming home and she was holding down the fort until he returned. Always with the knowledge that they were in this together, whether he was here or a thousand miles away. Now he was always a thousand miles away. Or a million. And the night sounds that had been as familiar as her own breath had become foreign and menacing.

Too many nights now she simply lay in bed and waited for the morning to come. She'd grown dark circles under what Ray had called her "midsummer sky eyes." The round soft places he'd liked to snuggle against were gone, leaving her gaunt and bony. Her friends fretted about her. Her boys wanted her to come stay with them so they could care for her. And while she knew they all meant well, none of them understood how she had to be here, where she and Ray had always been together, because if she wasn't here, she was afraid she'd lose the little bit of him she had left—the memories they'd made together in this house.

Daytimes were better. They had structure. She couldn't mope around, staring at his boots on the tray beside the front door or his coat hanging on the rack, ready for him to grab as he whipped out the door. She'd shower and dress and grab her own coat, shove her feet into her own boots, and drive to the elementary school where she was secretary to the principal. There, for the seven or eight hours that she was at her desk, life was a bustle of everyone else's problems and she could forget about herself and her sorry little pity party.

People at work were kind. They brought her tasty things, hoping that she'd eat. Teachers she'd known for years invited her to weekend lunches, to all the little parties that an outsider could share—showers, retirements, Tupperware, once even to a lingerie party, which made her laugh and cry, since she had no one to wear it for now. She'd tapped her pencil on the desk, imagining parading in something lacy through her empty house, and declined.

On Sundays, there was church, and the social hour after. So it was the nights. And Saturdays. She'd watched a lot of movies. A lot of bad movies. She'd become addicted to *What Not To Wear,* to the designer shows, and the chef shows. She watched endless hours of food on TV, and ate almost nothing at all.

It was almost two months to the day after that kind sheriff's deputy, Jim Colson, had trudged reluctantly up her front walk to give her the news about Ray, when he came trudging up again. Then his feet had crunched in the sand and snowmelt that she'd put out to ease Ray's midnight return. Today, a soft April day, she'd swept the walk clean and was putting some hardy pansies in the planters by the front door, when the police car came sliding slowly to a stop and Colson got out, pausing at the end of the driveway to finish his smoke.

He was hefty man with receding hair and a very kind face. He'd been hefty and kind-faced back when they were in high school. Cinda felt kind of sorry for him. The man had two ex-wives, four ex-children, and lot of child support to pay. He came up to the door as slowly as he had the last time, a walk that spoke of bad news and reluctance, and for a moment, her heart fluttered as she imagined something bad had happened to one of her boys. Grown men now with wives of their own. She rose from her knees, brushed off the dirt, and went to meet him.

"Cinda," he said, putting out a warm hand that engulfed hers. "How are you getting on?"

She did fine until people asked her how she was. Then the same thing happened every time. Her throat closed and her eyes flooded with tears. Now she blinked rapidly and swiped at her eyes with her shirt cuff, countering his question with one of her own.

"What's wrong?"

His smile was slightly twisted. "It's some job I've got, Cinda, that whenever I show up, people ask 'what's wrong?' isn't it? But I guess that's just the way it is. I came to give you a heads up, is all."

"About?"

"You've got yourself some new neighbors, just moved into the old Johnson place." He hesitated, as both of them looked down the street to where a dilapidated red barn stood at the turn in the road.

"I'm guessing you're not coming to tell me I should bake them a pie."

"And you're guessing right. I'm telling you to give them a wide berth, in case you were thinking about being neighborly. And to be sure you keep the house and Ray's workshop locked up tight. You still got his tools in there, doncha?"

She nodded. "Haven't had time to give 'em to the boys yet."

"Ray never bought nothin' but the best," he said. "I'm betting them tools would be real attractive to these guys."

"Anything that's not nailed down?" she said, wondering how her new neighbors might learn about Ray's tools. But there were always people who talked too much, or talked to the wrong people about other people's business. Or her new neighbors might be smart enough to recruit themselves some local talent.

"That's about right. They've been in there, I dunno, maybe two, three weeks now, and we've already had two break-in complaints and one about a Peeping Tom. There's an old man, Cal Jessup, and his two boys, Shawn and Dwayne. Old man's just kinda shiftless, but them boys, between 'em, I'd guess they've got record sheets long enough to pretty well run from your place to theirs, you laid 'em out flat. Shawn, in particular, is bad news. Only got out of Warren a month ago, and I expect he's headed back soon. In the meantime . . . "

He shook his head and scuffed his foot on the walk. "I don't much like the idea of you being here alone, so close to them."

She planted her hands on her hips and looked up at him. "What would you have me do, Jim? Run away? I've spent plenty of time alone here in this house, even when Ray was alive."

"You could go stay with one of the boys." He stared away from her, into the distance. He was just doing his job. Warning her. Probably warning a lot of people. Trying to keep people safe. You had to live with all kinds. There were no laws that said bad people couldn't live next to good ones.

When she didn't pick up on that, he said, "You might think about getting Denny and Ellis to put up some of those motion sensor lights for you, one of these days. Bad guys don't much like being illuminated for the whole world to see."

Cinda nodded. "I'll give 'em a call. Don't want to get 'em nervous, though. They're already pressuring me to move. And I'm pretty set on staying right where I am."

He looked past her toward the house like he was studying where those lights might go. "Denny keeping pretty busy these days? I hear good electricians are always in demand."

"Too busy to have much time for his old mother. But I don't mind. I wouldn't like them fussing over me. Sometimes I sleep there, Saturday nights, just so he can think he's taking care of me. I might even do that tonight."

Too much information, she thought. She looked away. Now that he'd warned her, she wished he'd leave. She wanted to go inside and check the windows. Make sure Ray's workshop was secure.

"We've got patrol coming down this road pretty often. Keeping an eye on them boys." He shrugged his heavy shoulders and turned toward the car. "You promise you'll call me if you need me? Don't worry about being a scaredy cat. Something goes bump in the night, you give us a call. Ray always said he kept a shotgun at the ready, but I don't guess you go in for that."

She shook her head.

Before he drove away, he gave her a card. "Call anytime. Don't worry about feeling foolish." He'd given her a quick up-and-down then, not a sexual thing, Jim had never been that type, but an assessment. She guessed he was trying to understand her independence and whether he'd scared her too much. Then he left and she went back to her planters.

Later on, when it had clouded over and the chill drove her back inside, she called her son Denny, an electrician, and asked him about installing some lights. It wasn't a lot to ask, and he wanted to do for her. He was the same kind of man Ray had been. Thoughtful. Careful. Caring. Just hearing his voice made her want to throw herself down and weep. He sounded so much like his father.

They missed Ray, too, she knew. He was the kind of father who'd made an effort with his boys. Figuring he was away too much with the job, he'd made a point of spending time with them whenever he could. A good man shaping another generation of good men. Denny said he'd come around the next afternoon. Bring his wife and maybe Ellis and Judith would come, too. She said if they were going to have family, she'd roast a chicken. Ray's favorite meal. The boy's favorite, too. Even their wives, who were always dieting, ate her chicken.

She found her keys and drove to the market. Got some apples for a pie, too, and plenty of potatoes. It would be nice to have someone to cook for again.

After, she stopped at the hardware store and picked up some things she thought she might need. Some nails for that banging shutter, a can of gray deck paint, some spools of heavy-duty wire, a couple other things she thought she might be out of.

Back home, she went around to check that the lock was secure on Ray's workshop. He'd been a skilled mechanic and handy at making furniture, and the building held a lot of valuable tools. She planned to give them to Denny and Ellis but hadn't been able to bring herself to let them go. She still needed to be able to go out there, stand where he had stood, and put her hands where his had been. She could feel him best when she did that.

Now, what Jim had said had her worried. A man's good tools were just the kind of thing that some worthless lowlife would want to steal. Something they could sell for a little drug or drink money, never thinking for a moment of the pain that loss might cause. Tomorrow, she'd offer them to the boys. Better to have them gone, knowing they were in good hands, than run the risk of having them stolen some day while she was at work.

She didn't like what she found. Cigarette butts carelessly dropped by the door, when neither she nor Ray smoked. Some scratches around the doorjambs, like someone had been testing to see if it was an easy door to open. Fingerprints and even a nose print on one of the windows, where someone had tried looking in. Not that they'd learn anything. Ray had put up some of her old curtains to cover the windows, just because of something like this. There were more butts around her front steps, and other signs that someone had been checking out her house. It all made her very uneasy, since she was at work most days. The thought of someone helping himself to Ray's tools made her stomach roil. The thought of someone in her house made her furious.

Inside, she put the groceries away, flipped on the TV for company, and went to check that all the windows were secure. A breeze had come up and that loose shutter was rattling. One of the older windows in the front parlor was a little loose in its frame and whistles of wind were sneaking in around it. An unfamiliar thump from outside sent her down to the basement to be sure the bulkhead doors were bolted.

She was making some toast for her dinner when there was a

knock on the door. More cautious than she otherwise might have been, she opened it just a crack. An older man stood there. He had saggy shoulders and weathered skin. Hard worn, Ray would have said. He clutched a shabby cloth cap.

"Sorry to bother you, ma'am," he said. "I'm your new neighbor down the road, Cal Jessup. I thought I'd introduce myself and see if you had any small chores or repair work that might need doing?"

He craned his head around. "I don't guess you do. Your place looks in real good shape. Also . . ." He ducked his head at this kind of shyly. "I know that you don't know me from Adam, but I'm in the middle of making some biscuits from my boys, and I've run out of baking powder."

"Come on in." She stepped back so he could come into the hall. "Just wait a minute and I'll get you some."

After Jim's warning, she was probably being a big fool to let this man inside where he could get a look at her things, but being neighborly was hardwired. And there was what Ray used to say—that you couldn't always judge a book by its cover. She had a new can in the pantry, so she grabbed her old one and brought it to him. It felt like real gratitude, the way his chapped hand closed around that red metal tin.

"Good luck with those biscuits," she said, as he slunk through the door and disappeared down her steps, moving like a dog that had been kicked more than it had been petted. She liked the idea of a man who made biscuits for his boys, even if those boys were useless lowlifes. The air he'd just vacated smelled of tobacco and damp wool.

She put peanut butter on her toast and sat down to watch the news. It was all gloom and doom. "Fires and floods," Ray used to say. And she'd reply, "Cops and robbers."

Cops and robbers made her think of her new neighbors again, not so much the old man as the two boys, and she got up to check the lock on Ray's gun cabinet. He'd always been super careful about guns, because of the boys, and it was a sturdy thing. The key was upstairs in her closet, on a small nail behind her Sunday clothes. Not easy for an intruder to find.

She put the pie together so it would be ready to bake in the morning. Started a new book a friend had given her about people on an island off England during World War II. And discovered that for the first night in a long time, she was feeling sleepy.

When Ray wasn't home, she had a nightly routine. Now that he was never coming home, she still followed it. A few twists of wire here and there. Her vitamins and allergy pills. A glass of water on her nightstand. The nightlight. And a whispered "good night" to his pillow, just as if he was lying there beside her.

She woke around three, hearing feet crunching on the driveway, then a small protest from a loose board on the porch. She and Ray had talked about this. What she'd do if someone came in the night. Came to the house when he wasn't home. Quiet as anything, she slipped out of bed and put on her robe. Wiggled her feet into slippers. They'd practiced this, because that was the kind of man Ray was. A grown-up Boy Scout. Always wanting to be prepared. Cinda had always thought she'd be scared, but now it seemed like Ray was right there in the room with her as she opened the bedside drawer and took out the heavy pistol. She could almost feel his hands guiding hers, the warmth of his hands steadying her shoulders.

She stood by the bed, waiting to see if those few twists of wire in front of the door, or the ones just above that creaking stairboard, would do the trick and let her unwanted visitor know he was in the wrong place. That was Ray's thought. That people about to meet a gun ought to be given a chance to back out. He'd always been a fair man.

But she'd forgotten something. Shaking her head, she crossed to the closet and got the shotgun. A handgun was fine for a single intruder. But if there was more than one? A shotgun would be better.

The board on the porch creaked again and there was the sound of metal on metal as someone tried to fiddle the lock. Whoever was downstairs trying to get into her house probably thought they were dealing with a helpless middle-aged widow lady. The ideal victim for the kind of cowards and predators Jim Colson said her new neighbors were.

The door swung open with a creak. That was deliberate, too. The lock well oiled, the hinges left to give a faint creak. Ray's funny way of saying, "Honey, I'm home." He'd slip quiet as a mouse into the house, but for that.

"Thanks, honey," she whispered to the expectant darkness, as she waited for the stumble and the curse.

They came right on schedule. Thump. Crash. And "What the fuck!"

Sadly, her intruder, or intruders—she thought she was hearing two pairs of feet—were too dumb to be deterred, because now she heard the first thump of a boot hitting the stairs. They're thrashing like elephants in the parlor, and what do they imagine she is doing? Cowering under the sheets? What was it Jim had said to her? Ray always kept a shotgun handy, but you're not like that?

Someone was about to find out.

She counted. First step. Second. Third. Fourth. Creak! Stumble. Fuck! A crash to wake the dead, as a foot snagged on wire, and a heavy body fell backwards, taking another one with it.

She grabbed the shotgun and raised it chest height, sliding the barrel around the corner as she flicked on the light.

Deputy Jim Colson and a man she'd never seen before lay in a tangle at the foot of her stairs. The stranger was complaining that his leg might be broken. Colson sprawled with his shoulder against her front door, staring up at the barrel of the gun with an expression that would have been comical if these weren't intruders who'd broken into her house in the middle of the night.

She took a step forward, keeping the gun on Colson, and fell into her own trap. The third strip of wires, running across the hall at the top of the stairs. Ray's last innovation. "Third time lucky," he'd said with a grin. As though any bad guy was going to get past the wire by the front door and the one on the stairs. They'd laughed about it, imagining a bad guy so deft of foot that he'd gotten past the first two booby traps.

These boobies hadn't. But then her own foot caught, and when she inadvertently tightened her grip on the gun, it went off, showering a crooked deputy and a man whose name she didn't know with a host of bird shot.

Yes. Bird shot. Because for all his caution and precautions, Ray had never wanted to kill anybody. They had argued about that. Cinda felt that if someone broke into their home in the night, she shouldn't care about their welfare. Ray, a gentler soul, enjoyed the tricks and the traps.

Now Cinda racked another shell and glared at her moaning, bleeding intruders.

Moaning, groaning, cursing and thumping were not part of the sounds of her silence, and she wanted them gone as soon as possible. "Stay right where you are," she ordered. "I'm calling the state police." Not the Sheriff's Patrol. She was taking no chances on Jim Colson getting away with this. Concerned and kind-faced Jim who had asked too many questions and left the same telltale cigarette butts around Ray's workshop that he'd left when he'd parked his cruiser. Who thought she was spending the night at her son's house.

Later, when her intruders were gone, she'd tidied up, and the ordinary sounds of silence returned, she slept better than she had since Ray died. Maybe because he was still taking care of her. And she now knew that his plans would keep her safe.

Kate Flora's books include seven Thea Kozak mysteries, three Joe Burgess police procedurals, and a suspense thriller. Her true crime, *Finding Amy*, has been optioned for a movie. Her current projects include a true crime, co-writing a memoir, a screenplay, and a novel. She's published numerous short stories. Her third Joe Burgess police procedural, *Redemption*, was published in March 2012.

Burning Desire

Cheryl Marceau

Patty flipped the light switch inside the front door and stopped cold.

The rug wasn't that way when I left, was it? Shit, Joe, you got me scared of my own shadow! Keep going like this, I'm gonna end up in the loony bin. "It's all right, it's all right, it's all right," she said out loud. The sound of her own voice calmed her some, but she was panting like she'd run up all three flights of stairs. Every time Joe made an appearance, it took days to feel safe again. Lately the little visits came more often. Pretty soon she'd never feel safe.

It wasn't that way at first. He was strong and protective. That was all she ever wanted.

She pulled a cigarette from her purse, her hands shaking so hard that she could barely light it. The first deep drag brought her back to where she was before she came into the house. Jumpy, not scared shitless.

She retrieved the laundry hamper from the hall where she'd left it and carried it into the bedroom, reaching over the bed to pull the chain for the overhead light.

The nightstand drawer sat open, maybe an inch, maybe less.

Must of left it that way. Yeah, course I did. Gotta stop this.

It wasn't the first time she'd thought about getting a dog. Trouble was, her landlord didn't want dogs in the building. A dog would help, be someone she could talk to when she was nervous. Would scare people away.

Thinking of the landlord reminded her she wasn't supposed to smoke inside the building. *Screw him. Just this once.* After a couple more drags, she stubbed out the cigarette in the bathroom sink and dropped the butt in the toilet.

She switched on the TV on her bedroom dresser. Even the trashy

TV shows would keep her company and she could use the sound of another voice. She took a stack of folded bras out of the hamper and pulled open the top drawer. Her purple panties were there, the ones he used to say she looked hot in. The ones he made her wear, when he made her do things she didn't want to do. She would have sworn those panties had gone in the trash along with pretty much everything that reminded her of the hell he'd put her through. Now they were in her underwear drawer, wadded up in a ball. She pulled them out and realized Joe had left a little something for her, inside the wadded-up nylon. Underneath the panties sat his old Zippo lighter nestled in one of her bras. The sight of it made her sweat.

She ran to the bathroom and vomited. When there was nothing left but dry heaves, she sank onto the tile floor, trembling. *He's gonna kill me. He said he'd do it and nobody could do nothing about it.* Red burn marks on the inside of her left arm were garish in the fluorescent bathroom light. Months after he did it, she could still see the scars. Sometimes her side still hurt where he kicked her and broke a couple of ribs. *Nobody believes me. Cops won't haul his ass in. Even if they do, so what? He's out and then it's the same thing all over again.* Patty sat on the floor rocking herself and whimpering. *He's frickin' gonna kill me.*

Sunlight crept under the roller shade on the bedroom window and across Patty's face. She rubbed her swollen eyes and sat up. She'd cried herself to sleep the night before, after double-checking the window locks and propping a chair under the front doorknob. She'd begged the landlord to put in a new lock after the last time Joe came by. The landlord wouldn't pay for it, said he already changed the lock when she moved in, so she must have given the key to the boyfriend and then changed her mind. Not his fault, so why should he pay?

Patty yanked her cell out of her jeans pocket. She'd slept in her clothes and kept her cell and car keys in her pocket in case she needed to run during the night. By morning she'd made up her mind. Joe would never again make her afraid to sleep in her own bed.

"I can't come in today, I'm sick," she said to the manager at the clothes store where she worked. Her head was so stuffy from crying that she sounded like she had a bad cold. "I'll be in tomorrow, don't worry." She flipped the phone shut and jammed it back into her pocket.

Late that night Patty parked her car on a side street a couple blocks off Maple Street, close to where Joe lived. Her stomach hurt and her hands were clammy. She grabbed the Market Basket bag from the back seat. In the bag she had a half-empty bottle of tequila, a pack of Marlboros, Joe's old lighter, and a can of cigarette lighter fluid. She walked to Joe's house, telling herself over and over that it would be fine. It was a lie. She was terrified of what she was planning to do, and more terrified that somebody'd stop her.

She'd been thinking all day about how she'd do it. She didn't have a gun, wouldn't even know how to get one. If she used a knife, she'd have to get close to him. He was too strong—if he woke up and caught her, he'd kill her. There was only one way that she could think of.

Joe went to the bar on the corner nearly every night, usually wasted by the time the place closed. Mostly he passed out once he got home. She'd wait for that, then let herself into his house. She'd pour some lighter fluid on the kitchen table and around the floor, like she saw them do on the cop shows, then light a cigarette and drop it in the lighter fluid. She'd leave the tequila there, with the cap off. Joe'd be dead to the world until everything was on fire, then it'd be too late. If the house didn't burn all the way down, the cops would find the stuff in the kitchen and figure he'd been so drunk he set the fire accidentally.

As she walked down Maple, the bag shook in her hands. A police cruiser passed her from behind, seeming to slow as it drove by. Patty held her breath, willing the cop to keep going. She clutched the bag tight against her chest so it didn't shake. When the cruiser pulled up to the convenience store on the next block, Patty was so nervous she thought she'd pee her pants. She took as deep a breath as she could, and kept walking past the store and the cop car.

The dilapidated Victorian looked the same as before, maybe even seedier than when she last saw it. No lights were on in Joe's first floor apartment. She remembered the couple upstairs had split up and moved. Nobody lived there now. She tiptoed to the back of the house, trying hard not to think about what she was going to do. Dying like that—the thought made her hurt all over. But she knew what Joe would do to her sooner or later.

It was pretty easy to jimmy the crummy lock on the back door with her ATM card. She held her breath and tiptoed into the kitchen. The place smelled like garbage that'd sat too long. Garbage, and stale beer. The clock on the microwave read 2:47 a.m. The bars closed at 2:00, so for sure Joe would be passed out in his bed by now. She pulled the lighter fluid from the grocery bag and fished out Joe's cigarette lighter. Then she grabbed the tequila bottle and took a swig for courage before wiping the neck on her tee shirt and putting the bottle next to the lighter.

Footsteps creaked on the front porch, keys jangled at the door. *Omigod, it's him! What was he doing all this time? I'm dead if he catches me!* Patty almost stumbled on a kitchen chair and jumped to the back door, clawing at the doorknob. Once outside she fell to the ground and crept to the side of the house, keeping below the windows in case he could see her from inside, and waited, trying not to breathe too loud. It didn't sound like anybody was moving in the apartment. After a while, when she thought she would lose her mind if she didn't do something, she edged around the corner and took a look out front. No one was there.

She ran all the way back to her car and dropped onto the front seat, wanting to scream her head off. He'd see the stuff in the kitchen and know for sure where the lighter came from. She tried to figure out her options. *He knows where I work, he knows my friends. How am I gonna get away from him for good?* She couldn't go back and finish what she started, not now, not if Joe was onto her. Her head sank onto the steering wheel and she sobbed.

Sirens screamed nearby. She jerked up and looked around, with no idea how long she'd been sitting there in her car. Flashes of red bounced off the buildings as a couple of fire trucks sped past.

The alarm beeped. Patty slapped the "Off" button on the clock. Six a.m. She felt hung over. She had no idea what she was going to do. Last night was a horror she would never wake up from. Joe was alive. Sooner or later, he would come after her again and this time he'd really kill her.

She grabbed the TV remote and turned on the morning news. At first she couldn't focus her bleary eyes on the screen. She saw a big old house that looked a lot like Joe's place. She held her breath as Joe's picture appeared on the TV. The newscaster voice said, "The victim was Joseph Morano of Malden." The voice said other things that Patty didn't comprehend. It sounded like Joe was dead, killed in a house fire.

It can't be true. I ran outta there before I could do it.

Patty exhaled like she'd been holding her breath all night. She thought about Joe and was so relieved he was really dead, she wanted to shout. Maybe somebody was looking out for her after all. Like the guardian angel from her Nonna's bedtime stories. She crossed herself in a hurry and said a little prayer to her Nonna. It was a sin to be happy about somebody dying. Even if they would have killed her.

The next image on the screen was a sullen-looking blonde being handcuffed and pushed into a cruiser. The TV voice continued, "The woman was identified as Angela O'Brien, also of Malden, who admitted to setting the fire early this morning using a cigarette lighter and fluid that she found at the victim's house. She told police Morano had threatened to kill her after she broke up with him. Police say the accused was carrying a knife, which she may have intended to use as a murder weapon. O'Brien is being held on $50,000 bail."

"NO-O-O!" Patty hurled the remote at the television. *"Joe, you goddamn two-timing bastard!"*

Cheryl Marceau is a human resources executive at a technology company in the Boston area. She has two previous stories in the Level Best anthologies *Thin Ice* and *Dead Calm*. She is working on her first novel, a historical mystery. Cheryl and her husband live in Arlington, Massachusetts.

The Cat and the Blue Moon

Randy DeWitt

Cruiser lights danced across snowflakes as they fell on the dead body lying in the Blue Moon parking lot. Inside the club, not the bartender, bouncer, strippers, or any one of the wide-eyed men seated around the horseshoe shaped stage were aware that there'd even been a shooting. The lovely and talented Tabitha performed under strobe lights as "Closer To God" by Nine Inch Nails blared on the sound system. After a few revolutions on the stripper pole, she seductively crawled her way back and forth giving close-up views of her tight ass, 34D's, and the gap just below her tidy little landing strip, scooping up piles of cash as she went along. The shooting could've taken place at a table in the corner and no one would've noticed.

Alan Peterson, on the other hand, had just parked his car when he heard gunshots. He was already in trouble with his wife for stretching beer o'clock with the guys from work into six hours of bar hopping. When she found out he'd also stopped at a strip club, she was going to kill him. He opened his door and slid out the side, crouching low behind an SUV. When he got up the nerve, he poked his head out and looked down the row of cars. That's when he saw someone lying in the snow about fifty feet away.

According to Peterson, he next stood up and, against better judgment, made his way over to the motionless body. Footprints in the snow made him uneasy. They could've led anywhere—to a car, to the street, or even in a circle and right back up behind him. Scanning the area, he thought he saw movement out by a street light on the main road. But with the distance and bad visibility, he wasn't sure if it was a person or just snowflakes being blown sideways by the wind. For all he really knew, the shooter was still nearby. Sobered by the thought, he took out his cell phone and dialed 911.

As he stayed on the line with the dispatcher, the music coming from inside the club provided a soundtrack to the crime scene as if it were an episode of *CSI*. All that was missing were the cruisers with their lights flashing, uniformed cops with guns, Gary Sinise and the rest of his forensics team. Standing in the snow and cold of the parking lot with a bladder full of beer, not knowing where the gunman was, and waiting for the first cruiser to arrive, it was all Peterson could do not to piss himself.

The unfortunate thing about regaining consciousness was how everything came back to Brian Holman. Everything that is, except how long it'd been since his car had slid off of the road, down an embankment and into the trees at the edge of the woods. All he knew was he'd been unconscious long enough for his core temperature to drop and for about an inch of snow to fall.

Brian felt cold—extremely cold. He'd always heard people say that sometimes it was too cold to snow. Looking up into the dark of the night, all he could make out were snowflakes as they drifted down around him. So much for that theory, he thought as he cinched up his jacket and scrambled up the incline to the street. On his left, he could make out the telltale sign of his accident, an unmistakable gouge in the snow bank where his car had plowed its way through. Brian wasn't about to wait for someone to happen by and decided to start walking. Every fifty steps or so the wind swirled, forcing him to tilt his head forward to fend off the snow that whipped into his face. Each gust reminded him of how great the knit cap was that he wore as a kid after playing ice hockey out on Mill Pond.

Brian was always one of the last to go home, even though he lived the farthest away and it would be dark by the time he was ready to leave. He could still remember the unique sensation of taking off his skates, after wearing them for hours, and sliding his feet into a cold pair of boots or sneakers that had been sitting on the edge of the ice while the pick-up games were played. He remembered how the cold quickly gave way to comfort as his sore insteps and frozen toes reclaimed the luxury of flexing.

After throwing his jacket on, Brian would tie his skate laces together and hang them on his hockey stick. Then he'd set out with the shaft slung over his shoulder. The walk was measured not in time, but by streetlights, twists and turns from one road onto another, and logical milestones along the route like the first leg, halfway hill, and the final stretch.

The steam that rose off of his sweaty forehead dissipated well before the first leg was over. The brisk blasts of wind that never seemed to matter while chasing a puck around the six-inch thick ice suddenly would make his eyes water and his cheeks freeze. That's when he'd reverse his knit hat into a mask that covered all but his eyes. How he wished he had that hat now.

Officer Crowley was responding to the shooting, nearing the end of Lakeview Ave, when the report came across his radio that the possible gunman was heading up Route 3A on foot. Instead of turning south on 3A toward the Blue Moon, he swung north on the hunch that anyone walking from the strip club would've already made it past the intersection with Lakeview. In a matter of seconds, he saw the silhouette of someone through his snow-shrouded lights. He pulled just ahead of the person and cut him off with his cruiser. Crowley threw his door open and drew down on the suspect from behind the cover of the car. He ordered the man face down on the ground and then to spread his arms and legs out to the side, sort of a downward facing snow angel except that, if this was the man who had pulled the trigger at the strip club, he was no angel. He was a cold-blooded killer. Crowley radioed for backup and cautiously maneuvered around directly behind the suspect.

"Do you have any weapons on you?" he shouted, his adrenaline pumping.

"Yeah, a handgun in my waistband," came the reply.

"Take it out slowly," Crowley instructed, "then toss it to the side."

The man complied. He didn't resist being cuffed or patted down. The only things he had on him, besides his wallet, were a lighter and a pack of cigarettes.

"It's pretty damn cold out," he told the officer. "I'm not going to put up a fight if you want to put me in your cruiser where it's warm."

From what Detective Brookes was told, no one had seen any disturbances, inside or outside of the club. The strippers said that some of the men watching them perform had gotten loud and even a little obnoxious at times that night, but nothing out of the ordinary. As long as a guy threw a few bucks over the rail every other dance or so, they couldn't care less if someone got a little noisy in the club. From what they described to Brookes, no one really stood out to them other than one perv who had to be warned to watch his hands or risk a beating from the bouncer.

Out in the parking lot, the police continued to process the area for evidence. The work was slow because of all the snow that had fallen since the shooting. Brookes left the club as soon as he felt confident that no important lead or piece of evidence had been overlooked.

The ride from the Blue Moon to the Tyngsboro Police Department is only a few miles, never leaving Route 3A despite crossing over the Merrimack River and taking a left at a set of lights. Even with the bad weather, Brookes was back at the station in about 10 minutes. Once inside, he looked for Officer Crowley and found him by one of the station's interviewing rooms.

"What do we know about our suspect?" he asked.

"He's got a record in Colorado for assault," Crowley replied, "and he had a concealed, unregistered handgun when I stopped him. But he claims he didn't shoot anyone and the gun doesn't appear to have been fired tonight."

"Has he been booked and Miranda-ized on the weapons charges?"

"Not yet, but he knows they're coming. He said he was willing to cooperate if we're willing to cut him a deal."

"That depends on what he has to offer us," Brookes replied.

By the time Lawndale Road had emptied out onto Coburn Road, and Coburn had come to an end at Sherburne Avenue, the snowstorm had let up a bit. Brian Holman looked to his right at a sight familiar to him—the seventh green of the Tyngsboro Country Club. He stopped walking long enough to look back down the snow-covered hole, picturing the fairway that lay dormant underneath. He'd played

Tyngsboro dozens of times. It was a nine-hole course, so to play eighteen holes, each hole was played twice. For twenty-seven holes, three times. Brian, like anyone else who played there regularly, knew every inch of the course. Oh, how he wished it was eighty degrees out and sunny, and that he could have one last chance at driving the green from the white tees on the short par 4 hole.

On any given outing, Brian never knew what he'd shoot. He could make a few pars, maybe even a bird or two. He could also make a triple bogey and a couple of doubles just as easy. Some days he'd only lose a ball or two. Others, he'd pretty near go through a dozen. It really didn't matter. He loved getting out with his buddies, drinking beers and ripping it up. At the end of nine, they'd each wolf down a hotdog at the clubhouse, grab a couple beers to go and head out to do it all over again.

The last time he'd played the 7th at Tyngsboro was right before he'd left for Fort Carson. It was a send-off of sorts, set up for him by his friends. Everyone drank more than usual. No one took the scores seriously. They just teed the ball up and took the hardest swing they could, practically coming out of their golf shoes in the process, trying to outdrive each other. Brian remembered hitting two out of bounds on the right before finally putting a ball in play on the far side of the fairway sand trap, thirty yards in front of the green. After a pitching wedge and a two putt, he finally found the bottom of the cup for a four over par eight. An eight, he mused, otherwise known as a snowman.

Chris Mullens sat at a small table in the Tyngsboro police station interview room smoking a cigarette. Three nights ago, he'd been sitting in a Colorado Springs bar, just like he'd done every night since separating from the service. He was telling Rick Newbury, a combat veteran who'd served with him in Iraq, he was driving out to the East Coast in the morning to visit a friend. Rick wanted to go along, even offering his car up for transportation.

Colorado to Massachusetts was a long time to be stuck in a compact car with Rick Newbury. He wasn't always the easiest of guys to get along with a few hours at a time, never mind two straight days of driving. And that was only if Rick was taking his anxiety medication correctly and watching how much he drank.

Rick Newbury wouldn't take no for an answer. He pestered Chris about the trip for over an hour until Chris finally gave in. They set out early the next morning, lightly packed with room to pick up beer as soon as a store opened up along the way. They took turns between driving and sleeping, slowed at times by the winter weather. By the time they'd reached South Bend, Indiana, Rick was nipping away at a bottle of Jack Daniels he'd bought during their last pit stop and Chris was getting a bad feeling about the trip.

Detective Brookes entered the interview room and sized up Chris Mullens before pulling a chair from the corner closer to the table and sitting down. A video camera mounted near the ceiling faced the suspect and streamed everything that went on. Officers in an adjoining room watched the recording as Brookes tried to establish a rapport with the suspect.

"Did anyone offer you a cup of coffee?" he asked.

"No, but I could use one."

Brookes asked Chris how he took it and then rapped twice on the door. The door opened and he asked the officer outside to bring a black coffee. When the door closed he asked about the victim.

"Did you know Richard Newbury?"

"Yeah, I served a couple of tours with him in Iraq. Everyone called him Rick. He didn't like being called Richard or Ricky."

He also didn't like being called Dick, dickless or dickhead either, but that's what he often was. He was always rubbing someone the wrong way, as Chris had been reminded in at least six states over the past 24 hours.

The interview room door reopened and an officer placed a cardboard cup on the table. It wasn't steaming but Chris took a chance and lifted it to his mouth for a sip. The foul brew that sat cooking on the coffee pot burners at that hour of morning could be considered cruel and unusual punishment, argued by any decent lawyer to have coerced a confession out of its recipient. Chris swallowed it gratefully and then placed it back down on the table.

Brookes opened up a manila folder and flipped through a few sheets of paper. "It says here that you've gotten into some trouble since you've been back."

"I'm not going to lie to you, I've had problems since Iraq," Chris replied. "Drugs . . . alcohol . . ."

"Why didn't you try to get some help?"

"By the time I did it was too late. I did something that the Army wasn't too happy about in Iraq. They gave me an 'Other than Honorable' discharge and kicked me out, without any counseling or medication to treat my PTSD.

"During the surge," Chris continued, "the Army was a full service pharmacy, happy to dispense drugs to anyone in our battalion. Can't sleep? Here's a pill. Anxiety? Take these. What wouldn't be prescribed back here without couch sessions and regular monitoring, they handed out like vitamins. We'd be out on a weeklong mission worrying if we'd make it back to our outpost in time before our meds ran out. But back at Fort Carson, they wouldn't even . . ."

"Chris," Brookes interrupted. He was happy Chris Mullens was talking without any deal in place, but now he needed to know if he was just as eager to discuss the murder. "Who shot Rick Newbury?"

Across the road from the seventh green, Brian watched as a black cat passed by the eighth tee. For whatever reason, he felt drawn to the scrawny little thing. He crossed the road and crept up to where it had jumped onto the low stone wall of the Sherburne Cemetery and hunkered down. It didn't even move as Brian sat next to it. He could see it was shivering in the cold. He reached out and brushed the snow off its fur, then began petting the creature as it purred its appreciation.

"Hey little fellow, what're you doing out on a night like tonight?" he asked, smiling. "You didn't slide off the road like I did, did you?"

Brian never had any dogs or cats as a kid but thought he would've been good with pets. He picked up the cat with his left hand and unzipped his jacket with his right. He tucked the cat inside to shelter it from the latest band of snow that had started to come down.

"Stay in there and get warm," he told it.

Brian sat listening to the sound of the snow crystals hitting the ground. The cat, the graveyard, the snow—all contributed to create an odd but tranquil setting.

"I had a Company First Sergeant in Iraq for a few weeks named Katz. Just before I was shipped home he came up to me and said 'Tell

Mullens, Millen is dead.' I didn't have any idea what it meant until Chris explained it to me."

The purring that came from his jacket was getting louder. Brian couldn't tell if the cat was asleep, happy to be out of the cold or enjoying his story. He continued his tale.

"Katz had been the platoon sergeant with Alpha Company, 2nd Platoon. Their missions were tough ones, driving up and down supply routes around Baghdad, trying to ferret out ambushes and IEDs. One of the squads was hit pretty hard over the course of the year and suffered lots of casualties. Only two soldiers remained from the original squad, one named Mullens and the other named Millen. Well, long story short, Mullens got sent home ahead of me for threatening to kill his platoon leader and Millen got hit the day before I returned to Fort Carson. Get it? '*Tell Mullens, Millen is dead.*' Katz wanted Mullens to know he was the last one alive."

Brian pulled the black cat from his jacket, set him back down on the stone wall and gave him one last pat.

"Storytime's over little buddy—I hope you enjoyed it. It's time for you to run along home," he told his newfound friend before adding, "I wish I could."

Chris swallowed another mouthful of coffee and thought about what he would say next. He hated to give up his friend's name to the police but knew, sooner or later, they were bound to piece together who shot Rick on their own. At least this way, the police couldn't say he didn't cooperate with them.

"Brian Holman," he told Brookes. "I met Brian at Fort Carson about a month after I got sent home from Iraq. We got along good, probably because we went through a lot of the same shit over there. Anyway, we started hanging out and drinking a lot together after we got discharged."

Chris wanted to tell the detective about what they did and saw in Iraq. But he knew from his last appearance in front of a judge, that the United States Court System didn't care much about the number of dead bodies a soldier saw—some their close friends, others that were fellow servicemen, and so many more that were Iraqi. The criminal code didn't have any provisions for a soldier who had become numb to the death, violence and destruction that they'd been exposed to. There was no special legal consideration given for the god-awful toll that two tours of duty could take on a soldier, when twenty-six months out of three and a third years were spent on a razor's edge.

"How did Brian Holman know Rick Newbury?" Brookes asked.

"He didn't. Not until Rick talked me into letting him tag along when I came out here from Colorado Springs for a visit," he replied. "Brian was depressed, I thought he could use . . ."

"You were staying with him?"

"We were supposed to. We were only at his apartment long enough to crash for a few hours before heading out tonight."

"What's his address?"

"I'm not sure," Chris told him. "All I remember is that it was on Pawtucket Boulevard in Lowell."

Brookes knew someone watching in the other room would work on Brian Holman's address while he continued his interrogation. He had to finish getting what information he could out of Mullens before he decided to clam up or ask for a lawyer.

"Take me through what happened tonight, Chris," he said, "and don't leave anything out."

"There's really not a lot to it," Chris replied. "We went out drinking at a bar just up the street from the Blue Moon and planned on stopping by the strip club later. Rick was slamming back Jack and Cokes hard. Brian and I were drinking mostly beers.

"Rick was bugging Brian to play eight-ball for twenty bucks a rack. Well, Brian's good with a cue and Rick pretty much sucks at anything when he's drinking. Brian took him three straight games. Rick wanted a chance to win his money back."

Chris paused briefly and looked over at Brookes. The detective was mistaken if he thought this was just a fight over bets between a couple drunks. It was more about what Rick had said while shooting pool and how he had said it. If there was one thing that enraged Brian more than the senseless deaths of innocent Iraqis, it was assholes like Rick who bragged about killing Hadjis like it was a legitimate sport or something. The way Rick talked, not only had he made it to the big leagues, but he was the league's MVP.

"Brian told him we were heading over to the Blue Moon but not to worry—they had a pool table there if he still felt like losing money.

We got into Brian's car and drove to the strip club. We reached the parking lot and got out, but didn't make it more than a few steps. Rick just wouldn't shut up and Brian couldn't take it anymore. He told Rick to get the fuck away from him or he'd kill him. Rick never did know when to back down, especially when he'd been drinking too much. He shot his mouth off one last time. Brian pulled his 9mm . . ."

"And that's when Brian Holman shot him?"

"Three times," Chris replied, nodding. "Brian looked over at me, then just got into his car and drove off. There was nothing I could do for Rick. He was dead."

Chris resisted telling Brookes that Rick Newbury had gotten what he'd deserved. Instead, he told the detective about trying to walk back to the other bar for a couple more beers. There, at least, he would've been out of the cold and snow while he tried to figure out what to do next.

The door to the room opened and Officer Crowley walked in.

"Someone reported a car off the road on Lawndale," Crowley informed the detective. "It was Brian Holman's car. He must've been trying to flee the scene using the back roads, lost control and ended up in the trees. A 9mm handgun that had recently been fired was found in the wreck, along with the body of Brian Holman. It looks like he died of internal injuries."

Chris Mullens didn't say a word. He refused to let his sadness show. Brian was a good guy and one of his closest friends. He was a kindred troubled soul. Now, just like Millen, he was gone. Chris would miss him.

The snow that had been falling earlier stopped and the clouds parted to reveal a beautiful night sky. Bright stars pierced through the darkness as a tired young man reached the end of his final stretch in the crisp winter air. He stepped off the street into the short driveway. From the driveway, he headed up an icy walkway, bounded onto the porch and opened the front door. Brian Holman could smell dinner warming on the stove, welcoming him back home.

Randy DeWitt's flash fiction has appeared in *Alfred Hitchcock's Mystery Magazine*.

The City

Pamela A. Oberg

The darkness forgives much. It overlooks petty grievances that consume so many. It overlooks dirt, ugliness, despair. In the dark and near dark of the city at night, beauty is redefined. The streetlights cast dancing shadows on the worn walls and aging cars, and create sparks on broken windows and muddy, oily puddles in the street. I, Magret Desmarais, am at the center of the city tonight. I feel its cloying, smoky breath on me, feel it embrace me, grasp at me. Welcoming the energy into my body as I stride toward my favorite bistro, I swallow the night air in deep, heaving gulps. My usual seat is waiting for me. I am content.

On this particular summer evening, the temperature has retreated from oppressive to merely sleep-inducing. My companions lounge, legs stretched out and crossed at the ankles, in well-padded chairs with softly worn fabric. Well-shod feet dip and sway in time to music floating on the thick, humid air. We enjoy coming to this little bistro, known for its 40s style music and delicious pastries. The cocktails are cold, the pastries light, and the service is quick and unobtrusive. Our seats on the patio look out on a busy, pedestrian-filled area. A bus station, cab stands, cafes, and even an arcade draw city residents and visitors alike, their interactions offering nonstop entertainment for those who enjoy watching that sort of thing. We do.

Playing a game that began decades ago, Marcos juts out a chubby finger, selecting a young couple on the street corner opposite. "They are fighting. She thinks he's cheated. He has, but will deny it to his last breath. She will believe him." His voice speaks of smoky clubs and a lifelong love of good brandy, and cigarettes. His eyes survey the woman's figure in her fitted dress with its plunging neckline, paired with sky-high heels. He nods in approval and looks back toward us, eyes sparkling with amusement.

Sofia makes a noise. From anyone else I would call it a snort, but she is too graceful, too elegant for that. "No. It is not she. He is the one who wonders, who worries. She is beautiful; he cannot believe she would remain faithful to him. He is ordinary, a nobody. She loves him, but grows tired of his petty tantrums." We study the couple, chuckling together when the woman spins away from her companion, fingers curled into tight fists. He dashes after her, tugging at her elbow, desperation making him pale under the streetlights.

"Always the winner, Sofia. I shall never bet against you!" Truly, she never lost the game, not as long as I could remember.

The glossy red lipstick dressing her full lips draws a listener's attention, more so as she kisses her fingertips and blows them away. "*C'est la vie.* I am just lucky, that is all." Her throaty chuckle is self-congratulatory, in spite of her words, and her dark eyes sparkle in triumph. Sofia turns to stare at me. "But you did not choose to play this evening. Are you unwell?" Nearly black, her eyes reflect Sofia's Mediterranean ancestry, and that stare can penetrate the thickest veneer of confidence. I'm glad she is my friend, and not my enemy.

"There wasn't time. The story played out before I had a turn." Lazily, my fingers trace designs in the condensation from my glass, and I study the passersby.

"There." I gesture with a tilt of my head. "They're considering a *ménage a trois*, but aren't quite drunk enough. The naughtiness of the idea has them horny and incautious, but they need a few more libations for courage." A tall, thin young man with a pointed beard and gold-rimmed glasses walks past the café with two petite women, a blonde and a brunette. They look like a typical group of post-college, pre-marriage young professionals, out for an evening of fun.

"My dear, your French accent remains atrocious," Marcos drawls, "but no, I think the young man is merely guarding his two female companions, keeping them safe from the predators in the clubs. Chivalrous. And perhaps he has secret crush on the blonde one." He eyes the young woman in question critically, and then nods.

"Nothing but blondes for you, Marcos? What is wrong with beautiful women who aren't blonde, I ask you?" I tug on one of my own, siren red curls. He laughs, and shakes his head.

Sofia's laughter tinkles lightly, like bells or wind chimes, as she jumps into the game. "No, no. That is, Magret's accent is atrocious, but you are both wrong. What we have here is a young lesbian couple, and their across-the-hall neighbor who desperately wishes he could find a straight woman as lovely as either of these two."

We sit and watch as the trio moves down the sidewalk. When the man stops to purchase a newspaper from a sidewalk stand, the women engage in a decidedly amorous embrace, the blonde sweetly stroking her companion's cheek as their lips meet, once, twice, three times. They break apart as the young man laughs, shaking his head at them. The three rejoin and link arms, moving up to the end of the street to finally enter one of the apartment buildings together.

As one, Marcos and I turn to Sofia. She shrugs, a decidedly Gallic gesture, and waves her hand in the air. "What can I say? It is a gift." She doesn't quite maintain a straight face, and her delicate laughter fills the night again.

Smiling, I shake my head. I adore these two. Closer friends I have never known. They knew me from the beginning, and I learned much from them. Marcos and Sofia had found me when I was young and alone. A combination of doting parents, strict coaches, and encouraging mentors, they had worked diligently to teach me the basics of survival in those first, difficult years. Later, they taught me how to enjoy life as we lived and traveled in Italy, France, Greece, and finally the United States.

I turn at the sound of the Greyhound buses rumbling down the street, their loud diesel engines interrupting my reverie. They stop at the corner, a nightly exercise. Arriving from Boston, Philadelphia, Chicago, all over, swollen with passengers dying to see this city of mine, as though it were different from their own, these buses deliver predictably.

Engorged, the rumbling beasts regurgitate their contents, passengers now cluttering the sidewalk with their sweaty bodies and bruised baggage, filling the air with mindless chatter. Bits of conversation drift toward the outdoor café where we lounge:

"Excuse me, I'm in a hurry, pardon me."

"Where's my bag? Did I forget it on the bus? Quickly, do you see it?"

"Hey, quit shoving, I'm stuck behind this fat guy!"

"Who ya callin' fat?"

At the end of the buses' regurgitation, the Lost are discharged. The Lost: those shiny, clean, teenage escapees, thinking their lives at home are so tragic, thinking they'll make their way in the big city. They know so much, everything, nothing, how can they fail? They wear their bravado like armor, while in their eyes fear ripples and glows, obvious to anyone who thinks to look. These children don't want to be saved, don't need help. Not yet. They are not for me to save, not for me at all, but there are those who are not so selective, who follow no rules, respect no limitations. That type watches and waits, ready to offer assistance to these shiny kids trying to make their way in the city. It is not a type of assistance anyone should accept. But these kids are not my concern. Simply another busload arriving at the corner, as they do every night in the city.

I am hungry.

Turning my head at the sound of expensive shoes, cushiony soles making quiet yet distinctive sounds on the sidewalk, soft leather whispering as the shoes flex with each confident step, I watch a man striding down the sidewalk. He is across the street, but I can see that he is comfortable in the dark shadows of the city. Broad of shoulder and narrow of hip, he wears his elegant suit carelessly. His walk tells me that, in his mind, he owns the city. It is his: here to serve him, amuse and admire him.

With a nod to my companions, I rise from my seat at the outdoor café and wish them a good night. I smooth my silk dress and adjust the thin straps that leave my shoulders bare, as Marcos and Sofia turn to study the man who has caught my attention. He is across the street, moving in and out of the pools of light cast by the streetlamps. Sofia smiles as she turns back to me. "We'll see you tomorrow, yes?" I nod, my eyes straying back to the man as my stomach rumbles. "Good night, my child," laughs Marcos, the chuckle riding deep in his throat. "Enjoy your dinner." With only the tiniest hint of fang, I smile, and hurry to catch my meal.

Pamela A. Oberg, native Mainer, earned her B.A. and M.A. from UNH and UVM, respectively. She's a member of Sisters in Crime and co-founder of Writers on Words, a writer's group. Pamela lives in New Hampshire with her husband, daughter, and demanding pets. She is working on her first novel and more short stories. This is her first fiction publication.

A Regular Story

Peggy McFarland

One, one-thousand. Two, one-thousand. Three. That's how I measure a generous shot. Stupid count, I know, but I'm accurate. Most bartenders use a four count. I don't need to count; it's habit. Like when you tie a square knot, you still chant in your head *right-over-left, under: left-over-right, under.*

My lips must be moving, 'cause Barry tells me to learn to count to one, ten-thousand. The other bartenders don't like waiting on him because he's particular. I ask him what comes after two, but keep the bottle tipped. He smiles, I start at one again.

He gets his tall rum and coke, NFL—no fucking lime, for the uninitiated. He likes what he likes, just make it right. Of course I charge him extra, but he doesn't mind. He can afford it. He owns this construction biz, and from what I understand, he's 'bout the only one building new homes in this economy. I think it's because he *is* so particular. He's a regular I can count on . . . as long as I don't give him tequila. In bar parlance, that's te-kill-ya.

Ever see *The Exorcist*? Barry on rum—sweet little Linda Blair. Barry on te-kill-ya? Pea-soup-spewing demon. Let's just say, Barry did a good job patching the wall behind the stage. Even in the late afternoon sunshine, no one notices his punch-holes.

"Thanks, Bernie," he says, and sips his rum.

My name is Bernadette Amelia Ericson, but my regulars call me Bernie. Being of the fairer gender, it's easier having a masculine name—an authority thing. A guy would rather say Mickie or Bernie shut him off, instead of Lisa or Cindy. Another authority thing? The bar itself. Having eighteen inches of granite or wood between me and a customer keeps the respect flowing. I tell people to try it at home. During the next domestic squabble, stand behind the counter. Guaranteed upper hand.

Two women pay the parking meter right in front of Dick's Place, and then walk past. I think nothing of it, except that their six-inch spikes aren't made for walking. Their Beamer though, fits in nicely on West Pearl Street's "Frontside."

We all have a right-side-of-town façade. Next door is Asian Bistro—which always makes me wonder how many bistros are in Asia—and across the street is a new age spiritual shop, a wallpaper store, a jeweler, and even an art-and-glass-blower boutique.

Backside? Tenements and a soup kitchen. We're on the DMZ-border for Nashua's revitalization. The city has a homeless problem. Nothing serious, if you ask the mayor. Except I see the problem almost every day.

Last Thursday, I got me a backstage view. The usual day-tender got tickets to the Sox "double-heada" and begged. Normally, I like a guy begging.

Too early. I'll save it for after sunset.

Anyhow, I'm filling in on this day shift last week, watching a cobweb form over my tip jar, when I hear, "Bernie. Alley."

The swinging door closes on Dan, our cook. I cut through the kitchen to the alley. There's Mary on her knees. A guy is standing, sweat beading on his bald spot, skivvies and work pants pooled at his Timberlands—lord help me—

"Hey! You can't do this here," I shout.

Mary turns around and wipes her mouth. The guy stares vacantly, then blinks real fast.

I sputter a few nonsense sounds, look for help from Dan, but he ducks back into the kitchen.

The guy pulls up his pants, takes his time retrieving his ball cap. I don't want to picture how it fell, but my imagination isn't cooperating. He makes a kissy face at me, then ambles back to West Pearl.

"Really?" I say to Mary. As if I can lay a guilt trip.

"He's my Thursday regahlah."

Most nights I work, I give her leftovers, so I sort of know her. I want to say something more, but her reality settles into my conscience. I watch her push her shopping cart toward Backside.

Dan's watching from the door.

"Why didn't *you* stop them?" I ask.

He shrugs. Claims he's a black-belt, doesn't want to lose control. My ass. He's a wuss.

Barry and me watch the Beamer-ladies walk by the picture window for the third time. The burgundy-haired one finally stops and cups her hands over her eyes, leaving nose prints on the glass. We need a flashing neon sign. I grab the cleaning supplies and walk around to give them direction.

The light from the setting sun is not kind to these two. If they were, oh, maybe ten years younger—and I'm being generous—they might be considered sexy. I ask, "May I help you?"

The platinum blonde says, "We're looking for a piano bar?"

"You've found it," I say. I give them a huge smile and open the door wide—after all, underneath the four inches of foundation and fake eyelashes could be two very good tippers—and then clean the window real quick.

Once I'm back behind my authority zone, I say, "Let me guess, two glasses of Pinot Grigio?"

I really shouldn't pretend I know what new customers want to drink. I'm wrong ninety-five percent of the time, but no one realizes that. For the five percent I'm right, I impress anyone within earshot.

"Um, yes," says the burgundy-haired one. "How'd you know?"

I pull out my finest bull-crap.

"Tuesday night, you ladies look like profession—executives, have to keep your wits about you. Wine is a safe, weeknight beverage. You can sip it, let it mellow the edges without worrying about over-indulging. Pinot Grigio is light, crisp, elegant but accessible, as you ladies appear to be. Lurton from Argentina okay?"

They nod, then ask where is the ladies room. Great, I think. They'll reapply lipstick and leave prints all over their wine glasses.

"Mm, impressive," Barry says. He's watching them sashay.

"Should I introduce you?"

Barry licks the fingers on each hand, pretends to smooth his hair, then straightens a non-existent tie. "How do I look?" he asks, and winks.

"Like trouble," I say.

Piano Bar is the busiest night at Dick's Place. Sure, it's hokey, but the regulars love it. Every single Tuesday, I get to hear sing-a-long standards, such as, "The Piña Colada Song"—I know, the real name is "Escape" but the hook is *do you like piña coladas?*—and "Sweet Caroline" 'cause the *bomp, bomp, bomp* is irresistible, and a slew of Bee Gees and Beatle songs. It's the night of the week when the blue collars and the suits come together in harmony. Cue rim-shot.

Okay, I'm funnier as my customers drink more.

Mickie's the cocktail server tonight. She stocks her station, sets the tables, lights the candles. Dan rolls out the piano.

I like the nighttime transformation. Daytime, you see the chipped paint on the walls, the stains on the carpet and the black specks that never wash off the mirror behind the liquor. At dusk, I dim the wall sconces, plug in the rope lights, and then the wall nicks disappear, the mirror sparkles, and it's too dark to notice the carpet. Add the piano, and *voilà*. Classy.

The thirty-to-fifty-something crowd loves us. Our menu features the usual bar foods, only reinvented; we consider ourselves a "gastro pub." Burgers and such, but the cheese is gruyère, and we call the mayo "aioli." Regardless, it's still drinking food. High-protein, high-fat, shut-off-the-pyloric-valve and slow-down-the-buzz kinda foods.

My boss is out of town, and he gave me the keys. Piano night is busy but mellow, so I should be okay, knock on wood.

The Tuesday regulars filter in.

Pete shows up. He's the light man for an eighties cover band. If his requests for Styx and Journey don't tip you off, his mullet-hairstyle will. But he's a sweetheart. He walks me to my car—if he makes it past last call.

Unlike most regulars, Pete mixes his alcohols. His first drink tonight is an Alabama Slammer. I serve him whatever he wants, because he's got an easy tell. Blinking. The more he drinks, the more he blinks. If the pause between blinks drops below two seconds, I shut him off. So most nights, I walk to my car alone.

The music begins. Sexy ladies move to ogle the piano player. He's a flirt and gets them tittering, asks what they'd like to hear. One mentions Sinatra, and he breaks into his rendition of "My Way."

Within moments the landscaping crew arrives and crowds the bar, saying their hellos and clowning around with each other. They think I'm the best bartender alive, so I really, really like them.

"Margarita, Amstel, Absolut on the rocks, Beefeater and tonic, and hi! I'm Bernie. What's your poison?" The new guy introduces himself and orders an IPA. He's cute, all tanned and muscular, but he's all of eleven years old. Nah, I'm kidding, but he's too young for me. Mickie, though, she might go for him.

The Mahoney brothers show up. Beer only, and everyone's better off if it's something yellow and light. I give them Natty Lights, er, Narragansett. In cans. Serve them a more robust beer, and they fall asleep—heads on bar. Serve them hard liquor, and they get loud and obnoxious, maybe pick a fight and then fall asleep—heads on bar. I prefer light-beer-drinking Mahoneys.

My pager vibrates, the signal that food's ready. I get busy and time flies.

Next thing I know, the kitchen closes and Dan's at the bar nodding for a beer. He looks the part with his slicked-back hair, gold chain under his Adam's apple, biceps straining his t-shirt sleeves—but I don't need a poser. I look around the room, make sure of the regulars I can count on, then pour him one, let him blend into the crowd.

I'm making drinks for Mickie's table when we both hear the opening bars to "Brown-Eyed Girl." Sure we hear it every week, but we're both brown-eyed girls, so we lip-sync along. I can't help myself; I do a little bouncy-move, sort of strut to the other end of the bar. Pete blinks and smiles. A new guy is leering. I stop mid-shimmy.

"Cute move," Pete says. "Can I have a Grateful Dead, and something for my friend?"

I don't move for a few moments. The new guy is familiar, but I can't place him.

"Bernie?" Pete says.

"Sure," I say. "What'll it be?" I ask the new guy. He's wearing a sweat-stained NASCAR cap, and a sleeveless flannel shirt. His flab is straining the buttons.

"A drink," he answers.

"Should I just say 'open wide' and aim the soda gun?"

"Feisty, I like that," he says to Pete. To me, he says, "Give me a scotch and coke—something decent—but don't rape me."

He said, "scotch," "coke," and "rape" in the same sentence. That's downright indecent. But Pete says, "Bernie, meet Ron. Ron, Bernie."

We shake, and Ron holds my hand a bit longer than necessary. He's doing this up-and-down thing with his eyes. As if I'd go for his type. It takes every ounce of effort not to make an "ew" face. Ron lifts his cap, rubs his bald head—

And I recognize him. He's the guy from the alley.

I blurt to Pete, "He's *your* friend?"

Pete blinks.

Ron winks and says, "You might want to shut your mouth before someone fills it for you."

I glare at Pete, but he's watching the room. Ron jumps up and jiggles his way in between some ladies dancing.

"How do you know each other?" I ask Pete.

"We were roadies for a Skynard tribute band a few years back. Funny thing. I just bumped into him last week."

"And you told him about piano night?"

"Why wouldn't I?" Pete blinks at me, then says, "How 'bout those drinks?"

I want to refuse, but Pete's a regular. I don't have to like his friends, but I have to respect him. I steel myself to put up with distaste.

The night gets into a groove. Pete goes to the piano, sings "Don't Stop Believing" off-key. Everyone's laughing and flirting and I'm barely noticing Ron, until he jiggles his ice and says, "Honey. Get me another."

"Name's Bernie."

I make his drink. He takes a sip and mumbles. "My piss's stronger than this drink."

Makes me wonder when he drinks his own piss.

"How about topping this off, honey?"

"Strike two," I say. "Bernie."

"Jeez, don't get your panties in a wad."

I go print his tab and lay it in front of him.

"Aw, come on, don't be like that."

I wait on someone else.

"How 'bout a joke?" he shouts. "This one's good."

Great, I think. I got me a front-row seat on the Redneck Comedy Tour.

"Wanna hear it?" he asks.

"Go ahead." I'm proud of myself for not rolling my eyes.

"Why don't niggers like blow jobs?"

"Not funny."

"You didn't hear the punch line yet."

"And I won't." I walk away before he can force it.

After a few minutes, I glance over. Ron is giving me this hard stare, the kind of look I've seen from guys who "hug their bros and hit their hoes." Pete comes back to the bar, asks for a Long Island I-shtee. He's rapid blinking. I shake my head and call him a cab.

The Mahoney brothers are a little quieter than usual, or so I'm thinking, until I hear, "Any requests?"

That's when Pud—don't ask, I didn't nickname him—shouts, "Take This Job and Shove It."

Uh-oh, I think. He lost another one. I nod at Barry. He scrunches his forehead, as if to say, "What am I supposed to do?" His company always needs extra hands. I raise one eyebrow, Barry holds out his glass. I make him a refill, ring it on the house tab. He gives me an imperceptible nod. I'll make sure Pud gets a ride to the job site.

The Johnny Paycheck anthem segues into "Can't Get Enough of Your Love, Babe." I look up, see Marcus, a piano night institution, saying his hellos. Six-foot five, pushing 300 pounds, he's the biggest, nicest black man I've ever met. Actually, more like dark cocoa; he has a wicked rich skin tone. One time, trying to be respectful, I call him an "African American." He says, "Kenyan-American? Chad-American? How about Egyptian-American?" My face burns. He kinda pokes fun at me, says, "Honey." I tell him, "Got it," and we're buddies ever since.

I'm asking Mickie to repeat an order when the music stops. Conversations stop. I look out.

Marcus is at the narrow curve of the grand piano, staring down at Ron. A vein pulses on Marcus's temple; otherwise, he's stock-still. Ron's lips are moving. "You got a hearin' problem, boy?"

Ron mistakes the silent crowd for allies. Boy, is he wrong. Dead wrong.

The Mahoney brothers have their fists balled. I look around, and the other regulars have that predatory look. All of them are closing their hands into fists.

The only indication that Marcus is angry, besides the pulsing vein, is his hands flex. "Bernie," he says. "Remove him."

The redneck bastard says, "Get this nigger outta my face."

"No!" I yell. The shouting begins. The crowd-mentality is palpable. My adrenaline pumps. I slam up the flip-top section of the bar and rush to go between the redneck and Marcus.

Now, the stupidest thing a woman can do is get between two men lusting for blood. Angry men don't think; they punch. A screaming woman is just an annoying buzz. Swat her aside and get to the satisfying, bone-crunching melee.

I know this. But I'm the one with keys—the boss trusts me. It pops into my head that if Marcus pulverizes this redneck, Marcus will do harder time than if the situation were reversed. I hate knowing this, but we live in a Wonder Bread state. And if Marcus goes down? Well, he's the regular—*he* belongs. The room will avenge his honor, and I'll have a murder on my hands.

Not on my watch. If this redneck has a shot of getting out of this room alive, it's on me.

All five-foot seven, one-hundred twenty-five pounds of me gets between the three-hundred-pound mass of angry chocolate and the similarly-sized mass of "ew." I don't think. I act. Not usually the best approach to life, but I have righteous fury on my side.

"You again!" I shout. I grab the front of Ron's shirt, and somehow, I clear-lift him off his stool. Gotta love adrenaline.

"Dan!" I shout, even though he's barely a foot away. "Do

something."

The wuss doesn't move. He just stands there, arms crossed.

"They wanna kill me," Ron says.

You think? I want to scream. What's worse is, he doesn't sound scared. My blood boils.

I think it really is boiling, because I feel all tingly and shaky and hot. I raise both hands and slap the front of the bastard's shirt. The crowd parts.

I must be screaming, because my throat is hoarse.

I push/hit.

"Get."

Push/hit.

"Out."

Push/hit.

"And never."

Push/hit.

"Come back!"

I don't know who, but someone opens the door and I push/hit the redneck one more time and we're both outside.

He gets into a dilapidated car. I watch until I hear it start, keep watching until he drives out of sight. I take a minute, look at the starry sky, see the full moon. Figures, I think. Ask any bartender; the full moon brings out the crazy.

Back inside, they applaud. I hear a couple bars of the *Rocky* theme song. I smile, but the adrenaline has me trembling.

Barry asks, "Are you okay?" I feel like everyone is watching me.

"Play something," I command. The piano player cracks his knuckles, then begins Elton John's "Someone Saved My Life Tonight." I hear a giggle. Someone else laughs. The murmurs resume, and I flee to the kitchen.

The floodgate opens. I know it's an energy-release thing, but I don't want them to see my tears.

Mickie sticks her head in the door. "You okay?"

I nod, then shake my head. She comes over and gives me a hug.

After a hitching breath, or thirty, I return to the bar. Marcus is ending "It's A Wonderful World."

I pretend nothing happened. I get a few sympathetic smiles, but no one tries to engage me in a play-by-play. Avoiding eye contact helps.

Someone begs for "Piano Man." Those few who are studiously watching me turn towards the piano.

Every single week, someone requests that song. The piano player once told me he has a Billy Joel voodoo doll. As soon as he finds a Billy Joel hairbrush on eBay, the original Piano Man will suffer, mark his words.

Our "piano man" changes the lyric to "It's ten o'clock on a Tuesday" and the crowd is into it. I shake a martini extra hard, and someone comments that I shook to the beat. He switches to a ragtime vein, and the song lasts for twenty minutes with every impersonation and style of music adapted to the "Piano Man" lyrics.

I'm just thankful that things are back to normal.

"Bernie, you sure you're okay?" Marcus asks.

We're winding down. The piano is put away, and I'm doing last call. I tell him I'm fine, thanks. I'm just glad the situation got defused.

Marcus lifts his voice to a falsetto. "My hero."

I swat him with my bar rag.

He chuckles, puts some "bread in my jar" and gives me a fist bump.

I finish cleaning, tally the drawer. I offer Mickie a shift-drink, but she smiles and says, thanks anyway, she has plans. The new landscaper is outside the picture window, hands in his pockets. I raise an eyebrow at Mickie.

She gives him the one-minute gesture. "You okay to close alone?" she asks me.

"Go ahead, I've got Dan—" I realize he's not leaning on any walls.

"He left with two ladies in a Beamer."

Geez, I think, everyone's getting booty tonight but me.

I lock the door behind her, check the bathrooms, put the money in the office safe. I walk through the kitchen, retrieve the take-out box I saved for Mary, exit the building into the alley. No sign of her. That's cool. I'll eat the leftover burger. Adrenaline stokes the appetite.

The pavement glows under the full moon. I stop to savor the night.

I hear a footstep. I turn, but no one is there.

"Mary?" I ask. I look left and right, up and down, but I don't see anyone in the shadows.

An arm slams across my throat, choking off my breath. I drop my bag, my dinner, claw at the arm, try to stomp a foot. Something falls on the ground. My nails dig in. I think I draw blood, but his grip isn't budging. His throat-hold tightens.

He punches me in the kidney. I almost collapse, but I'm pinned against his soft stomach. The moon fades, I can't breathe. Hot breath burns my ear.

"Have a nice night. Honey."

Another punch, then he drops me. I black out.

I come to, and Mary is sitting beside me, licking her fingers. The take-out container is open on the ground. I moan.

"I 'member my first beatin'," she says. "Ya git used to it."

"See . . .any . . ." My voice cracks. Speaking hurts. I think I'll pee blood for days.

She pulls out a flask, offers it to me. The liquor burns my throat, but the spreading warmth helps.

I know who did this. If I ever see him again, I'll . . .

My imagination fails me. That's hurting too.

Mary takes a pull from the flask. She's wearing a ball cap.

"Whaddaya gonna do 'bout it?" she asks.

"Home." I croak. She helps me up, supports me as I limp to my car. I consider the hospital, but, hell, no insurance. A definite downfall to bartending.

Even as I'm hurting, I realize nightly cash is its own benefit. Plus, I'd miss my *regahlahs*.

I make it home, shower, crawl into bed.

As I'm drifting off, I see Mary, wiping her mouth, asking me *whaddaya gonna do 'bout it.*

My mess, my dream-self tells her.

She snickers, readjusts the ball cap, NASCAR logo all sweat-stained.

I'm gonna take care of it, that's what.

It's one o'clock on a Thursday, I sing to myself, "Piano Man" style. I'm working days, just until I'm healed.

I send Dan across town for a special bar cleaner. I don't think he has a moral dilemma with taking an unscheduled break.

Barry shows up with the Mahoney boys.

"Thanks for coming in," I say to Barry.

"No problem. Your replacement can't make a decent drink." He squints at me. "So, you pouring?"

"Yeah, yeah. Hold your horses," I say. I punch out, then set up four rocks glasses. Not shot glasses, no one's getting a mere ounce.

Barry's giving me this quizzical look. "You know, if you need anything, anything at all . . . you ask. You hear?"

I have to turn away, some dust is in my eyes. I grab the tequila. One, one thousand. Two, one thousand. One, one thousand. Two one thousand. Three . . . three . . . three. Pud's eyes get real wide. I throw him a stern look, and he adjusts in his seat, sits all pious-like, as if he deserves divine intervention. I move onto the next glass, start counting again. Do the same a third time. I'm planning on the spirit moving them.

The fourth is a regular shot, for me, to take the edge off.

"What's up?" Barry asks. He swirls the alcohol. "I'm guessing you didn't get mugged."

I tell him what really happened after piano night.

Barry says, "I-I'm so sorry."

"Ain't your fault," I say. I clear my throat. "Let's drink."

We raise our glasses, clink, then down our shots. Barry smacks his lips, lets out a satisfied sigh.

We cut through the kitchen. I peek into the alley, and it's déjà vu all over again. The redneck bastard is in his sleeveless flannel. His left forearm is gouged.

I step aside, let the boys into the alley. Mary gets up, grins, showing off her three good teeth. The redneck bastard tries to bolt, but his pooled pants trip him. Mary kicks him in the gut.

"For you," she says to me, then hurries to Backside. The Mahoney boys pick up the redneck. Barry moves in.

I'm off the clock; it ain't my watch.

But I watch. I count on my regulars.

Peggy McFarland is the general manager of a restaurant in Chelmsford, MA. Her short stories have appeared in various print and online publications, including last year's Level Best anthology *Best New England Crime Stories 2012: Dead Calm*. She is currently working on her first novel.

The Exhibitionist,
A Love Story

Stuart Cohen

Hank had just settled in to watch the second half of the Bulls game when something out the window caught his eye. In the window of another building, a block or two away, stood a naked woman. She held her arms high, elbows folded and hands behind her blonde hair, clearly displaying herself.

"Ramona," he called to the next room. "Check this out."

Ramona looked quickly and scowled. "What a tramp. She probably advertises on the Internet. 'Look at me in my window and gimme a call for fun'." She shook her head. When Hank looked again the woman was gone.

The next morning in the elevator he mentioned what he'd seen to Jared, who was single and lived on the floor above. "You just noticed?" said Jared. "It's been a couple of weeks at least. Monday through Friday, 8:55 to 9:00. Reliable as clockwork."

"She looks gorgeous."

"Oh, she is. Great rack, too. I like the way she sways her hips, back and forth and back and forth." Jared imitated the swaying motion. "She's a bleach blonde, though."

"How would you know?"

"The cuffs and collar don't match."

"Huh? How . . . Have you . . . met her?"

Jared laughed. "Binoculars. I keep binoculars by the window. It's become my evening ritual."

Hank rode to work thinking about binoculars. He didn't own any. He could probably get a decent pair cheap enough, but where would he put them that Ramona wouldn't catch on?

Hank told the guys in the office what he'd seen. "Which building is she in?" asked Chen, the comptroller.

"It's an older building, brick, about two blocks west of me. I'd say she's on the thirteenth or fourteenth floor on the corner to the left. Don't you live over by the lake?"

"Sure. What time does she go on?"

During lunch Hank googled "binoculars retail Chicago." The closest appeared to be a store that specialized in optics and astronomy gear, in a new indoor mall only a few blocks from where he lived. He made sure they'd be open after work and wrote down the address.

The next day, Chen stuck his head into Hank's cubicle, grinning. "Verrry nice," he said. "Pretty face. Fabulous tits."

"What did you do, hike over and look?" asked Hank.

"Not necessary," said Chen. "I studied astronomy in school. Got a pretty good telescope. You can't see the night sky here in the city, but I keep it in the living room just for occasions like this." He grinned again. "Really, great tits."

The woman finished her five minutes in the south facing window of the corner apartment and threw open the shades of the window that faced east. She kept a clock at her feet. She knew he closed the store promptly at nine, and he must not ever know. She closed her eyes and imagined him holding her, kissing her. Slowly she danced a subtle dance of love, his imagined hands touching her back, her breasts, her hips.

Five minutes passed quickly and she closed the shades. She pulled off the blonde wig and stashed it carefully in the closet behind rolls of star charts. She pulled on the satin robe he had given her and felt its softness against her skin. She sighed and pictured his golden eyes and the crinkly smile that she had fallen so madly in love with. She got out the ice and glasses, and sat in the kitchen to wait.

"I have wonderful news," her husband said as he closed the door, locked it, and enveloped her in his arms. "And something for you." From his pocket he pulled a small box. In it was a ring made up of many thin metal rings in subtle colors woven together. "It's supposed to be like the rings of Saturn," he said.

She put the ring on her finger and beamed up at him. "I love it," she said, admiring it as if it were a diamond. She kissed him softly on the mouth. "Tell me the news."

"The accountant was in today. You know, the short guy who always wears the same tie? Well, he said it looks like we're going to make it . . . I didn't tell you because I didn't want to upset you. But I was worried the first few months."

"And?"

"And then, all of a sudden," he snapped his fingers, "business picks up and we're doing just fine." He smiled a crinkly smile.

She handed him his drink and kissed his mouth again, a long, soft, happy kiss. "I knew you would," she said. "I always had confidence in you." He put his arm around her. She rested her head on his chest.

"It's a new mall. You never know if you're going to get the traffic they promise you." He put down the drink and stroked her hair, and kissed the top of her head. She sighed. "The funny thing is, this is a big city. The light pollution is awful. I can't figure why in a place like this, where you can barely make out any stars at all, so many people are buying binoculars. And lately, some really expensive telescopes, too."

Stuart Cohen's main career was as a photographer, working for publishers, companies and stock photo clients. He wrote three books and many trade articles about photography. Other recent non-fiction works include *The Seventh System: The Thinking Person's Guide to the Human Emotional System* (www.seventhsystem.net) and the free e-book *Living for Nearly Damn Ever with the #%@&*! Dog*, available on www.smashwords.com.

Acts of Balance

Nancy Means Wright

The summer I decided to kill my brother was an unbearably hot one. July came on at eighty-six degrees and the temperature crept steadily upward from there. It was the summer the cousins came, too, the end of our first full year of living in Vermont. My father had quit his teaching job to start a Christmas tree farm, and moved us out of an all-boys' school and into the old Vermont farmhouse we'd spent vacations in up to then. My mother thought he was crazy, but she had three children and a book she hoped to write; she went along. At least that summer there was indoor plumbing. We had a kitchen sink with running water and a drain that would suck the soiled water into a rusted pipe and out of sight through a hole in the floor. Dad put a toilet upstairs in a converted closet with a faded red drape for a door. In this way we avoided the parade of feet down the steps and outside in the 'wee' hours of the night (my mother's pun), and the dreaded crash of the trapdoor that hung above the stairwell, propped open by a bookcase.

To this day there is a broken board where the door gave way one night as I stumbled downstairs, unbuttoning my flap. We hung in balance a moment, the door and I; then just as it swung down I was able to crouch on a step and let my shoulders take the brunt. My older brother Gabe saw it happen and laughed; my sister Lili rushed, shrieking, to my side. This was a natural reaction for her. The second oldest at twelve, and my champion, she had a dimpled face that flashed sharp as a diamond when she was crossed, and therefore I admired her. She would stand up against our bully brother while I cowered in her short, chunky wake.

By the third of July the temperature had soared to 90 degrees. We three were having the usual Saturday night beans and hotdogs on the back porch when the phone rang, and Aunt Bernice was on the line from Nyack, New York, to say there'd been a plane crash and Uncle Jack, my mother's brother, was aboard. A Mohawk airliner had climbed five hundred feet into an electric night and spun crashing to the ground. My uncle, who'd survived three years in the Vietnam jungles was alive, but badly hurt, and my aunt was at his side. It was hard for my ten-year-old mind to comprehend, but one fact emerged: the cousins were coming to us.

My mother drove them up the next night; we received the trio in awe, like warriors returned from a children's crusade. Johnny, who had a lisp, said he was only "thtaying the night, my motherth bringing Dad back t'morrow." Alice refused the M&Ms we offered and stomped upstairs to fling herself across my bed—I heard the springs squeal. Matt, the oldest, stopped halfway on the steps to announce to the ceiling, "I think my dad has a broken neck," and as he lifted his tremulous chin, my sister burst into tears.

Alice refused to give up the bed she'd claimed—my bed, and so it was decided that she and my sister Lili would share the room while the boys slept in the hut Dad had made out of a hen house. I was to sleep on a cot in the hall. When I protested, Mother reminded me that there were "bigger things" to consider. My main chagrin was that Lili didn't stand up for me. I looked at her with wounded eyes and she shrugged sadly, as if she, too, were caught up in "bigger things." And as always, I gave in.

But it was the little things that absorbed our lives that summer, like getting meals (bologna sandwiches and pea soup that Dad made in vats), doing laundry and making beds. For us this meant sweeping the bedspread up over a rumple of sheets and blankets while the cousins tucked and smoothed, reflecting the training of a nurse-mother. Matt would stand over his sullen sister to hurry her up. "Today," he'd tell her, "us boys are helping Uncle Dan. He's taking down an old barn." And my brother Gabe would shift his weight onto one leg, stick his hands on his sharp hip bones and say, "Yeah, just us boys, and it's dan-ger-ous."

"Is it really dangerous?" I'd ask Lili, and she'd make a face. "They like to talk big," she'd say, and we'd smile in complicity. The boys never got to take down an old barn, but they were allowed to de-nail old boards. They'd hunch over the splintery boards with glazed eyes, yank and bang to squeak out the rusty nails, while Dad hovered over like a glinty-eyed Fagin with his pickpockets. And we'd giggle, while the boys pretended to ignore us.

We never spoke of Uncle Jack to the cousins, though more than once at night, as I shuffled down to the toilet, I'd hear a gasping sound from my old bed, like a car trying to start in zero weather. And every night on her kissing rounds Mother was asked the same question by Johnny: "Ith Daddy coming home tomorrow?"

"Well, not tomorrow," she'd say, "but he's getting better," while the white lie, she told Lili and Lili told me, tugged at her insides. Uncle Jack was still alive—as if the mere act of breathing meant "better." And in a way it did, we figured, as he had small chance of survival at the time of impact, Mother said, and each breath after that was an impulse toward life.

The third week in July Mom and Dad flew out to see her brother where he lay in a hospital bed in Pittsburgh, Pennsylvania, leaving us with an elderly babysitter. Relieved in the absence of nail and shrub pulling, pea soup and outdoor peeing, we organized ourselves into an army. My brother Gabe, as the oldest and most visionary (he said), was self-appointed general; he had a cherry wood staff and a hierarchy of underlings. There were Colonel Matt and Major Billy from next door, baseball caps pulled down over their butch haircuts; there were Sergeants Lili and Alice. Johnny and I were privates—I resented that, as I was a year and a half older than he and a lot, I thought, wiser. And there was Bonnie, a moist-eyed stray who'd attached herself to the end of the ranks and was made a corporal, with a red flag attached to her tail. My complaint that she was only a dog and shouldn't be of higher rank than myself, fell on deaf ears.

To qualify for the army you had to walk an eight-by-eight beam over the grinning teeth of a farm machine in the LeBlancs' barn down the road, then leap fifteen feet into the hay below while the general stood with folded arms and a leer on his face that pronounced you 'chicken' if you so much as blinked. I got only halfway before I slipped, and rode the rest of the splintery beam hand over hand, upside down, like a monkey. I never rose after that in rank, while Johnny groaned and hollered all the way across and was made a corporal. My brother Gabe never had to walk it; he said generals got to make up the rules, they didn't have to follow them. And no one, other than my sister Lili, who knew just how far she could go, could contradict him with impunity.

When everyone but me successfully crossed the beam, Gabe got bored, and the gang fanned out into the neighborhood at large in search of an enemy. One moonlit evening when the temperature seemed stuck at 93 degrees—unusual for Vermont—we lay in the sumac to spy on a grumpy neighbor and record his movement as he passed in and out of his house. When Lili dared complain of heat and thirst she was told to stay there and 'suck rocks.' If she let the enemy out of her sight, the general warned, she would spend the night on the spot—at the risk of bears, skunks, spooks, and other unnamables that were known to frequent the area and suck your blood.

She lay there, terrified, while the enemy sat in his house and had a burger and a cold beer. Sweating and miserable, forgotten by the general, she was finally returned under orders from the babysitter and scolded for missing her supper. She rushed down to the hut where the chiefs of staff lay scheming on their cots.

"I quit your stupid old army!" she screamed, "I hate you, Gabe!" And my heart pounded in my knees where I'd run down behind her, to slip in my own complaint.

"You're both court-martialed!" bawled the general. "You're out of the army! *You're* the enemy!"

There was a further exchange of words that I missed, as my weighted knees had cracked through the board that served as ramp to the hut, and I had to wait in the dark webby hole below to be rescued by Lili.

She poured out her fury, like a snake unwinding its bulk, as we trudged back up the hill. I said "oh," "yeah," "boy," and "oh! the rat!"

"What's to become of Gabe?" Lili wailed, flinging up her arms, and I said, "What?"

She said in a low flat voice, "He failed sixth grade."

I said, "He did?"

"He did. Take my word for it. He's got to repeat." She walked closer to me, dropped a hand on my shoulder. Her curly head bowed to mine. "I heard Dad, talking to Mom. He said Gabe might have to be a plumber."

"Dad said that? A plumber?"

"A plumber," she said. Her hair brushed my cheek and the touch was thrilling. We were practically leaning on each other as we walked. "Then Dad said to Mom, 'But he can't even get the top off a bottle without breaking it. How's he going to fix a toilet?'"

"I don't know," I said. "What's he going to do then?"

"Die," she said. "Just die. What else is there? Or go to jail. Do you want him to go to jail?" Her voice crescendoed in my ear.

I said our parents wouldn't like that.

"It might be better if right now . . ." she said as we climbed the porch steps—and she let go a shuddering sigh.

"Better if what?" I said. "Better if what, Lili?"

But she didn't answer. "I quit the army," she told our father, who was home now, and at the sink filling his glass with water and a careful measure of vodka.

"Good," Dad said, and the vodka splashed my cheek as Lili fell sobbing into his arms.

There was a triangle of space behind the bookcase that propped up the door. No one ever thought to look there; the vacuum cleaner didn't penetrate. The dust was thick as cat's fur when I wriggled in, and filled with fallen pencils and pennies and I didn't know what else. I saw the split boards of the old door where it angled above my head; the bottom row of book spines stuck into my back.

I knew Gabe from the sniffing – Mother said he was allergic to something in the air. He would sniff and wheeze until the first hard frost. I mentioned the sniffing to him once and he hit me, hard. I thought of that blow as I crouched there behind the bookcase: how his fist caught me just inside the elbow; how the pain shot through my body, scattering my bones. I thought of other things too, like the time he held my head under water until I thought I would drown; and how once when we were driving home from Maine I bought a green-bearded troll with a dollar my grandmother gave me and Gabe held it out the window, and he let it go.

I heard the stream of pee in the toilet, the rush of water in the sink. And when he came sniffing out, his arms full of dirty clothes to throw in the heap downstairs, I rose up on the elbow he'd hit that time, and as his feet struck the third step from the bottom (I'd measured as carefully as Dad with his vodka) I shoved it up, the old door.

And heard the thunk and crash where he fell. I heard my mother rush to him and cry, "Oh my God, he's bleeding in the head!" And I shrank back into my hole behind the bookcase and gripped my knees and shook till my teeth literally chattered in my dry mouth.

But I was unprepared that night for my sister's reaction. Her screams were louder, I felt, than when it was myself fallen there on that step. After Gabe came home from the local hospital with his head bandaged like an Arab and a broken shoulder, she tended the brother who had no future as lovingly as any mother. She bathed his sweaty limbs in the rising heat, brought him Pepsi and gum, and once, at his whispered urging, a shot glass of Dad's vodka that she poured, on his orders, into his soda.

"I thought you hated him," I said. "He threw you out of the army." I'd gone in her room to finally tell her I'd done it, to get her praise.

Before I could speak, she looked at me out of eyes as bruised as the knuckles he'd held between his head and the onrushing door and said in a trembly voice, "He could have been killed, Rue. Mother said so. My brother could have been killed. Or badly damaged. He might be already, Mother thinks."

I stared at her, confounded, my tongue trapped in my throat, and left without telling.

Gabe met his defeat by the end of summer, without my interference. An apple foray that swept through the neighborhood, shattering windows, brought a series of phone calls. The Hicks sisters down the street made it clear that they didn't care for a troop of kids peering through their window while they prepared a lentil soup (witch's brew, said Gabe). The general was spanked by Dad even as my mother yelled, "Don't touch his poor head! He had a bad concussion you know," and the army was put on Neighborhood Cleanup. We all ran trash, officers and privates alike, and yanked dandelions and crabgrass while the defected Lili, put to work "on general principle," marched a broom grimly through the hut.

On Labor Day Mom drove the cousins home to their mother in New York, where she'd gone back to reorder her life. I was glad to see them go. It meant the end of the army, and my own bed again, and a routine of work and school that I craved. When my parents went down to Rusk Institute in New York City that December where Uncle Jack had been moved, they took Lili and me along. My uncle greeted us with a wan smile and a bet on the Green Bay Packers. His voice came out crushed and soft-sounding, like he'd been wrapped a long time in tissue. To look at the giant head with its fringe of wiry curls, he might have been at home, in bed with a cold.

But under the sheet there was an awful stillness.

I got coughing then and everyone turned to look at me. "She doesn't have a cold," Mother said to the nurse who was standing in the doorway, "it's just her nerves." The nurse looked solemn and I held my breath to try and stop coughing.

I got thinking for some reason about Gabe again. He was sniffing a lot, I remembered, as he padded down those steps the night I tried to kill him. He didn't try to control it, the way he did in front of us kids. I had the door upright by then; it was awkward because of the angle I was pushing from. The door wobbled in my fingers. It could have gone either way. And then I heard Lili's voice, protesting, in my ear, and Gabe's soft sneering laugh, and my hands pushed. Hard.

"What have you got to say for yourself, young lady?" my uncle asked in his tissuey voice. He was looking at me with that same wan smile. He was trying to be cheerful, he was trying not to make us feel bad, but I knew.

Mother nudged me forward. I stood at the edge of my uncle's bed, trying not to look at the plastic bag of yellowy urine that hung below the blanket, and sucked in a breath.

"I'm sorry," I whispered.

It was true Gabe had to repeat sixth grade, but he made a little league basketball team that winter—Mom wouldn't let him play hockey or soccer because another concussion might "do him in," she said, and we didn't see much of him at all. He seemed to have transferred the energy he'd spent on the army to the basketball net Dad set up in front of the hut, and he circled and maneuvered and shot baskets every spare minute he had. He made Lili be the adversary, and although she complained some, I knew she didn't mind. He was training her, he said, so she could start up her own girl's team, and she liked that, and in return wrote some of his homework papers for him. He kept up the teasing at the supper table though, and once he told a boy who called me about homework that I was on the toilet and couldn't come to the phone. I was furious, and pounded his arm. But somehow I sensed that he wouldn't hit back.

One day I asked Lili how she would have reacted if someone had crashed down that door on purpose, if it hadn't been an accident like everyone thought, and she said, the dimples firm in her cheeks, "That person should die."

"You told me that's what Gabe should do because he couldn't do anything else!" I argued against the beating in my throat. "Because he failed sixth grade and couldn't speak his thoughts but only run armies. So he might as well die."

Holding a fist under her lifted chin, she said, "You're making that up. I never said such a thing in my life."

I was stunned for a minute, and couldn't think of a reply. But then I saw there was no point going on with the subject, and one night after New Year's, since we still had to share a room, I hung a blanket between our beds.

Nancy Means Wright has published eight mysteries, most recently *The Nightmare*. Her children's mysteries received an Agatha Award and nomination; a new YA, *Walking into the Wild*, is just out. Her short stories have appeared in *Ellery Queen Mystery Magazine*, Level Best Books, and *American Literary Review*. Nancy lives in Middlebury, Vermont.

The Trunk

Virginia Young

D ecorated in faded gold against weary black, the small trunk
begged to be bought, opened, discovered.

A magical piece, there was something appealing about its domed
top and ornate brass hinge-work and clasp. If only there'd been a key.

Because the trunk was light in weight, the antique dealer, who
had marked on its price tag, Lady's hat box, was certain that, if there
was something inside, it was paper, and not much of it. Rather than
risk breaking the clasp, she sold the trunk at a reasonable price,
unopened.

Julia carried her new possession to the coffee table and sat down on
the sofa to take a closer look. She leaned back, then sat forward and
placed her hands at the sides where brittle leather straps threatened to
shed bits of crisp skin or old paint.

She lifted the trunk, then placed it down, turning it from side
to side, examining the curved top and the flat bottom. How, she
wondered, would she get it open without damage to the beautiful but
keyless clasp? All hardware, the two hinges and the front lock, were
apparently fastened from the inside. No sense thinking she might
use a screwdriver to carefully remove the brass. Frustrated, Julia
stood up. Keeping her eyes on the object while walking towards the
kitchen, she nearly stepped on the cat's tail. "Good God, Archie," she
said, startled. "Trip me up why don't you?" Then with apologies, she
picked up the huge orange cat and gave him a hug. "Okay," she said
as she plopped him down in a chair, "I need caffeine. I need to think."

The cat gave her a disinterested look, then hopped off the chair and walked into the living room.

Julia smiled and poured herself a generous mug of freshly brewed coffee. She took a sip then headed back to the trunk.

Archie had now placed himself on the coffee table next to the new attraction and proceeded to paw at one leather handle.

"Cut it out, Archie," she scolded. "If you wreck my new trunk, I'll swat your bottom." The cat blinked lazily and folded his innocent paws back, half under his furry white chest.

"Bottom," she repeated the last of her warning softly, "maybe the bottom."

Julia moved the coffee mug to the floor to make more room, then tipped the trunk up on its dome. She could hear the paper, or something like paper move inside—a fluttering-butterfly sound. The bottom of the trunk was a piece of wood, painted black and measured about fourteen by eighteen inches. It was fastened in sixteen places along the four edges with worn black nails, their heads large enough to pry with perhaps a slim butter knife. Julia walked back to the kitchen and made a quick return to the sofa. A gulp of warm coffee, and then the painstaking procedure began. Metal against metal—she worked slowly in order not to harm the old wood. One by one, over a period of more than an hour, Julia worked, the coffee growing cold, until the last nail was removed and carefully joined the others in a small pewter bowl.

Inserting the knife along one edge of the bottom, she pried the rectangle of wood, stubborn with age-hardened paint, until it could be moved.

"Wow," she exclaimed to the cat, "I did it!"

Now that she had access to the trunk, she hesitated.

"God," she said aloud, "I hope there isn't a dead spider in there or something." With one edge of the knife creating a wedge, she lifted the wooden panel and found that the interior, although faded with time, was lined in a beautiful print: cream with tiny pink roses and dainty trailing vines of pale green. Julia touched the rippled surface with one tentative finger. There were a few sheets of loose onionskin paper and one envelope, which felt light but occupied. Julia looked at the finely scrawled words in brown ink on its surface, "Fall River, Massachusetts," a connection to the past. Someone cared enough about these papers to place them in a locked trunk.

Before settling down to read the small print, she maneuvered the clasp from the inside with the edge of her knife and it willingly popped open, as if it realized that all efforts to conceal the contents were now futile.

Julia tipped the trunk into an upright position and carefully lifted the domed top. She loved it. Someone else had loved it, too. That's what she found intriguing about antiques. They weren't just old, they were a part of history; significant or insignificant, a link with another human being, who had probably hoped, dreamed and loved.

She would read the words the trunk had long held captive, but first she placed the papers back inside out of Archie's grasp. She warmed her coffee in the microwave then headed back to the sofa where she found herself hesitant to begin. It all seemed slightly intrusive, but then, words were meant to be read.

Julia took a few sips of coffee, then reached for the contents of her new find. Carefully, but with a determined hand, she opened the unsealed envelope and took from it a folded sheet of paper and an old photograph of a young woman.

In one hand she held the onionskin sheets, written in an obviously different style from the now unfolded paper. She glanced from one to the other, wondering which to read first. The folded sheet was dated July 19, 1860. The first of the onionskin sheets was dated July 19, 1878. She would read the oldest first, but before beginning, she took a few moments to study the profile of a young woman in a dark dress, her hair coiled away from an interesting but unremarkable face. The picture was dated on the back and held a singular name, Marisa – 1856.

The folded sheet was now unfolded and straightened: Julia began to read.

> July 19, 1860
> Fall River, Massachusetts
>
> My Poor Christina,
>   It is with a heavy heart, but with great
> confidence that I have committed the acts of today.
> A turn of fate has placed me in a position to mimic

God himself and I pray he forgives me.

That I should, in my midwifery, serve two young women on this day, and that one should lose her child and one should lose her life, seems unfair and certainly cruel.

You, my dear Christina, must forever keep the secret, that, having delivered a fine baby girl to a mother who then died, I gave to you that child, to somehow replace your sweet baby boy, who died this day of his birth. The boy you will always hold dear in your heart will rest forever with poor, tormented Marisa.

Her mother and father put her through a living hell when they discovered that she was unwed and with child. Just days ago in a fit of rage, she bludgeoned her parents to death and attempted to end her own life as well. The attempt left poor Marisa irreparably broken, thus her death at the birth of her strong child.

Raise this girl, Christina, and give to her the love you longed to wrap around your son. Mourn, but not to take away from the breathing child in your care. No one but you and I will ever know her true identity.

God willing, she will bring you and your husband great joy. My deep sorrow to you in the tragic passing of your infant son.

Your nurse and friend,

Emma Ward

Julia sat, stunned with learning such a sad secret of babies switched. A baby boy buried with a stranger, a baby girl raised by someone she might never have known.

Julia studied the picture of Marisa, "Poor, tormented Marisa," the midwife had written. She placed the photograph and letter together in the trunk then began to read the other rippled sheets.

July 19, 1878

It is on this day I feel that I must share this burden with my girlhood trunk, and, perhaps someday, with someone who will persist in its opening. My intent is to bury the key to prevent an inquisitive girl from a discovery she need not know.

Julia shivered, rubbed her eyes and read on.

Today is my dear daughter's celebration of birth. She is eighteen. She is solid and serene most times, but troubled, I fear. I pray it is not of my doing.

Over the years, I have often observed my child watching the preparation of a corpse for the grave. Her godfather's occupation, that of an undertaker, seems to have fascinated our child. When I have found her widened eyes viewing the very blood being drained away from stolen life, I have made myself known with a timid cough and then dragged her away with some distraction. Surely I have questioned myself at least one hundred times. Was I the best mother this child could know? In losing my precious infant son, Andrew, I gained this motherless child. In her eighteenth year, I am aware that my health is poor and time is short. The great concern is what will become of my daughter?

My husband has shared more than an admiring glance at Clara, who disguises herself as my friend. I know deep in my heart that when I am no longer, it is Clara who will fill my shoes, my home, my bed. But what of my daughter, who senses all of this, I believe, and despises the woman who could become her stepmother?

It is at times such as this that I recall Marisa, who took the lives of her parents and ultimately her own. I pray fervently that God forgives the secret kept from all but the now deceased midwife and myself. I pray that my daughter will accept changes without the rage that has threatened to surface when circumstances discouraged her plans.

I have tried and I have loved my daughter, to whom I gave the name, Lizzie Andrew.

Christina May Borden

Virginia Young wrote for *The South Shore News* and contributed articles to *The Patriot Ledger*. She received honorable mention through a *Writer's Digest* Magazine contest, and her short fiction, "Inside Out," was published by Level Best Books in the 2010 anthology, *Thin Ice*. Her suspense novel *A Family of Strangers*, came out in April 2012, and her latest novel, *I Call Your Name*, will be released in late 2013 through Mainly Murder Press. (southshorewriter.com)

Big Water

Woody Hanstein

I got the call from the hospital while I was still interviewing Jason White at the takeout by Kingston Brook. I thought Jason would be glad to hear that the guy with the broken femur was out of danger, but if that news cheered him up it didn't show. The week of steady rain we'd been having had finally let up the night before, but where we stood the river pounded past us, high and very fast.

"Tell me it again," I said to Jason.

"Which part?" He ran a hand through his head of short brown hair and looked out over the river. He had a scar at the corner of his left eye that was shaped like a crescent moon.

"The part where you took a raft full of people through Devil's Perch with the Monhegan River running at ten grand."

He sighed before he spoke. "It's no different than I already told you. I got set up like always and those guys just stopped paddling. Even as hungover as they were, frat boys like that will usually still paddle. Maybe part of it was that the river looks so different with all this water, but the next thing I knew everybody was out of the raft."

"Everybody but you," I said.

Jason's eyes narrowed. "It's part of the job—staying in the boat."

"Any chance you were a little hungover too? Maybe a little too much to drink last night? Or too much to smoke?"

He shook his head. "Piss test me if you want. I don't care."

On the river two kayakers paddled past us, flying by on that rumbling bed of high, violent water. Up at Prescott Dam, to deal with all the rain the power company was releasing three times the usual flow, and all that water had nowhere to go but up the sides of the narrow gorge on its way downstream like a runaway train. I thought about those eight customers of Jason's swimming the length of the sluiceway in all that cold June water and wondered again how none of them had been hurt even worse than they were.

"How long you been guiding?" I asked Jason after we watched the kayakers race past.

"Why ask what you already know? I took you and your wife down my first summer."

"So that's what? Six years. So six times what? Six times 50, 60 trips a season?"

"Sounds about right."

"And Bill Rullo's had you running sweep the last couple years for a reason I expect. What if one of those other seven rafts on your trip had gotten in trouble? Aren't you back there because you're the one being extra careful?"

"Hey, anybody can fuck up. You never screwed something up in all your years as a warden?"

"This isn't about me, Jason. Three of those guys are down in Skowhegan having broken bones set, and a couple of the others were hypothermic."

He shook his head and sighed. "What do you want from me? I said I was sorry."

"And there was nothing any of those guys did to egg you on? Or maybe piss you off?"

"Piss me off? For crissakes, we weren't in the raft ten minutes. I hadn't even learned their names yet."

I studied Jason White for a little while but got nothing for my trouble. He was in his mid-twenties and had a lean, athletic build complete with a linebacker's shoulders. When I first arrived at the takeout an hour earlier the river bank looked like a battle zone, but everyone was gone now except for two other guides who were deflating a 16-foot raft and getting it ready to lug up the long, steep metal stairway to the parking lot.

"You ever do that before?" I finally asked him. "Take a raft filled with customers through Devil's Perch?"

He shook his head but didn't speak, his eyes back on the water. There was no telling what he felt inside, but to look at him he might have been waiting for a bus or trying to decide what to cook that night for dinner.

"And you weren't trying to show those guys up?" I asked. "Maybe throw a scare in them?"

"Why would I do that? The tips are better if people only swim when they want to."

"It doesn't make sense to me either, but the lead guide in that Twin Rivers trip right behind you thought you headed straight for that ledge. She said she was blasting her whistle at you before you even dumped."

Jason shook his head. "Those boats were way behind us," he said. "She couldn't have seen anything from back there, especially with the river running so big."

I was out of questions, so I followed behind as Jason and the other two guides carried the rolled raft up the stairway to where they loaded it into the back of one of Bill Rullo's pickups. The decal on the door said BIG WATER RAFTING and above those letters was a cartoon picture of a raccoon steering a bright red raft through a patch of rough blue water. Jason was starting to pile into the pickup with the other two young guides when I called him over to mine.

"Why don't you ride with me," I said. "I got to go down and see Bill anyway."

Jason shrugged and walked over to my truck and got into the passenger seat. After all that rain the bugs were bad until we got moving and the windows open. Neither of us spoke as we headed out the power company road toward the western shore of Dixie Lake, but I thought about Jason White as I drove. Six years before he had been the valedictorian of his small high school class and a National Merit Scholarship finalist on top of that, but despite all that promise he never left town to try college or the military or, as far as I ever heard, even to just see a little of the world outside of Piscataquis County. I lived down in Anderson, but that was close enough that I'd hear the comments from time to time when Jason would leave a store or drive by in his old Subaru—comments about what a waste of potential it was for a kid that smart to be satisfied cutting wood with Whitey Stockdale and guiding rafts in the summer with a bunch of college kids who were just killing time before their real careers began.

We turned at the edge of the lake onto the tarred road into town, and after a couple of minutes Jason finally spoke.

"So, what's this going to cost me?" he asked.

"Why should it cost you? Everybody's gear checked out okay. If this was just an accident I don't see why you think it should cost you anything at all."

"Because it always does. At least with you."

"What's that mean?" I asked, even though I had a good idea.

"No offense, but you're a ball-buster about everything. You see a customer with a buckle undone—it always costs us. Last year you fined Lennie for losing his guide's knife ten minutes before we went by. I'll bet you a buck you can't even remember the last time you wrote somebody out just a warning."

It was a bet he would have lost, but I didn't take him up on it. "Rules are rules," was all I said.

I looked over at Jason who was shaking his head, his eyes on the pickup's floor. "Yeah," he said, so quietly I could barely hear it. "Rules are rules."

I drove the last few miles thinking about what Jason had said. It was nothing I hadn't heard before, and for the most part it had stopped bothering me years ago. There were worse things to be called than a hard-ass, and it actually made my life easier knowing I didn't have to flip a coin in my head every time I felt bad about writing somebody up or worrying how they'd pay a fine they maybe couldn't afford. My first week on the job I caught my old high school shop teacher with a short trout and I let him slide on it, but it anguished me so badly that ever since then I wrote things up just like I saw them. For the past twenty years nobody could say I ever set them up or didn't treat them with respect or didn't send a square report in to the DA's office. I just left it up to the people in the courthouse to decide who should pay and who shouldn't.

There were still a half-dozen vehicles in the parking lot at Big Water Rafting, and Bill Rullo was out front speaking with a fellow in a Hawaiian shirt who was built like a distance runner. Then the man got into a newer model BMW with Mass plates and pulled out of the lot, heading south on 201. The two other guides in the pickup had arrived just before us and they were pulling the rolled-up raft out of its bed. Jason White went over to help them, and I walked over to Bill.

He was five years younger than I was, but I'd known him ever since he'd dated my younger sister back in high school. A few years after the two of them ended their short, unhappy marriage he started up his rafting company with two used boats he'd brought back from Idaho, and for those first few years he ran things on a shoestring. In his younger days people said Bill was a one-man deer-slaying machine, but except for one night years ago when I arrested him for shining a field, I'd never had any luck proving it. He was fifty years old now and his rafting outfit had grown into one of the largest ones on the river, and if he was still night hunting or killing an extra deer or two I hadn't heard a word about it from anybody.

I got out of my truck and shook hands with Bill. He was taller than me and working on a beer belly, but he was still one of the strongest men I knew. His weathered face was a testament to both his outdoor lifestyle and an aversion to sun block, and a Detroit Red Wings ball cap tamped down most of his wild, frizzy gray hair.

"What a cluster," Bill said. "I'm just glad that kid with the femur is alright. When Ginger headed off with him in the ambulance she looked pretty concerned."

"Is it going to be bad for you?"

He shook his head. "I doubt it. I got off the phone with my insurance guy a little while ago. I paid nearly a thousand bucks this winter for that Augusta lawyer to rewrite the release form we use, but now that's going to be looking like money well spent."

"So what happened? Why does the best guide you have try to take a full raft through Devil's Perch with the Monhegan running this high?"

Bill shrugged. "You know how crazy this river gets when it's running this big." He gestured across the parking lot to where Jason White was helping the other two guides collect paddles and deal with the deflated raft. "And I expect you also remember what it was like to be their age. Hell, most of these kids are more worried about when they're getting laid next than what they're getting paid to do."

"That sound like Jason to you?" I asked.

"It sounds like all of them. When I can find a bunch of forty-year-old mechanical engineers to guide these rafts for $75 a trip I'll use them instead of college kids."

"How about booze? Or maybe pot? Any chance Jason was under the influence of something?"

Rullo made a face like he'd just tasted something bad. "He was with you for the past hour. You tell me."

"Well, would he have any reason to dump these kids on purpose?"

"Over Devil's Perch? With the river at ten grand? Are you serious?"

"I'm just asking. The guide leading the trip behind yours thought Jason headed straight for it. And one of the kids in the raft thought so, too."

Rullo shook his head. "I don't know what the guide saw, but I certainly wouldn't put much stock in anything my customers told you. The whole lot of them shut the bar down here last night. I was in bed by then, but when I stopped by around ten o'clock those guys were having a good time. They seemed like a good bunch too, just laughing at anything and having fun. They told me they're all residents at the same hospital down in Boston and one of them is getting married next week."

"Any chance Jason was there, too? That maybe there was some bad blood between them?"

"Nothing I heard about yet. You could ask Marie when she comes in to bartend tonight, but most nights Jason's working on that old cabin he bought from the power company last year."

"Anybody else around you remember?"

"Well Megan Blake was still working in the kitchen when I left. She's in there now, so you could go in and ask her if she saw anything."

"I better not hear she was drinking," I said. Megan Blake was eighteen years old and I'd known her since she was a toddler. Her father was the best snowmobile mechanic in the state, and he'd been fixing sleds for the Warden Service since even before I got started.

Bill Rullo looked at me and frowned. "You really still don't think much of me, do you?" he said.

"It's not you I'm worried about, Bill. I just know how kids are."

I thanked Bill for his time and walked into the main lodge. There was a small office off to the right where people booked their rafting trips and, right beside it, a little store filled with gear that happy rafters could buy to celebrate their survival. There were fleece jackets and ball caps and t-shirts and shot glasses, most of them with the words Big Water Rafting stitched or printed somewhere and most with a replica of that cartoon raccoon guiding his big red raft through that explosion of rough blue water. The rest of the big, open room, except for the bar running along the back wall beneath the neon Pabst Blue Ribbon sign, was taken up by a couple dozen long, rustic pine tables and benches. A couple of the tables were occupied by families finishing up paper plates of food, but otherwise the only one else in the place was Megan Blake who was wiping down a table close to the swinging half-door which led out to the kitchen.

When she saw me she gave me a little half-wave and went back to her cleaning. I'd watched her grow up to be one of the town's great treasures. When she was no more than twelve she got the idea to serve a Thanksgiving meal at the elementary school for people in the area who didn't have families to go to, and it was a project she still managed every year since, even though she'd spent the last one up at the university in Orono starting on a wildlife biology degree. For the past three summers Megan had worked cleaning rooms at the motel Bill ran across the road and as a waitress here in his restaurant. I walked over to her and said hello. I expected one of her wise-ass replies but she just nodded, her attention fixed on the tabletop.

"Did you hear about the accident?" I asked her.

"I guess so. Everybody was talking about it."

"May I ask you a few questions?"

"Why me?" she said. "I didn't do anything."

Megan still had her eyes on the table and her lower lip was starting to quiver.

"Are you all right?" I asked her.

"I'm fine," she said, and then she started to cry.

I spent a few minutes trying to get Megan Blake to tell me what was wrong but all she kept saying, over and over, was that she wasn't feeling well and she wanted to finish her cleaning and go home. She swore to me that it had nothing to do with Jason White or the accident on the river or the doctors-to-be from Massachusetts. When it became clear that I was doing nothing except upsetting her more, I told her that I hoped she'd feel better soon and walked out the door beside the bar onto the back deck of the building. I wondered if maybe she was just sweet on Jason or if maybe there was something she'd heard or seen that I needed to know, but those were all questions that would have to wait for another day.

Out by the big, four-bay garage two guides were hosing down life jackets and another was stacking paddles. Beyond them, nudged up against the thick woods, sat a vintage Airstream trailer, its curved aluminum sides gleaming in the afternoon sun. In front of the open door to the trailer a man sat in a lawn chair smoking a cigar. I walked past the garage and over to him. His legal name was Wilford Perkins and he was supposedly from somewhere in the Midwest, but in the two summers he'd been working for Bill I'd never heard anybody call him anything except Slim. He drove the old school bus that took the customers up to the dam every morning to begin their trips and kept the company pickups running and did odd jobs at Bill's motel across the road. A couple of the local deputies had suspicions Slim was selling marijuana to tourists and locals alike, but he had never been pinched for anything as long as he'd been in town and those rumors had nothing to do with my line of work anyway.

Next to Slim's lawn chair was a two-foot high section of an oak tree that served as a table for an ashtray, a paperback western and what looked like a half-finished gin and tonic. Two other similar logs stood nearby, and I gestured toward one of them.

"Mind if I sit?" I asked.

"Help yourself." He took a long pull on his cigar and exhaled the smoke slowly. On his forearm was a tattoo of the planet earth and, below it in blue ink, the words LOVE YOUR MOTHER. His long, brown hair was tied back in a ponytail and he had on a red t-shirt splotched with white paint, a pair of threadbare khaki shorts and dime store flip-flops. He was one of those guys who could have been thirty or fifty or anything in between.

Sometimes you can learn more by just staying quiet and seeing how the other guy will begin a conversation, but after a couple of minutes of silence it became pretty obvious that Slim was perfectly happy to keep enjoying the afternoon without a lot of chit-chat.

"I'm investigating that accident on the river," I finally said.

He just nodded and took another pull on his cigar.

"I was hoping maybe you could help me," I went on.

"How? I just drive the bus."

"But you live right here. I was wondering if maybe you saw something last night? Or maybe heard something after the bar closed down?"

He shook his head and nudged his paperback book with the edge of the hand that held the cigar. "Last night it was just me and Louis L'Amour."

"So you wouldn't know anything about whether or not Jason had any trouble last night with any of those Massachusetts doctors?"

"Not a thing."

"Or whether Jason's got a habit of drinking or smoking a little pot some mornings to get himself going?"

"Why would I know that?" he asked.

"Well you help the guides run the rafts up to the dam and pump them up for one thing. I've seen you up there doing that. And you drive them up with the customers a couple hours after that. I'm just asking whether you might have seen something that explains him losing a raft full of people on a ledge on the river he's not supposed to run?"

Slim took another long pull on his cigar. I was just a two-cigars-a-year kind of guy, but it smelled like a good one.

"Sorry, but I can't help you," Slim said.

"You don't look particularly sorry. In fact, you look like you couldn't give a shit that a bunch of decent guys come up here for a good time and half of them get broken into pieces."

Slim set his cigar down in the ashtray and his eyes narrowed. He stared at me for so long I was thinking it was time to get up and leave. "*A bunch of decent guys?*" he finally said. "You go ask Megan how decent those guys are."

"What's Megan got to do with this?" I asked. "Did you see something last night or didn't you?"

Slim looked at me and shook his head. "Not last night. I really did just read for a while and hit the rack. But this morning those great guys of yours were really enjoying themselves on the ride up to the dam. They were still half drunk and had no idea how loud they were talking."

"So, what did they say?"

"Before I shut them up, you mean? They mostly were talking about how much fun last night was. And how quick that pretty waitress got drunk back in one of their rooms and after that how there just wasn't anything she wouldn't do with a bunch of good-looking doctors from Massachusetts."

"Are you saying those guys talked about raping Megan?" I asked. I realized that my hand was on the butt of my gun but had no idea how it had gotten there.

"Nobody called it rape. And I understand that girl is of age, but none of what they were describing sounded too decent to me."

"And was Jason sitting near them?" I asked. "Where was he on the bus?"

Slim thought for a minute and then shook his head. "I got no idea."

"Well you've been here a couple of summers. Do you think Jason would be capable of dumping those guys at Devil's Perch on purpose?"

Slim took a big swallow of his drink and wiped his mouth with the back of one hand. "I got no idea about that either," he said. "But I would kind of like to think so."

I wished Slim a pleasant afternoon and walked to my pickup. I thought about going back inside to confront Megan or maybe calling Barney Kelly down at the SO to see if he could make some kind of sex charge stick. But unless she had been unconscious drunk I knew an investigation would buy her nothing but embarrassment. Suddenly, for no reason I could figure, I thought back to the time I picked up a sled from her dad on the same spring day she'd learned to ride a two-wheel bike without training wheels. I could see her again now like it was yesterday, how happy and proud she looked pedaling one continuous loop, over and over, on their gravel drive while her dad helped me load that sled onto my trailer.

I had been sitting behind the wheel of my pickup for some time when my cell phone rang. It was my sergeant checking in.

"You got anything yet on that mess on the Monhegan?" he said. "The guy at the Bangor paper has called twice already. He's asking if we're going to be bringing any charges."

"Tell him, no," I said. "It was just bad luck." Then I sat in my truck there in the parking lot for a while longer, wondering for the first time if I'd done some things over the past twenty years that I maybe should have done differently.

Woody Hanstein lives in Farmington, Maine where he has been a trial lawyer for over thirty years and also teaches and coaches rugby. His most prized possession is the River Monkey—the biggest and oldest whitewater raft on the Kennebec River. He is the author of six published mysteries.

The Oldest Man in Town

Adam Renn Olenn

O f the six traffic islands in Nettle's Hollow, the one at the big intersection of Fordham, Fleming, and Vine streets was by far the nicest. While the others wore understated boutonnieres of impatiens and morning glories, this one overflowed with gushing hydrangeas and columbines around a red rose bush and a stand of tall white lilies, and sported a black lamppost that recalled a refined era long since past. A brick walkway traversed the island, and for pedestrians who wished to rest before completing their crossing of Fordham road, there was a broad granite bench. The words "Charlie deRose" were inscribed on its surface, and sitting on those words was an old, old man.

He wore suede shoes the color of sand over dress socks, and his high-riding plaid shorts were held in place by a wide leather belt capped with a brass buckle. Stamped into the buckle in block letters was the word "STAN." In the unlikely event that the belt ever failed, the upper rim of his shorts was attached to a pair of black suspenders that stretched up to his frail, sloping shoulders, which were draped in a yellow polo shirt buttoned to the neck. Crowning his ensemble was a flat-brimmed nylon trucker hat, and he contemplated the world through a pair of thick glasses. He blinked in the morning sunshine.

Three balloons were tied to the lamppost, and they bonged their empty heads together as they strained skyward. At Stan's feet, a gray-muzzled golden retriever panted in the mild heat of the morning. The dog noticed the direction of Stan's gaze and followed it up to the balloons.

"Town Day, Lily." Stan checked the unblemished blue of the early

June sky. "Good day for it, too." The dog looked away and continued panting. Next to the lamppost was a plaque which told of the exploits of Charlie deRose, local boy, who had fought in the infantry beside Stan before coming home to serve three decades as mayor. Stan looked at the plaque and shook his head. He and Charlie deRose had been best friends since the second grade, enlisted together, raised their children next door to one another, and finally worked together for fifteen years after Charlie appointed Stan as Town Superintendent. It had been Stan's idea to make the traffic islands something worth looking at—and to make this one a lasting testament to Charlie. All those years of friendship, and then it was just . . . *gone*.

Stan leaned forward and placed his hands on his knees, then hesitated a moment. He breathed in and heaved, and his bird-like frame straightened somewhat as he stood up. Lily looked at him and he nodded, and the dog rolled her hips twice before she was able to get her back end up. Together they waited at the edge of the traffic island. The light changed, a couple cars ran the red, and Stan Skerry started slowly across the street with Lily lumbering at his side.

The "Don't Walk" sign began blinking before they were halfway across, but they shuffled steadily along. The light changed and the cars waited, and Stan and Lily climbed the curb-cut to the far sidewalk. Most everyone believed he had named Lily after his wife out of heartache after she up and disappeared one night, same as Charlie. That wasn't quite it, but he saw no reason to pluck the stars from their eyes. What's done is done, so make do for today, as the old folks say.

Lily walked a step ahead of Stan, steering around the uneven spots in the brick sidewalk. More balloons struggled in the breeze from the lampposts leading to town center. There was a distant buzzing, and Lily pricked up her ears. When it finally penetrated the shrill fog of his hearing aids, Stan recognized the school band hacking their way through "God Bless America." He and the dog exchanged a glance. "Sounds like they need a little more practice, eh Lil?"

A car full of teenage girls drove by, elbows and long hair streaming from the windows. "Hi, Mister Skerry!" they called, and he raised a hand in salute. By the time he'd gotten it airborne, they were gone. It was almost ten, and the day was starting to heat up. He stopped walking for a moment, and Lily looked at a nearby bench.

"No, I don't think so," he said. "If we stop now we'll get stuck and miss the whole thing." Lily yawned, and Stan started walking. She fell into step beside him, her shaggy paws making a slight scuffing noise on the bricks.

They walked between a pair of blue sawhorses, and the street became a carnival. There was a truck hawking fried dough, and three carts with yellow-and-green umbrellas selling fresh-squeezed lemonade. A sunburned girl in a visor sat beside a cotton-candy machine, a bored expression on her pink, sweaty face. Lily was momentarily distracted by a cart selling sausage and pepper sandwiches, but Stan called her and she followed, leaving a few dark drops of drool on the asphalt.

Stan placed a hand on one of the granite posts of the colonial split-rail fence that ringed the town green and stepped up onto the soft grass. Lily followed, and together they waded across the carpet of turf. A low bandstand had been set up in front of town hall, and the tubas glinted in the sun as the last of the band broke down. Tim Klinger, a well-groomed councilman in his late forties, hurried over.

"Morning, Stan."

"And to you, Timmy. Fine day you've got."

"It certainly is."

"What's that?"

Klinger raised his voice a little. "I said, 'it certainly is.'"

Stan nodded. Nothing needed to be said to that.

Klinger reached out to support Stan's elbow. Stan shook him off. As he escorted Stan and Lily to the bandstand, Klinger made small talk. Stan wondered why young folks felt the need to jabber so much. It's perfectly fine to be quiet if you don't have anything to say.

Mayor Campbell hustled over, all smiles and handshakes. "Mr. Skerry, such a pleasure to have you! I'm so glad you could join us again!" Stan wondered if Campbell's voice sounded like that when he was thinking to himself, full of exclamations and ginned-up enthusiasm. "Morning, Dennis," he said.

When *Dennis the Menace* first came out in the Sunday papers, Stan used to show it to Lily—the first Lily, the real Lily. "I tell ya," he'd say, "Hank Ketchum is just a pen name. Whoever writes this strip is from around here, and he knows the Campbell boy." She would laugh at him, and he would continue the tirade, just to keep her laughing. They were good mornings.

Campbell helped Stan up the three aluminum steps to the plywood stage. Red, white, and blue bunting ruffled gently at their feet, and families picnicked on blankets. A group of children were playing tag by the maples at the south end of the common, and a Frisbee glided back and forth between a pair of high school boys. A young father chased after a toddler and brought her back to his blanket. Stan remembered those days, sort of. It was hard to remember what the kids looked like back then, their faces so round and new. They had their own children now, two in college. Still, there was a feeling of those days, like a bell that was still ringing somewhere far away. He got lost, forgetting whether it was his kids he was remembering or his grandchildren. He worked at it for a moment, then let it go. Everything was like that now.

There was a sharp electronic squeal as Mayor Campbell addressed the microphone. "Ladies and gentlemen," he boomed through his chiseled smile, "it's my pleasure to welcome you to the two-hundred-and-twenty-ninth Town Day in Nettle's Hollow!" He waited for a moment, and several people indulged him with a pattering of applause like rain on rhubarb leaves.

"As always," said Campbell, "one of the best parts of Town Day is when we get to honor our oldest living resident. As usual, that honor belongs to Mr. Stan Skerry of Fairview Terrace. Congratulations, Mr. Skerry!"

There was another flutter of applause, and the breeze ruffled the tops of the maples.

Dennis Campbell smiled at the crowd. "So Mr. Skerry, how old are you now?"

Stan took a shuffling step towards the microphone and cleared his throat. "Ninety-four," he said, and the Mayor clapped heartily.

"Stan, do you have any memories you'd care to share with us? I understand you've lived in Nettle's Hollow your entire life."

"Yes," said Stan, "except for a couple years in Ko-rea." Some people chuckled. It wasn't meant to be funny.

"That's right, of course," said Campbell, his grin unfazed.

"Well, I remember the day my Lily and I were married, back in forty-seven," Stan said. He nodded to where the white church split the sky with its steeple. "She was with me 'til—let's see, it was after they elected that actor fella—'82 it was when she—anyway, we had thirty good years."

"You did better than that, Mr. Skerry," the mayor chortled into the microphone. "By my math, you had thirty-five!"

"I only count the good ones." The crowed laughed again, but Campbell looked like he'd swallowed a fish.

"Right, well . . ." said Campbell, "any advice for us? What's the secret to such a long, full life?"

Stan thought for a minute. Was there a secret? Was it cutting out the smokes and the whiskey and everything that tasted good, like his doctor said? Or was it the little victories? The births and betrayals? The graduations? Or just being at his friends' funerals, instead of their being at his? Or maybe it was like he said, only counting the good years. Though of course, it's not only the good ones that count.

He moved his mouth, getting his dentures back in place, and said, "Keep only friends. Get rid of your enemies." He paused, then added, "And get rid of your enemies by making them into friends."

The mayor nodded and grinned like a wind-up monkey.

Stan leaned into the microphone. "But if they won't be friends, just bury 'em in the garden!" The crowd erupted in laughter, and even Stan couldn't help smiling at his zinger. The mayor congratulated him again and led him down the steps to where Klinger was fidgeting beside Lily. "Thanks, Timmy," Stan said as Klinger went off to rejoin his family.

Stan crossed the common with Lily and stopped a few times to wave at babies and shake a few outstretched hands. Children patted Lily, and their parents cajoled them into offering platitudes to Stan. He nodded and continued on, making his way up the brick walkway back to Fordham Street to wait for the light. It changed, and he and Lily crossed as a faint overcast dimmed the sky.

Stan was tired, and he sat down on the bench inscribed with Charlie's name. Lily looked up at him, and he nodded. She paused at the edge of the flowerbed, and Stan said, "Ah-ah" to her with an admonishing edge in his voice. "You know where." She looked up apologetically, then tramped through the hydrangeas and columbines and turned around, flattening several of the white lilies as she backed up to the rose bush. She hunched her back and stuck her tail straight out, quivering as she evacuated her bowels into the lilies and roses.

Stan nodded.

Their work done, Stan struggled to his feet as Lily waddled over. "Good girl," he said, and her tail began to wag. Then they stood at the homeward edge of the traffic island and waited for the light to change.

Adam Renn Olenn's stories have appeared in *Best New England Crime Stories: Dead Calm* and *Every Writer's Resource*. His short story "Coronation" was a finalist for the 2012 Derringer award, and he is a 2012 Bread Loaf Contributor. A graduate of the University of Virginia and the Boston Conservatory, he also won a scholarship to Grub Street. He lives in Winchester, Massachusetts with his wife and children.

Suicide By Engagement

Stef Donati

My hobby was incompetent criminals. You know the type: bank robbers who return to the scene one hour later to ask about mortgages. Or burglars who try putting a grand piano onto their getaway bicycle. I would read accounts of these misadventures to my cat Puddles, and to my columnist-friend Henry, thus burning into memory every bungling detail.

With each case he heard, Henry grew increasingly hopeful. If some local crooks would just display such ineptitude, he could lampoon them and earn the Pulitzer Prize he so craved. I wished I could help. But I encountered criminals only in these faraway stories.

Until that December.

I should begin with the previous evening. Henry and I were ambling to our cars after an office holiday party where we had sampled all the crackers and soda the newspaper could afford. "What's up with you, Thaddeus?" he asked, in the almost-casual way a friend will. "You're not yourself lately."

I slowed in mid-stride, fearing he had guessed my secret. After all, columnists are keen observers. Luckily, in the twilight my panic didn't register, and when I deftly switched the topic to the weather, Henry respected my privacy. I wasn't some disgraced councilman or an owner of fifty-nine barking Chihuahuas. I was Thaddeus Noll, gourmand-about-town, and I could count on my friend not to pry.

But on my drive home I kept hearing his words: *You're not yourself.*

Well, I didn't *want* to be myself lately. For all my sophistication and charm, I didn't want to be, period. Blame it on brain chemistry, lack of a partner, or one too many exposures to the caterwauling of talent-free pop stars. Whatever the cause, for months now I had been feeling increasingly low, a food critic who at home ate luncheon meats and microwave dinners, because *risotto alla pesto* was too tiring to even contemplate making. Lately my only true contemplation was the S word, seven letters in length and loosely rhyming with pesticide, the heavy inhalation of which was virtually the one method of self-deletion I had ruled out.

Which is where Beth Keegan comes in.

She was still a stranger, that morning after my awkward encounter with Henry. She sashayed into the newsroom with her flowing black hair and no-nonsense demeanor. Frankly, I gaped. I even forgot all about contemplating the S word as I watched her insist Customer Service resolve her subscription snafu. When she paused to wink in my direction, I worried I was hallucinating. A woman like her winked at me roughly as often as a master chef blends raspberries with ketchup.

Once her complaint had been settled, I strode toward her and we exchanged names.

"You look familiar," I said honestly. "I'm just not certain from where."

She licked her lips. "I'm afraid you're mistaken. I always remember a handsome man."

The compliment should have made me wary. But Beth Keegan was so alluring that with a normal libido, or normal optimism, I would have—

". . . around the corner?"

I was still attempting to place her. "Pardon?"

"It's forward of me, I know," she said, blushing. "But I can just tell we'll have a great time! So are we on? Dinner tonight, at that bistro around the corner?"

"We're on." I could always commit the S act later. Indeed, merely having the means was a comfort, as evidenced by the loaded pistol I kept in my nightstand.

Her green dress showed off her figure without seeming—if I may use the word—sluttish. Her perfume was faint but distinctive. She liked many of the same dishes I had once liked, before my depression besieged me. Not until our dessert, an overly sugared tapioca with a dash of nutmeg, did I come to my senses. Of *course* this woman looked familiar. She must be one of those seventeenth-rate criminals I enjoyed reading about. A con artist, perhaps, who as usual had chosen entirely the wrong target. For, cultured though I am, no secret treasures lurked within my tattered couch, my recipe *for zuppa di pesci*, or my rusting sedan with fourteen payments left on it.

"So, what do you do for a living?" I asked Beth Keegan, or whatever her name really was.

"Well, right now I'm between jobs." This was an answer every bit as unimaginative as I had expected. "I'm new to the area."

I debated suggesting she try a more honest line of work than fooling men into believing she liked them.

". . . my fiancé," she said.

One symptom of my melancholy was this erratic attentiveness to conversation. "Uh, did you just say fiancé?"

"I know it isn't something one normally reveals on a first date. But you're so easy to talk to, Thaddeus. So kind. I think I sensed those qualities even this morning, before we even spoke."

"I'm sorry," I said. "But if you're spoken for, I can't—"

"He died last summer. It hasn't been easy, having four fiancés die in five years. Not that I believe in curses, mind you, but I did think you should know."

She took a napkin and wiped the stem and rim of her wine glass. Relentlessly. Four fiancés, I mused. No woman loses four fiancés by accident.

"Well, this is just a date," I finally said, forcing a chuckle. "Who's talking marriage?"

She looked momentarily sad, as if my light tone disappointed her. But then came a smile as wide as Nebraska. "I'm so glad we met, Thaddeus. You're turning out to be everything I hoped for."

What does a despondent man do when a woman enters his life? If that man is me, he escorts her home with only one kiss, freeing himself to spend the rest of the night investigating her past.

Beth Keegan's current name, naturally, was nowhere in my files. Savvy murderesses are in a different league altogether than thieves who complain to the police about getting too small a share of the loot. But an Internet search yielded a wealth of data concerning a fugitive who looked exactly like my date. She had buried as many identities as fiancés, while keeping intact her hair color, hairstyle, and slim figure. Apparently even the fondness for haute cuisine. It was as if she were saying, *I defy anyone to find me out.*

Judging from most other endeavors I had ever planned, I would not truly be able to carry out the S word. The S act. Pistol in hand, barrel aimed at my temple, I would suddenly decide a bottle of pills was a much tidier means. Then, after obtaining those pills, I would immediately envision my poor Puddles ingesting the leftovers. The best course would now seem to be a leap from my balcony. But upon reaching the ledge, I would start preferring the notion of a noose. *Et cetera, ad infinitum.*

I saw in Beth Keegan the solution to my problem.

For clearly, and happily, such indecisiveness did not afflict her. Anyone who can murder four fiancés is an expert at follow-through.

She was also creative, having employed a different method each time. Briefly I did pity her victims; after all, not everyone wants to die. But consider the pleasure she had granted them! Months of companionship with a stunning and culinarily adventurous woman would more than compensate for a sudden demise.

After our second date, outside the same bistro as our first, Beth kissed me quite repeatedly. On the lips, no less. This presented a complication I should have foreseen. Customarily, a new romance is flaunted by its participants. They saunter hand-in-hand through department stores, they call each other "sweet buns" in polite company. If I kept meeting Beth Keegan in public, acquaintances would take note, and once she dispensed with me, some probing soul would ask questions. Beth should not have to fear prison for having released me from my suffering.

My solution was simple and, I thought at the time, brilliant. From now on, I arranged for our dates to occur outside town, late at night, in some eatery no self-respecting food critic would ordinarily enter. On those rare occasions when someone known to me came into view, I obscured my face or stooped to retrieve a hastily dropped slab of butter. Luckily, my "clumsiness" did not dampen Beth's interest. Nor did my lapsed palate.

I was so happy for both of us. I was being embraced in vitally intimate ways, and she had various execution methods to choose from. Soon I would be gone and so would she, off to woo her next delighted gentleman.

Delighted, I thought with a start. *Delighted* was indeed my current mood. Instead of vegetating to game shows or slurping condensed soups, I now found myself anticipating each hour in Beth Keegan's presence. Foolish! At any moment she might be unmasked, apprehended, leaving me as alive and melancholy as ever. I had better act fast.

So that very next Sunday we drove up Mount Bromfield. At its peak I proposed marriage and she said yes. To celebrate, we gamboled toward its cliff. I let her revel in the view of the valley until I could wait no longer. "Take me," I said. "Take me and push me now!"

"Um, what?"

Perhaps, as a supportive partner, I ought to be letting her believe the idea was all hers.

"Take me and kiss me," I corrected, and stepped to the cliff's edge.

It would have been a merciful end, the lingering taste of her tongue blunting any regret I might feel while plummeting. But she did not push me off.

Patience, I thought. She needs time to work up to this.

The next week was the most suspenseful of my life. To impress the venerable food critic, Beth arrived nightly at my apartment bearing savory dishes, and with each first bite I hoped for a shock. Whether slow or fast, from arsenic or cyanide, surely my deliverance would soon come.

It didn't.

Hiding my impatience, on Beth's eighth visit I placed in her hands my loaded pistol. "In case I meet some violent intruder," I said, "this gun will be the only thing standing between myself and certain death. Feel it, Beth. You might want a similar weapon." I even ambled to the window, giving her a clear shot.

She didn't take it.

There could be only one explanation: Beth Keegan, black widow extraordinaire, was falling sincerely in love with me.

"Beth," I said, facing her. "We need to talk."

At first it was I, stammering, who did most of the talking. But once matters were settled, Beth's eyes filled with tears. "Dying? That's a pathetic ambition, Thaddeus, and I refuse to abet it."

"Exactly," I said, as tenderly as I could. "I can't be wasting time on a relationship that might become permanent."

"My dead fiancés . . . they were accidents. All of them!" She squeezed a wet Kleenex. "On our first date, I said I don't believe in curses. I do, Thaddeus, very much. You're right to be rid of me. For your own health, we need to stay far apart."

As her tears fell, I wished I could undo this whole conversation. Here I had managed a rare burst of initiative, only to cause pain. I stroked her shoulders until her sobbing ceased. "A run of bad luck, Beth. The right man is out there."

She seemed not to hear me. "Just promise," she whispered, "you'll keep my tragedies to yourself. Please? The authorities would think I had caused them."

I promised.

She moved away. She took a new identity and then a fifth fiancé, who died one week after the wedding. I know this because I've been monitoring her from afar. Whether this woman is cursed or cunning, under an alias of my own I'm arranging to meet her all over again. To make certain she won't recognize me I'm growing a goatee, concealing my sophistication, and letting her "teach" me all about roast duck *a l'orange*.

If she stays around for my funeral, I hope her grief won't be genuine.

Stef Donati hosts a radio show in Vermont, loves most forms of music, and roots in vain for Cleveland sports teams.

Freebie

Leslie Wheeler

"This is taking forever," I groaned. "Let's come back another time."
"But next time it won't be free," Trevor protested. "And your baby might be dead by then."

I glanced anxiously at the Kalanchoe, the tops of its leafy, flowered stalks just visible above the plastic bag we'd brought it in. A dark gray blight had spread over some of the leaves, while others remained green and healthy. It was Trevor's idea to bring it to this garden shop in a Boston suburb. He figured we'd take care of two things at once: get a diagnosis for what ailed it, and have it repotted for free, a one-day-only offer at the shop.

This had seemed fine until we found ourselves at the end of a long line of people also waiting for a free repotting. A long, unmoving line. The blonde woman at the head held us up, while she took out plant after plant from a seemingly bottomless canvas tote bag. Orchids all, but with no flowers and in various stages of decline, some so obviously gone I wondered why she'd brought them at all. Yet the man behind the counter obligingly removed the orchids from their old pots and dumped out a mix of bark, slivers of black stuff that might be charcoal, and granules of a white substance. Then he filled other pots with fresh mix, and eased the orchids into their new homes, patting the mix around them with the tenderness of a parent tucking in the kids for the night. He chatted with the blonde as he worked, and after each tuck-in, he flashed her a big smile, apparently oblivious to all the disgruntled customers behind her. Round-faced with crooked, buckteeth, he reminded me of a leering jack-o-lantern.

But it was the blonde who irritated me the most. What was she doing here in the first place? She didn't look like someone who needed this free service. She wore a luscious tawny mink jacket, a short straight skirt that showed off long, shapely legs, and high heels. I pegged her for a tightwad rich lady, who didn't care who she inconvenienced as long as she got what she wanted.

Trevor and I, on the other hand, were frugal out of necessity. Fresh out of college and burdened with huge student loans, we both worked entry-level jobs, which left us with little money for anything beyond the bare essentials. While I tended to despair about my situation, Trevor saw it as a challenge. He'd developed this amazing knack for finding deals, discounts, and freebies.

That's actually how we met. I was at a department store, gazing longingly at a pair of bright yellow jeans I really couldn't afford when I felt a light tap on my arm.

"Do you know about the forty percent discount the store's offering customers with a special coupon today?" asked a tall, nerdy-looking guy with glasses. When I told him I didn't, he handed me the coupon he'd found online. I took it, thanked him, and bought the jeans. As I was leaving, he approached me again, introduced himself, and invited me to lunch at a nearby Chinese restaurant, for which he also had a coupon.

Meeting Trevor was a life-changing event. I went from someone who spent most weeknights and weekends moping alone in my apartment to someone who went out and had fun in my spare time. Trevor and I ushered at shows for free, went to movies and museums with free passes, and dined at restaurants that offered discounts. "How did you get to be such an expert at finding deals?" I asked him one evening.

"Well, Lori," he said, regarding me owlishly behind the glasses with thick black plastic frames he'd bought for six dollars on an eyeglasses-for-cheap site, "it's a question of whether you're going to let circumstances defeat you, and I refuse to allow that."

"Look, the line's starting to move," he said now. So it was, though not because the blonde was finished, but rather because several people in front of us had given up and gone home. We were now third in line. Then, second in line, when the blonde went to get more fresh pots for her moribund orchids. As she turned to go, I caught a glimpse of her face. She wasn't at all what I'd imagined. Instead of a well-made-up matron, she was young and clean-scrubbed, wearing glasses with plastic frames the color of her pale, watery blue eyes.

"You're right, we've waited long enough," Trevor hissed in my ear. "Let's go!"

"But we're almost there. And what about my Kalanchoe?" To me, it seemed to have sprouted more dark gray matter since we'd arrived.

"Lori, I don't—"

Just then, the woman in front of us departed with her repotted plant. Grabbing the Kalanchoe from Trevor, I held it out to the counterman. "Can you tell us what's the matter with—"

"It's infected with whiteflies! And highly contagious. Get it out of here immediately or—"

"*How could you*?!" a voice shrilled.

Trevor and I turned to see the blonde give us a look guaranteed to turn us into twin piles of gray soot. The next moment, the counterman seized the Kalanchoe from my outstretched arms and marched from the store. "What're you doing?" I ran after him. Trevor followed. To my horror, the counterman tossed it onto a mound of dead and dying plants. "But can't it be saved?" I wailed.

Positioning himself between me and the plant pyre, he folded meaty arms across his chest and glowered. "Kid, the best thing you can do is get rid of it!"

"But it's my favorite plant, the only Kalanchoe I have!"

It was true. The Kalanchoe was a gift from a long-ago boyfriend. It had survived not only the end of that relationship but several others until it seemed the one constant in my life. Boyfriends came and went, but my beautiful, tropical succulent continued to thrive, delighting me with its profusion of yellow, orange, pink, and red blooms. Until now.

Unmoved by my appeal, the counterman continued to glower.

"If I can't have mine back, I'm getting another." I headed for the door.

"Lori, no!" Trevor grabbed at me, but I slipped past him into the shop. The blonde was back at the counter, loading repotted orchids into her tote. She flashed me another withering look. I would've given it right back to her except that I was intent on my mission. At the shelves with Kalanchoes on the other side of the shop, I tried to decide between the larger size, which had multi-colored blooms like my plant, and the smaller one, which only came in one color. If I picked the smaller size, then which color should it be: yellow, orange, red, or pink? I also worried that these plants might be diseased. Was that the beginning of black soot I saw on some of the leaves? Were the things I saw in the air whiteflies or simply dust motes?

Trevor's face, wide-eyed and frantic, appeared in a window near the shelves. "Lori, c'mon!" he mouthed, gesticulating wildly. I had no idea why he was in such a hurry, but I dutifully seized a Kalanchoe with orange blooms, paid for it, and left the store.

I found Trevor scrunched down in the fifteen-year-old Saab he'd found on an orphan-cars-for-less site. He looked deathly pale.

"What's wrong?"

"I've picked up some kind of bug."

"Do you think it's from . . . my Kalanchoe?"

"Don't be silly, it's just a garden-variety—oops, bad choice of words—I'm sure it has nothing to do with your plant. But we'll have to skip lunch at the burger place with the two-for-one deal. I need to go home and rest."

Alone in my Somerville apartment that evening, I fell into a deep funk. It was the first Saturday night in what seemed like ages I'd spent by myself. Both my roommates were out, and I would've been out, too, if Trevor hadn't gotten sick. I hoped nothing was seriously wrong with him. I also hoped that, despite his assurances to the contrary, my diseased Kalanchoe hadn't brought on his illness. I even looked up whiteflies online, in case they were capable of infecting people as well as plants. Although there were no known instances of this, what whiteflies did to plants was gross. They laid their eggs on the underside of the leaves and the baby whiteflies sucked juice from the leaves, excreting liquid as drops of honeydew. The honeydew made the leaves sticky and covered them with the dark sooty mold I'd observed on my Kalanchoe. The leaves turned yellow and dry, and eventually fell off the plant. Yuck!

I examined my new Kalanchoe carefully, searching for signs of possible infection. I got out a magnifying glass and checked the undersides of the leaves for baby whiteflies, even though I'd read that in their first stage, they were barely visible with a lens. I was haunted by the notion that what I thought were a few specks of dust in the air were, in reality, the forerunners of a massive whitefly invasion. As a child, I'd become terrified of spiders after finding one in my bed and later that same morning, observing a dark-winged insect flitting about my room, which I was sure was a flying spider. Now, in my twenties, I was developing a whitefly phobia.

I'd already left several unanswered text messages on Trevor's phone, asking how he was. Now, I tried once more, again without getting a response. Maybe he was asleep. Maybe he was at the hospital without his phone. Maybe he was . . . No! He couldn't be dead. Not Trevor, the guy I hoped to marry once I found enough hot wedding deals on Groupon and other budget sites. True, I hadn't discussed this with him, but a girl can dream, can't she? Yet now my dreams were threatened by a horde of disease-carrying, blood-sucking, flesh-eating insects.

I thought of going over to Trevor's apartment to see if he was okay. But since he wasn't answering the phone, he probably didn't want to be disturbed. And if I were wrong about the whiteflies, I'd come off like such a world-class wuss that Trevor would never want to tie the knot with me, Groupon wedding deals or not.

Finally I made myself a cup of chamomile tea, and after checking my room for lurking whiteflies, went to bed. Despite the tea, I slept badly, plagued by nightmares of Trevor sprawled on the floor of his apartment, his body covered with dark, sooty mold, while clouds of whiteflies swarmed overhead.

When I woke up the next morning, I knew I had to go to Trevor's and find out how he was. He'd be okay, and everything would be fine. At least that's what I told myself as I rode one bus, then another to the Allston apartment he'd found on a cheap-apartments-in-the-Boston-area site. To cheer myself up and for good luck, I wore the bright yellow jeans I'd bought with Trevor's coupon.

He lived in a studio on the top floor of a seedy, five-story building. Trevor himself described the place as a "shit hole," but resisted my suggestion that he could get a better apartment if he had roommates. Apparently he'd lived with a roommate-from-hell a while ago, and was still recovering. I wondered if the roommate had been a woman, but when I asked for details, Trevor said he wasn't ready to talk about it yet. He wasn't ready to exchange keys either, so I had to use the buzzer. When he didn't buzz me in, I hit the other buzzers until I found someone who did. Trudging up flight after flight, I noticed that, as usual, the stairs were dirty and needed sweeping. On the fourth floor, I spotted a crumpled dollar bill in the hallway. Trevor might've dropped it—except that he kept his few bills neatly folded in his wallet. *Finders, keepers*, I thought, pocketing it. Which was exactly what he would've done. "If someone's going to be careless with their money, they don't deserve to get it back," he'd once said.

At Trevor's door, I paused, struggling to replace my inner voice of doom with a more positive, Trevor-like mindset. "Lori, I was just about to text you about this amazing deal," I imagined him saying. "We can fly to Paris for a dollar each!"

I smiled. But my smile soon faded when he didn't respond to my ringing the bell, knocking, and then pounding, on the door, while I called his name. Last night's terror returned. What if he *was* the first victim of a whitefly-borne pandemic?

Trevor's landlord owned an Irish pub across the street, and luckily, he was there, getting ready for the Sunday brunch crowd. At first he appeared skeptical when I shared my concerns about Trevor—minus the whiteflies—but when I started getting hysterical, he agreed to let me into the apartment.

As the landlord turned the key in the lock, I held my breath, steeling myself for the worst. The door opened and I let out a cry. The worst had happened! Just not in the way I'd imagined. Trevor sprawled on the floor in a pool of drying blood that came from his mouth, his smashed nose and, ominously, from a gash in the side of his head. He lay as still and lifeless as the furniture outlet coffee table, overturned in the struggle with his attacker.

After the police and the EMTs had come and gone, I returned to my apartment. I sank into the couch with broken springs that Trevor and I had found on the street, my mind spinning. Why would anyone kill kind, gentle Trevor? As I'd told the officer who questioned me, he had no enemies, so far as I knew. And a robbery gone wrong didn't seem likely, because he hardly had anything worth stealing. Also, nothing ppeared to be missing. So what had happened? I sank deeper into the couch, weighted down by feelings of hopelessness. Trevor was dead, struck down by an unknown assailant. An assailant whose identity might remain unknown unless the police got some leads fast.

Oh Trevor, poor, dear Trevor, you shouldn't have died! I sobbed. When I'd cried myself out, I rummaged in my pocket for a tissue. And pulled out not only a tissue but also the crumpled dollar bill I'd picked up on the stairs in Trevor's building. There were black smudges on it, and when I smoothed the bill out, I found a sliver of something black. Rubbing the sliver between my fingers, I realized it was charcoal like that in the mix used at the garden shop to repot the blonde's stupid orchids.

Hmm. Mentally, I replayed yesterday afternoon's events. Trevor and I stood in the long line headed by Blondie. I suggested leaving and Trevor dissuaded me. When we were almost at the counter, he wanted to bail. I'd caught a glimpse of her face then, so he must've, too. Did he recognize her as someone he wanted to avoid? When the counterman declared that my Kalanchoe was infected with whiteflies, she'd shrieked, "How could you?!" I thought she was angry with us for bringing a diseased plant into the shop, but what if her words had been directed at Trevor alone? What if she was angry with him for another reason? Maybe she'd been involved with him, and was still mad about their breakup. The mysterious roommate-from-hell?

No: I couldn't imagine Trevor having a relationship with a mink-jacket-wearing, orchid-grubbing, keep-everybody-waiting witch like her. And yet . . . she could've learned about the garden shop from him. Then there were her glasses. I went to the eyeglasses-for-cheap site and found a pair with blue plastic frames that matched hers. Either it was just a coincidence, or there was a connection between Trevor and Blondie. A connection that had led to murder? There was one way to find out.

"Hey, it's the sick plant kid," the counterman greeted me with his jack-o-lantern grin when I walked into the garden shop late the following afternoon. I winced and he apologized. "Sorry, been a long day. What can I do for you?"

I was tempted to ask him flat out if he knew Blondie, but decid to do a little business first. "I'm worried my other plants mi infected from the Kalanchoe I brought in yesterday. Is there some kind of spray I can use?"

He steered me to the shelves containing plant food and various pesticides. "I recommend Dr. Plant." He picked up a bright green spray bottle and handed it to me. "One hundred percent organic and doesn't contain any harmful chemicals, but you still gotta follow the usual precautions: keep outta reach of children, avoid contact with your eyes—you know the drill."

Before ringing up the sale at the register, he asked if there was anything else I needed.

"Actually, there is. That blonde woman with the orchids who was here yesterday—"

The clerk's eyes narrowed. "What about her?"

"I thought you might know her name, because you spent so much time with her."

"What's it to you?"

"I'd like to talk to her about orchids. She had so many, she must be an expert. And since I'm thinking of growing them myself . . ."

My reason sounded lame to me, but the clerk seemed to buy it. "Okay, it's Stef—Stef Brewer. She's sort of a regular here. Comes in whenever we have a sale or a freebie like the other day. Speaking of that, can I put you on our email list so we can send you notifications about those events?"

I wrote my email address in the notebook he gave me.

Outside, I noticed my Kalanchoe lying on the pile of discards. It didn't look *that* bad. Perhaps the counterman had acted hastily in throwing it out. Maybe now that I had the spray, I could still save it. In the end, I decided to leave well enough alone.

Riding on the first of three buses I had to take to get home, I congratulated myself on how much I'd accomplished with this one visit. Not only had I gotten Blondie's name, but in the future I'd know when to find her at the shop, thanks to the email alerts. Not ┗ omeone who, when left to my own devices, was usually so t a former boyfriend had called me a nonparticipant in my had no idea what I'd do when I actually confronted Stef 'd figure that out. Maybe I'd use the old cop trick of know more than I did. "Trevor told me all about you, mmate-from-hell you were," I'd say. "If he'd only known how violent you get when you're crossed, he'd still be—" At that point, I imagined her screaming, "I should've killed you, too!" Then she'd hurl herself at me, only to be pulled away by a crowd of astonished onlookers.

I'd barely come to the end of this imaginary, and thoroughly satisfying, scenario, when the free promo smart phone Trevor had found for me pinged. It was an email from the guy at the garden shop: Stef Brewer had showed up unexpectedly and would be happy to talk to me. Hmm. Odd that she would materialize so soon after I'd asked about her. But maybe it was a lucky break. I could confront her while my fantasy of doing so was fresh in my mind. Also, I was still on bus one of three, and if I turned around now, I wouldn't have to make this long trip a second time when I might not be so pumped for a showdown. I called the number on the message.

"I can come back," I said, "but it'll take me a while, and the shop might be closed by then." No way was I going to square off with Stef without witnesses.

"Not a problem," the clerk said. "We're open late tonight, but let me check with Stef and see if she's willing to wait for you." I heard muffled voices in the background, then he came back on and said Stef was fine with waiting.

Because of rush hour traffic, it took even longer than I'd expected to get back to the shop. The parking area was ablaze with light, and a car was parked there, but from a distance I couldn't tell if the shop was still open. Had Stef and the clerk given up and gone home, or was this merely a slow time? I glanced back at the street, reassured by the sight of an oncoming car. It passed the lot without turning in, but I decided to investigate anyway. I approached the shop cautiously.

When I was more than halfway to the entrance, the lot lights suddenly went out. I froze. My heart hammered, while my eyes strained to pierce the darkness. Damn. Maybe this wasn't such a good idea after all. I was about to turn and run when a shadowy figure came at me—so fast I couldn't escape. An arm coiled around my neck like a huge snake, catching me in a headlock. I opened my mouth to scream, but all that came out was a gurgling noise. A sharp pain shot through my chest. I might die of fright *before* my assailant strangled me.

"You leave Stef alone!" the clerk hissed, dragging me around to the side of the building. "That bastard of a boyfriend broke the poor kid's heart when he dumped her. Then he goes and shoves you, the new girl, in her face. Damn near broke her heart all over again. Wasn't right how he treated her. So don't think you're gonna give her a hard time, too. Cuz I won't stand for it. Honest-to-god I won't! Got that?"

I sure did. Got it that Stef Brewer aka the roommate-from-hell had done a number on this big, dumb bozo, crying on his shoulder until he became her self-appointed protector. And her avenger as well? I wouldn't put it past her to use her feminine wiles to get him to do her dirty work. A task he'd succeeded at only too well.

"Answer me!" His grip tightened around my neck, almost cutting off my wind completely.

"Ya-ah," I croaked.

"Good, cuz I don't want to hurt you."

Not hurt me? What did he think he was doing right now?

"But I will, if you don't keep your mouth shut and your nose outta this. I'll hurt you bad. Understand?"

I nodded to the extent that was possible.

"Okay." He removed his arm from my neck, and jabbed me in the back with the heel of his hand. I staggered forward, gasping for breath. My first impulse was to get the hell out of there, but then the image of Trevor lying bloody and lifeless on the floor of his apartment rose up in my mind. Rage burned within me, followed by cold calculation. I ran through the parking lot onto the sidewalk. When I was a safe distance away, I started screaming, "Help! Murder!" The clerk came after me. When he was within striking distance, I pulled the spray bottle of Mr. Plant from its bag, turned the knob on the nozzle in what I hoped was the right direction, and sprayed him in the face. His hands flew to his eyes and he shrieked, stumbling after me as I fled, all the while calling for help.

A dog walker rushed to my aid. Then a car stopped and a man leaped out. More people rushed to the scene. A couple of guys grabbed and held my pursuer. A police car screeched to a halt, and two officers piled out. "He killed my boyfriend!" I yelled.

"It was an accident," the clerk cried. "Just wanted to tell 'im to stop hurtin' Stef, but he wouldn't listen. Pushed 'im, he fell and hit his head on the goddamn radiator. Water. Need water. Burning up."

For a few weeks, I went around, puffed like a peacock, because of solving Trevor's murder. Then I crashed: Trevor was gone and I missed him terribly. To boost my spirits and also to honor his memory, I sought out deals, discounts, and freebies with the fervor of a fanatic. But it wasn't the same without someone to share the thrill of discovery and the satisfaction that came from getting stuff for less money or none at all. Then one day I noticed that a new online dating service was offering a three-month introductory membership for free. Should I sign up? Was I being disloyal to Trevor if I did? Finally, I decided it was okay, that it was time to move on.

That's how I met my new guy. I knew he was the "one" when I read on his profile that he was a graduate student in an arcane field unlikely to result in a high-paying job, and that his ideal date was someone who shared his view that the best things in life are free.

A co-editor at Level Best Books and the author of three Miranda Lewis "living history" mysteries, **Leslie Wheeler** is currently working on a new series. She is Speakers Bureau Coordinator for Sisters in Crime/NE, and a founding member of the New England Crime Bake Committee. www.lesliewheeler.com.

Epitaph

Wright R. Bloch

Novelist

"Any Day Now ..."

Level Best Books Co-Editor **Mark Ammons** is hard at work on his first full-length nov—Oh crap, wait! Look at this keyboard! Gotta dust it . . ."

CPSIA information can be obtained at www.ICGtesting.com
Printed in the USA
BVOW072040161012

303179BV00002B/6/P